The ache deep inside her was starting to affect her head. If she were thinking straight, she'd be running for the nearest exit.

"Now, Caroline," he said in that smooth, talk-you-out-of-your-knickers voice of his. Just the sound of it sent sparks shooting along her nerves.

"The key," she repeated firmly.

With a rueful smile, he dropped it in her palm. "Worth a try."

"And that's all it was worth." When he didn't move, she added, "If this is inconvenient, I can always use the ladies' powder room downstairs."

He stepped back. She didn't dare touch him—they wouldn't even make it through the door, let alone all the way to the bed, if she did.

J.R. however, didn't believe in fighting fair. He whispered in her ear, "If you need any help, just holler."

THE BRIDE'S REVENGE

ANNE AVERY

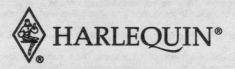
HARLEQUIN®

TORONTO • NEW YORK • LONDON
AMSTERDAM • PARIS • SYDNEY • HAMBURG
STOCKHOLM • ATHENS • TOKYO • MILAN • MADRID
PRAGUE • WARSAW • BUDAPEST • AUCKLAND

ISBN 0-373-29218-X

THE BRIDE'S REVENGE

Please address questions and book requests to:
Harlequin Reader Service
U.S.: 3010 Walden Ave., P.O. Box 1325, Buffalo, NY 14269
Canadian: P.O. Box 609, Fort Erie, Ont. L2A 5X3

To Angel Strong Smits
who kindly loaned me her notorious great-uncle,
Sam Strong, a Cripple Creek millionaire and infamous
womanizer who died in a barroom argument at the turn
of the century. A jury eventually determined that the man
who shot him acted in self-defense.
Doubts linger, however.
For this story, I have gleefully exploited
both Sam's peccadilloes and the doubts.

Chapter One

Life was good.

J. Randolph Abbott, III had always thought so, and with good cause. After all, he was one of Fortune's favorites and always had been. Right from the moment he'd popped into the world almost thirty-two years earlier he had been blessed with everything a man could possibly desire, and things had only gotten better with every year that passed.

He had loving parents with money and all the right connections, flagrant good looks, charm, wit, a Harvard education, an independent income, growing fame as an investigative reporter for the *Rocky Mountain Tribune,* and—not least among the many gifts for which he was duly grateful—irresistible sex appeal. Not to mention an undeniable talent for putting that appeal into eminently satisfying practice.

He thought of the previous night and looked up to

find his beautiful bride of some two months or so studying him from her place at the opposite end of the long dining room table.

At the sight of her, his chest swelled with love and proprietary pleasure. She was a splendid creature. Glorious! She loved him and he loved her, and—best of all—she was his, all his!

The thought added lustre to the already fine morning and whetted his appetite for the breakfast he could smell cooking in the kitchen. At the thought of breakfast, he glanced at his empty coffee cup.

"Would you like some coffee, darling?" his bride said, just as she did every morning. She had a lovely voice, one a man could enjoy listening to even over the breakfast table.

"Yes, thank you," he said, and smiled as she rose from her chair, then crossed behind the first of the four chairs set in an orderly row along that side of the table.

He really did love watching her move. She was so tall and graceful, so elegantly sure of herself. Even this early in the morning she was neatly dressed and perfectly coifed—the flawless image of a proper wife.

The rich, mink-brown hair that had spilled with such abandon over his pillow last night was now done up in a smooth chignon that left two soft tendrils to curl at either side of her face—not enough to be improper, but enough to tease a man's fantasies.

Her full, soft, marvelous breasts were decently bound and covered under her high-collared, tailored shirtwaist. Unfortunately. He loved her breasts. Loved looking at them, loved fondling them. Just the thought of them was enough to distract him from his work, even in the middle of the newsroom's mad clatter. Whenever he remembered how they tasted, too, he stopped functioning for a good quarter of an hour, every time.

Breasts like that, though, a man could be forgiven for getting distracted. Especially when they belonged to him. *Especially* when he'd only had two months to enjoy them. Or was it three?

Three months or three years, he'd still be thinking of them. Any man would. The way her corset thrust them up and out was guaranteed to catch a man's imagination. The mutton-chop sleeves and starched, pleated front of her shirtwaist only emphasized their tempting curves.

Her corset had very little to do with that delicious nineteen-inch waist, however. Unlike other women he knew, Caroline never had to strain to tighten her laces so she could fit into the narrow-waisted skirts that were the fashion these days. Fortune had been as kind to her as she had been to him.

But, then, he hadn't expected anything else. Not when it came to the woman he had chosen to marry.

The scent of her perfume, delicate, yet with a tantalizing darkness in it, caught his attention as she stopped beside his chair.

Eyes modestly downcast, she picked up the silver coffeepot that was set six inches from his saucer, and filled his cup. Gracefully and without spilling a drop.

"Thank you, my love," he said, and smiled again to let her know he appreciated her care.

"Of course, my love," she said, and neatly added

two cubes of sugar with just a touch more force than was strictly necessary. *Plunk! Plunk!*

"Would you like me to stir it for you, too?" she asked.

His smile widened. Such a jewel of a wife!

"No, thank you. I can manage just fine."

He ran his hand possessively over her hip. Beneath the layers of twill skirt and muslin underskirt and lacy muslin drawers, he could feel the curve of her but not the warm, yielding flesh. He liked knowing that he was the only man who would ever know just how soft her skin was there, and how eagerly she responded when she was touched.

The sound of footsteps in the pantry made him drop his hand.

"Here we are, then," said Mrs. Priddy brightly, backing through the swinging door, her heavily laden tray held high. "Fresh biscuits, toast, eggs just the way you like them, bacon, sausage, and a nice bit of steak, done to a turn. More than enough to set a man right for the day ahead, and that's a fact."

Unruffled by the interruption, Caroline returned to her place. J. Randolph watched her go, savoring every step she took.

When Mrs. Priddy set the loaded tray on the table near him, he gestured for her to fill his plate. He didn't want to take his eyes off his wife.

He had known Caroline was going to be his from the moment he first spotted her at that tedious soiree at the governor's mansion. He hadn't even intended to go, but it *was* at the governor's mansion, which meant easy access to men with information and influence he could use. A good reporter never missed a chance to expand his contacts, and he was a damned good reporter. One of the best.

Once he'd spotted Caroline, however, he'd forgotten everyone and everything else.

She'd been talking with several of Denver's golden youth, the bright, rich young men and women whose parents ruled the city and the West. The electric lights, normally so unkind to women's beauty, had made her flawless skin glow and showed her perfect figure to advantage. She'd been dressed in something green, he remembered. The gown had left her shoulders bare and revealed just enough of that magnificent bosom to set a man's eyes popping. Her eyes—the color of fine old brandy, though he didn't know it then—had been alight with laughter. She'd seemed so self-possessed, so perfect, so...*alive*.

Just then, as if she'd felt his gaze upon her, she'd turned and glanced his way.

He'd fallen in love with her, just like that.

He'd spent the next half hour arranging a formal introduction, and the rest of the evening making her laugh. It didn't hurt that she knew who he was and admired his work, or that she not only possessed great beauty and charm, but was also gifted with a keen intelligence that had kept him on his toes.

At some point in that memorable evening, he'd realized that the only thing lacking in his life was the proper, adoring, intelligent wife, and that Providence, as was its responsibility, had dutifully provided the best possible candidate when it sent Caroline Rhodes his way.

Until that moment, he'd never given much thought to taking a wife. His life was busy, fulfilling, and productive, and there were always plenty of pretty, proper young ladies available to escort to the theater when he wanted to observe the social niceties, and even more pretty, improper young ladies to amuse him when he did not. If he'd thought of marriage at all, it was more in the nature of something one did, eventually, because it was the respectible thing to do, and because a man needed children to carry on his name.

With one sparkling glance, Caroline had changed all that, and he couldn't be happier.

Ignoring the fragrant temptation of the steak and eggs and other goodies on his plate, he watched as Caroline daintily served herself from the tray Mrs. Priddy held.

His only real regret at marrying had been the thought that he'd have to give up the energetic bed sports he enjoyed so much. Or at least, he would for the first few months when no decent man would even think of visiting the female friends who'd kept him company before he'd tied the knot.

The trouble, he'd thought, was that well-bred young ladies of the sort one actually married and who eventually became the mother of one's children were raised to believe that sex was something a decent woman endured because she had to, not because she liked it. Sex, so their training went, was necessary to produce babies. But once the babies had come, the sex could be discreetly forgotten, or offered only when one's husband could no longer be ignored.

At least, that's what his married friends had told him. He'd heard too many tales of dutiful lovemaking and, all too soon, inventive excuses to avoid it, not to know that that was how things worked.

But of course, it hadn't worked that way with Caroline. Not with him. He should have known that it wouldn't.

Despite her ladylike upbringing, his wife had proven to be a marvelously enthusiastic bed partner— quick to learn, eager to explore, and more than willing to revel in the physical delights that were a woman's natural gift as much as any man's.

Better still, after the wonder and uncertainty of those first few weeks had worn off, Caroline had proven to have a talent for invention that rivaled an expensive, clever courtesan's. What man could possibly ask for more?

With a little inward sigh of satisfaction, J. Randolph took a sip of the excellent coffee, then opened the morning's edition of the *Tribune*, which his bride had neatly folded and laid at the right side of his plate, just as she had on every other morning since their wedding.

The sight of the front page made him smile.

There it was in neat bold type: his byline, J. Randolph Abbott, III, right beneath an eye-popping headline in 38-point type and right at the top of an article that was going to start a firestorm of debate in the state's gold-domed capital building.

Despite the threats of angry mine owners and a battering physical attack by one of the owner's hired thugs that had left him limping for a week, he had dug up the kind of hard evidence that showed how mine owners sacrificed their workers' safety in the cold-blooded pursuit of greater profits. If this first in a series of articles didn't start a public outcry for better laws to protect the miners, then his name wasn't J. Randolph Abbot, III.

With a modest smile of satisfaction, J. Randolph propped up the paper so he could read while he ate, took another sip from that perfect cup of coffee, then dug into his steak and eggs and bacon.

Life was really *very* good indeed.

She should have poured the coffee into his lap instead of his cup.

Caroline Rhodes Abbott glared at the open paper, which was all she could see of her husband except for the top of his head, then unfolded her napkin with a *snap!* and angrily spread it on her lap. Her husband never even glanced up from whatever had grabbed his attention in that damned paper of his.

Three months, five days, and sixteen hours of marriage and already he was taking her for granted. He hadn't wanted a *wife,* a *partner;* he'd wanted a maid, butler, housekeeper, party planner, social escort, and willing bed companion, all rolled up into one neat, inexpensive, and appropriately decorative bundle.

Pour his coffee indeed! The man would happily fight three vicious bruisers who'd leave him battered and bloody and limping for a week, but he couldn't pick up a coffeepot that wasn't a foot from his own cup?

Knife in hand, Caroline attacked the steak on her plate.

All right, she'd admit that some of it was her fault. She'd started marriage off on the wrong foot entirely by being too eager to please him and take care of him. *She* was the one who'd offered to pour that very first cup of coffee. But it hadn't taken even a week for him to start considering that loving gesture his God-given right! Not even a week!

Blame it on her mother. Blame it on the privileged world into which she'd been born. Both believed that a woman's role in society was as the dutiful, loving handmaiden to the men in their life—first to their fathers, then to their husbands, and eventually to their sons. That was the way her mother lived. That was the way her grandmother lived. And that, by and large, was the way all her friends lived, too.

But it wasn't the way she'd intended to live her life, which was why, at the age of twenty-one and three-quarters, she'd left her family's comfortable, upper-class Baltimore home and come all the way out here to Denver and the wild, wild West.

She'd wanted to see more of the world than just the drawing rooms and watering holes of the rich that were all she'd ever known of it. She'd wanted Adventure with a capital *A,* and she'd been willing to give up comfort and security, if she had to, to find it.

She'd been convinced she'd found that Adventure when she'd met the famous J. Randolph Abbott, III, a man who had forsaken the same privileged background she'd known in order to make his own way in the world. And what a job he'd done of it, too!

She'd heard of him long before they met at that soiree at the governor's mansion. Who hadn't? His byline on an article was enough to make rich men sweat and powerful men curse over their morning coffee. At no small risk to himself, he'd taken on corrupt politicians, unscrupulous businessmen, and defended the causes of the common working man so ably that he was credited with having forced the state legislature to pass some much-needed laws to protect workers against their employers.

The friends with whom she'd been staying—her family had threatened to cut off the income from her trust fund if she'd even dared think of staying in a hotel on her own—had been full of tales of his Adventures, all of them of the capital *A* variety, as far as she could see.

J. Randolph Abbott, III had become something of a folk hero among her friends, though not necessarily among their parents, the people he was most likely to skewer in his articles.

She'd been dazzled at meeting him, immensely flattered when he'd pursued her, and completely swept off her feet when he'd proposed. Somewhere in there— she wasn't sure just when or where—she'd fallen in love with him.

Behind his paper, J.R. muttered over something that displeased him, then turned the page without ever glancing up.

Irritated, Caroline stabbed her steak with her fork and sawed off another bite.

Three months and five-plus days of marriage had taught her there was no use trying to talk to him over the breakfast table. Once she'd filled his coffee cup and Mrs. Priddy his plate, he was incapable of anything other than grunts, mutterings, and an occasional slurp of his coffee until he'd worked his way through the *Tribune* and its chief rival, the *Denver Times*. Only then would he emerge and realize that she was still sitting at the other end of the table.

Her father had been morose in the morning. Her husband was just plain oblivious to anything except his food and his papers.

Her family hadn't been thrilled about their engagement. Not at first, anyway. They'd wanted her to marry George Davies, a fine young man who would step into his father's shoes as head of the family banking and industrial empire when that worthy gentleman eventually retired to his orchids and good works.

But George was far too proper, worthy, and dull for her tastes, and she'd been quite certain he wouldn't have approved of adventures, even of the lowercase variety. She hadn't even considered marrying George.

She hadn't really planned on marrying J.R., either, but once he'd set himself to charm her, no woman could have resisted him. And once she'd fallen in love... What was a well-bred young lady to do when the man of her heart could make her insides melt with just one sparkling glance? There were limits to the Adventures she was willing to try, and indulging in an illicit affair, even with the man she loved, was one of them.

Besides, she was beginning to be a little desperate over those same Adventures. Denver, it turned out, was *not* the rowdy, reckless, shoot-'em-up place she'd imagined. Not to put too fine a point on it: The place was a major disappointment.

There'd been no covered wagons, no wild Indians, no buffaloes, no gun fights, no cattle stampedes, and not even one handsome, ruthless, dark-eyed bandido intent on kidnapping and ravaging every decent young woman he found. There'd been absolutely *no* Adventures.

Instead, she'd found electric lights, telephones, hot and cold running water, bathtubs and flush toilets and central heating. She'd found electric trams and opera houses and theaters, lending libraries and subscription musicals and art galleries, restaurants and department stores and exclusive ladies' shops stocked with much the same things she would have seen in Baltimore. It hadn't taken her a week to realize the biggest difference between Denver and Baltimore was that Denver's buildings were newer and its public facilities a whole heck of a lot more modern.

The disillusionment was enough to make a grown woman weep.

When a camping expedition into Rocky Mountain National Park had fallen horribly short of Adventurous—camping in tents didn't count if your hosts brought along their butler, two cooks, and a raft of servants to see to their guests' comfort—she'd seriously considered running away entirely and seeing where that got her.

And then she'd met J.R. and that, as they said, was that.

Here, she'd thought, was a kindred spirit, a man

who understood that there was more to life than knowing which fork to use at a formal dinner. True, he hadn't taken her along on any of his Adventures, but then, how could he? They hadn't been married yet.

But he would! He hadn't said so, but she'd been sure of it. No man who respected a woman's intelligence and opinions as much as J. R. Abbott respected hers would ever deny her the chance to realize her dreams. Hadn't he taken her advice about checking into the background of that smooth-talking con man who was beguiling "investors" with his promises of riches to be dredged out of the South Platte with his "secret" new technology? She'd been right and he'd been more than happy to admit it. Proud, even! And then there was that scandal of the "preacher" who was skimming from the collection every Sunday. If it hadn't been for her, J.R. wouldn't have had that story until the man was halfway to California. Why, he'd even credited her in his article about it, citing a "reliable source" as the crucial link in all of it!

When she'd accepted J.R.'s proposal of marriage, she'd been convinced that she would be one of the lucky ones to have it all: a comfortable home, an adoring, handsome husband, and the adventurous life she craved, all rolled into one neat marital package.

She couldn't have been more wrong.

It hadn't taken her long to realize that J.R.'s notions of how marriage worked were darned near as stodgy as her parents', at least when it came to what *she* would be allowed to do.

There were, of course, no limits on what *he* could

do, so long as he was discreet about it. And that only added to her growing disgust with the whole darned mess.

With a self-important rustling of newsprint, J.R. tossed aside the *Tribune* and picked up the *Times*. She had a glimpse of her husband as he scowled at the bright red headlines plastered across the front page of the *Times* before he disappeared behind it.

He hadn't so much as glanced toward her end of the table.

Caroline glared at the biscuit she'd just picked up, then at the pot of jam at the opposite end of the table where he'd put it to work helping prop up his paper. Disgusted, she threw down the biscuit and scowled at the empty stretch of starched white damask that divided them.

Damask! At the breakfast table!

Not that he'd deliberately put her in this gilded cage. Oh, no! He hadn't even thought about it, which only added to the crime as far as she was concerned. He'd simply assumed, in that thick-headed, infuriatingly complacent male way of his, that he was the center of the universe and she just one more star set into orbit about him.

Even the delights of the marriage bed—and she'd been pleased to discover they were many and varied—weren't enough to compensate for the choking sense that she was prisoner in her own house, and that her chances for Adventure had ended the minute she'd let him slip that fine gold band on her finger.

Worse, J.R. hadn't even tried to understand. When she'd explained that she, too, wanted to have Adventures, he'd laughed and told her that a department store glove sale ought to be adventure enough for any three women. She'd almost hit him. Almost. Adventure didn't include brawling with one's husband, no matter how pigheaded he got.

But there were, she was learning, other ways to catch a man's attention. And some of them were an awful lot of fun.

She thought of what they'd shared in bed last night and felt her face grow hot and the muscles between her legs—muscles she hadn't even realized she had a few short months ago—squeeze in a disconcerting and delightfully suggestive way.

She looked at her biscuit, then at the distant pot of jam.

An idea formed.

Caroline smiled, picked up the biscuit, then rose and made her way to the head of the table and her oblivious husband.

"I'm going to take the jam pot, love," she said. "I hope you don't mind."

"Huh?" J.R. emerged from behind his paper, blinking in confusion.

Her smile widened. "The jam."

"Er…" He peered at the assembled plates and pots and serving pieces, bewildered.

Without looking at him, she pulled the jam pot toward her, then carefully spread a large dollop of strawberry preserves atop the biscuit. She flattered herself that no one, and certainly not her husband, would guess the jam she spilled on her fingers was a carefully calculated maneuver.

Out of the corner of her eye she watched him watch her delicately lick the spilled jam off the tip of one finger, then another and another. She could tell the instant his breathing stopped, caught the upward bob of his Adam's apple and its consequent plunge as he swallowed.

Daintily, she took a bite of the biscuit.

He was starting to pant ever so slightly.

"Mmmm," she said, and licked her lips.

"You...uh...you missed a bit right there."

"Really?" She took another bite, making sure to leave a dab of jam at the side of her mouth. She pretended not to notice.

His eyes locked on her mouth. The panting was noticeably louder. This close, she could see the swift, shallow rise and fall of his chest under that expensive tailored jacket and perfectly starched white shirt.

"Delicious," she said, lowering her voice to a sultry purr. "Would you like some?"

Before he could gather enough of his wits to answer, she leaned close and held the jam-covered biscuit to his lips. The tip of her breast brushed his sleeve, but she pretended not to notice that, either.

He noticed, though. He was long past the point of being able to pretend he hadn't.

"Take a bite," she said.

He took a bite, chewed, swallowed. She doubted he'd tasted anything. His gaze was fixed on her with such unblinking intensity that she was starting to have a hard time breathing, too.

His mouth was so beautifully, temptingly masculine it made her heart squeeze with wanting him.

"You have a bit of jam at the corner of your mouth," she said, leaning closer still. "Right here."

When she licked it off, he gasped, then came surging up out of his chair like a bull after its tormentor.

The biscuit—what was left of it—went flying. In one move he wrapped his arm around her waist and pulled her down on the rug.

She had just enough time for a short, triumphant laugh before his mouth crushed down on hers and she forgot about everything except the glory of wanting him, and of being wanted in return.

Chapter Two

"**Y**our hair's come undone," said J. Randolph Abbott, III, tugging on an errant lock.

"Mmmm," said his wife dreamily. "It wouldn't have if you hadn't pulled out half the pins."

Her head was pillowed on his breast, right where she could hear his heart beat. He smelled of starch and shaving soap and man. He'd tasted of coffee and strawberry jam.

At the memory, she smiled.

"I love your hair," he said, looping a lock of it around his finger. "You have beautiful hair."

He brushed the ends of it across the tip of her nose, making her laugh.

They were still lying on the rug with her indecently sprawled on top, legs spread wide. Her rucked-up skirts were the only thing that preserved a scrap of modesty for either of them. He didn't seem to mind. In fact, he was looking rather smug. Rather as she must look, Caroline thought, though he had an advantage. He wasn't staring at his underwear carelessly tossed on the floor not a foot away.

Although her drawers, like most women's, provided an opening for hygienic purposes that would have been more than ample for their recent, more athletic endeavours, he'd ripped the lacy muslin right off her in his haste. He'd never been quite that violent before and she'd found she rather liked it. It gave the act a new and deliciously dangerous flavor that added to the pleasure.

"I suppose," he said regretfully, "that we ought to get up and make ourselves decent before Mrs. Priddy comes in to clear away."

"She won't come until I ring for her."

Which was just as well, because she didn't have any intention of letting him up just yet.

She propped herself up on his chest, pressing her pelvis hard against him in the process. His pupils dilated so much his eyes looked black.

"I've got a job," she said, suddenly rather breathless at the thought of it.

He blinked. "A job?"

"With the *Times*. Oh, not a *real* job, not yet!" she added hastily. "But Mr. Blackmun said he'd be happy to see some pieces whenever I had something appropriate."

He raised his head off the floor. "Appropriate?" The single word carried a world of suspicion in it.

It was, she told herself, simply the way he was. Good investigative reporters like him were born suspicious.

Still, it did make her a little uneasy.

"Society pieces, just at first. I figured it was the easiest way to get my foot in the door." She shoved a little higher on her elbows, making sure she kept him pinned right where he was. "Eventually I'd like to write about women's issues—labor laws, working conditions, health concerns. The sorts of things you do, only from the female perspective."

J.R. sat up so abruptly she tumbled off him. He got to his feet without offering her a hand up.

"My wife does not need to work!" he said in the tone Moses must have used when he came down from the Mount.

She scrambled to her feet. "Yes, I do! I didn't leave Baltimore and come all the way out here just so I could go to ladies' teas and embroider doilies!"

"But you *did* marry *me*," he said, clearly offended.

"I didn't stop being *me* when I did, though!"

"What's that supposed to mean?"

"It means I want to do more with my life than pour your coffee and iron your shirts!"

"You don't iron my shirts! The laundry does!"

"That's not the point!"

Since she wasn't sure she could put the point into words, she retrieved her mangled drawers and wadded them into an untidy ball, instead.

The sight of the underwear distracted him for a moment and softened that hard glint in his eyes.

"The point is," she persisted, "that I didn't marry you just so I could keep your house and bear your children."

He wrenched his gaze away from her underwear. "Well, of course not! Nobody said you did, least of all me!"

She almost relented when he added, "You married me because you loved me!"

"I married you because you're normally an intelligent man—"

"Normally?"

"…who recognizes that a woman has a brain, too. I married you because I admired your work and your courage and your integrity, and because you seemed as interested in my intelligence as…as the rest of me!" she finished, brandishing her mutilated knickers.

Again his gaze flicked to the underwear. "Uh…"

"I want to work, darn it!" she said, stomping her foot in frustration. "I want to get out and see the world and do interesting things that matter, just like you!"

"What?"

"And I *don't* want to spend my time thinking about glove sales!" she added triumphantly.

He gaped. "What do glove sales have to do with anything?"

"You said they ought to be enough adventure for any woman. Well, let me tell you something—they're not!"

"Well, of course not. Besides, there's other sales, and teas with your friends, and—"

She hit him right between the eyes with her wadded-up drawers. Next time she saw her brother, she'd have to thank him for teaching her some of the finer points about pitching a baseball.

"Now that's enough!" he roared, batting the drawers aside. They fluttered to the floor, landing so the opening at the crotch was glaringly evident. His face turned red.

"I've been a reasonable and generous man," he said, "but this is going too far. I will *not* allow my wife to work. I especially will not allow her to work for a newspaper. *Any* newspaper, let alone the *Times*! And I will *not* be assaulted in my own home and at *my* breakfast table!"

"Your breakfast table!"

"That's right." He drew himself up tall and his chest expanded to intimidating proportions. His eyes sparked with a martial light. "Furthermore, I will be calling that cur, Blackmun, today and telling him that my wife will *not* be writing anything for him, not even so much as a recipe, by God!"

"J.R.!"

"No!" he said, and strode from the room like a man who thought he'd won the battle *and* the war.

His exit, she thought sourly, giving her drawers a frustrated kick, would have been more impressive if he'd remembered to button his pants first.

J. Randolph was as good as his word. He called the *Times* editor first thing that morning and sternly informed the man that his wife did not stoop to writing for hire, and *especially* not to writing for the *Times*! Caroline knew because she got hold of Blackmun not fifteen minutes later.

When she'd indignantly protested that her husband had absolutely nothing to say in the matter, Blackmun had chuckled and said he'd take five column inches on any society fling she cared to write about so long as he had it by noon Wednesday so he could get it in the Sunday edition. She had no idea what five column inches were, but she'd have agreed to writing a book if that's what he'd wanted. Even after discreet inquiries revealed that five column inches wasn't much at all, she refused to lose hope.

It was a beginning. Not an impressive beginning, but one couldn't have everything.

She didn't say a word when J.R. informed her over dinner that he had spoken with Blackmun and forbidden the editor to hire her. He made the mistake of interpreting her silence as acquiescence. She didn't try to correct him. Not then, anyway.

That night, clearly bent on showing her she was forgiven, he kissed her a couple of times, then tried to rouse her by trailing wet kisses down her throat, then fondling her breasts. She rolled onto her side with her back to him and switched off the light.

"Not tonight," she said, and pulled the covers up to her chin.

He muttered something under his breath, then switched off the light on his side of the bed, rolled over so his back was to her, and burrowed under the covers.

It was a long time before either one of them finally fell asleep.

She managed to resist his advances for two more nights, but by then she was suffering as much as he was. Their lovemaking that night was fierce, hot, and frequently repeated. But even as she rushed headlong for that first sweet release, Caroline knew it was just a lull in the battle, not surrender.

*   *   *

A week passed, then two.

She stopped pouring his coffee at breakfast. After three days of morosely eyeing his empty cup until Mrs. Priddy finally appeared and filled it for him, J.R. finally gave in and started pouring it himself. Half the time he slopped some on the tablecloth, but she didn't care. Let *him* pay for the extra cleaning and ironing. *He* was the one who was working and earning the money, wasn't he?

They still made love every night, but something had gone out of it and Caroline couldn't figure out what. Trust, perhaps. Or the confidence that had come from thinking they were equals in everything, not just the bedroom.

Neither one of them smiled much anymore, and neither made the slightest effort to apologize or try to bridge the gap that was widening between them. J.R. seemed to think she'd come meekly to heel eventually, and she was determined to show him just how wrong he was.

She had no intention of giving up newspaper work just because he said she should.

Besides a number of little pieces—fillers, Caroline had learned they were called—the *Times* picked up an entire article about a ladies' luncheon for forty hosted by Mrs. Andrew Moffat, wife of a former governor and millionaire businessman. Unfortunately, they didn't give her a byline.

J.R. didn't even notice, but it *was* the society pages, she reminded herself, and without a byline there wasn't any way for him to know it had been written by his wife unless she told him.

She kept quiet and kept on writing.

When J.R., grimly working his way through the *Denver Times* over breakfast, saw the piece about the disturbance at Miss Julie's, he flinched. When a quick scan of the article showed his name was included among the gentlemen whom the police had found in the parlor of one of Denver's finest brothels when they'd raided the place two nights before—trust the *Times* not to miss *that* fact!—he set his coffee cup down so abruptly that half the contents slopped over the edge and onto the tablecloth.

J.R. looked up guiltily. His wife hadn't noticed the coffee—she was too engrossed in her own perusal of the *Tribune*.

Ever since he'd had to put his foot down over her absurd plan of writing for the *Times*, she'd insisted on having the morning papers as soon as he had finished with them. He hadn't much liked it. Always before she'd been happy to read them after he'd left for work. But he was a fair man and, in the interests of marital harmony, which was more than a little strained these days, he'd given in to her demand. Now, he was very grateful he had.

The only reason he'd been at Miss Julie's was that a man who'd promised him some useful information for a story he was working on had chosen it as their meeting place. They didn't want to be seen meeting privately, the fellow had nervously insisted. People might suspect.

Since Julie's was a very respectable place, as such things went—he'd patronized her establishment a time or two himself before he'd met Caroline—J.R. had agreed to the fellow's terms. It was just plain bad luck that the police commissioner had chosen that night to raid the place.

The commissioner and Julie had been on the outs for some time. Everyone knew that, though rumors varied as to cause. Some said Julie had stopped granting him reduced rates, others that he'd taken exception when she'd declined to entertain him herself. Whatever the cause, Gallagher had gotten even by raiding the place on the flimsy pretext that they were after an accused felon who'd slipped out of their grasp.

The felon, if he even existed, had continued to elude the police's grasp, but J.R. had not. If it hadn't been for a friend of his at the jailhouse, he'd probably have spent the night at the expense of the city. As it was, he'd been late getting home. Very late.

To his dismay, Caroline had been in the parlor reading when he walked in. The eager, worried way she'd rushed to him had been extremely gratifying. But the concern in her eyes had quickly turned to frost when she'd gotten a good whiff of the mingled odor of cheap perfume, cigars, whiskey, and jailhouse sweat that lingered on his clothes and skin.

With what he preferred to think of as good sense rather than outright cowardice, he hadn't tried to explain where he'd been or why. She hadn't asked. He wasn't sure why it made him so damned nervous that she hadn't. Wives weren't supposed to pry into their husband's affairs. It was one of those unwritten rules or something.

He hadn't gotten any sex that night, and not much last night, either.

J.R. glared at the article in the *Times*. It wasn't really all that big, and it was on an inside page at the bottom near the fold, but that was no guarantee Caroline wouldn't spot it.

Under the circumstances, discretion was definitely the better part of valor. He folded the paper neatly, then tucked it under his arm as he rose from the table. She'd never notice if he took it to work with him rather than leaving it here as he usually did.

Caroline looked up as he stood.

"Delicious, my dear, as always." J.R. gave her his best, most seductive smile. He'd swear the paper was burning a hole in his side. "Thank you."

His wife's gaze dropped to her paper dismissively. "Thank Mrs. Priddy. She's the one who cooked it."

The smile vanished. "Of course."

He hovered for a moment, uncertain. Used to be Caroline would always come to see him off. She'd be smiling and radiant and adoring, and her kisses always carried a tantalizing promise for the night ahead. She'd fiddle with his tie, too, which he'd known was simply an excuse to get her hands on him one last time before he left.

He thought of that morning she'd seduced him, right here at the breakfast table, and felt a tentative stirring in his trousers. Then he remembered the revelation that seduction had led to. The stirring stopped. His heart hardened.

A man had his standards. If he didn't have the courage to stand by them—and in his own house, too!—then he really couldn't call himself a man. No gentleman would let his gently-bred wife demean herself by working, and certainly not by writing for that scandalous rag, the *Times*.

She'd see he was right eventually. All he had to do was hold fast and she'd come round. And if she didn't want a goodbye kiss, it was her choice. He wasn't about to stoop to walking all the way down the table to beg for one.

As he'd known he would, J.R. took a bit of ragging in the newsroom that morning. The tale of his incarceration had been common gossip, of course, and not all that interesting—a good newsman was expected to end up in jail from time to time—but the *Times* article brought out the jester in everyone.

By midafternoon things were beginning to settle down, though, and he was able to concentrate on his job. For that reason, he didn't think a thing of it when he was called to the phone.

"Abbott, here," he said crisply.

"Did you really think that stealing the paper this morning would keep me from hearing about your little…peccadillo?"

He bolted upright in his chair. "Caroline?"

"You were at a brothel?"

"Now, now. I can explain—"

"I sat up waiting for you, imagining all sorts of horrible things. That you'd been shot, or run over by a runaway wagon, or beaten to a pulp by some monstrous men, and you were in a...a *whorehouse?*"

"Caroline!" He glanced over his shoulder and found half the newsroom had stopped what they were doing to listen to his end of the conversation. He leaned closer to the receiver and lowered his voice. "Watch your language! You're a lady and—"

"I'm your *wife,*" she shouted, "and everybody knows it!"

J.R. grimaced and held the receiver away from his ear.

"Five different people dropped by this morning to commiserate," she raged, "and they all brought that article along just in case I hadn't seen it! I've had more than a dozen sympathy calls, half of them from women I hardly know and definitely don't like. And now you tell me I'm supposed to be a *lady?*"

Actually, she was screeching like a harridan from one of Denver's less savory brothels, but he wasn't about to tell her that.

"Ah..." Out of the corner of his eye J.R. caught two reporters, a copy boy, and an editor edging closer. He turned his back on them and hunched over the mouthpiece, the receiver tight against his ear. Deafness was better than having everyone think he was the kind of man whose wife screamed at him. "Darling—"

"Don't you darling *me!*" his sweet wife shouted back. "So it's wrong for me to get a job, but all right for you to be caught consorting with prostitutes and the riffraff of Denver, is it? Well let me tell you something, Mr. J. Randolph Abbott the Third, you're wrong! Got that? *Wrong!*"

He pulled out his handkerchief to mop a brow suddenly gone damp with sweat.

"Caroline, dearest, if you'd only let me expla—"

That's as far as he got before she slammed the phone down in his ear.

By the time J.R. left the newsroom that evening, he'd almost convinced himself that the incident was nothing more than a little misunderstanding that would soon blow over. After all, he'd done nothing wrong. In fact, he was the injured party in all this, which made him feel distinctly put-upon.

Fortunately, he was man enough to rise above such things. By now, Caroline would have cooled down sufficiently that she'd be ready to listen to reason. His sweet, beautiful wife was far too intelligent to let this get any further out of hand.

Once he'd had a chance to explain, she'd apologize. He, of course, would be gracious and forgiving about the whole thing because that was just the way he was. Why, he might even take her out to the theater tonight! That would show her he didn't hold a grudge. It would also give her a chance to dress up a little and maybe show off that diamond necklace he'd given her as a wedding gift. She'd like that. He was sure of it.

He was wrong.

When he turned the corner half a block from his house, he found the normally placid street abuzz. A gaggle of bystanders, heads tilted to watch something that was hidden from his view by trees, were clustered before a gate about halfway down the street. *His* gate, he realized with dismay.

Panic struck. Had something happened to Caroline? Had she fallen? Been attacked? Had someone broken into the house with the intention of taking the silver and hurt her in the process?

At the thought, J.R. started running. Caroline would be all right. She *had* to be all right! But if she wasn't, if anyone had hurt her, he'd make sure the fellow paid for it, by God! He'd beat the bastard to a pulp. He'd hang him from the highest tree he could find. He'd—

Something fluttered from an upstairs window. The crowd laughed.

J.R. slowed to a walk, then stopped dead when another item sailed out the window. It was absurd, of course, but he'd swear it was a pair of his own drawers.

It couldn't be. Caroline wouldn't—

He thought of her earlier that afternoon, screaming on the phone.

Maybe she would.

For a moment he considered walking away, but J. Randolph Abbott, III had never walked away from a difficult situation in his life, and he wasn't going to start now.

The crowd didn't notice him at first, but then one of the neighbor boys turned and spied him.

"Hey, Mr. Abbott! We were wonderin' when you'd get home!"

At that, the crowd turned as one, then, with many

knowing grins and stifled snickers, parted to let him through.

Head high and nostrils flaring, J.R. strode forward. He pretended not to hear the whispered comments from all sides, but he couldn't block them out.

"That's him!" said one woman in a stage whisper audible to everyone. "That's the one got caught in that raid at that fancy house."

"Imagine! And them not six months married!" said another, just as clearly.

Toothless, tottering old Mr. Joseph from three houses down the street gave him a playful poke in the ribs with his cane. "Got caught, didja? You'll learn! Man's gotta be careful 'bout that sorta thing, y'know!"

J.R. cast him a fulminating glance but didn't stop to argue. A man didn't stoop to defend himself from common rabble like this, no matter how ill-informed and stupid they might be.

Because he was looking up at an open window on the second floor—his bedroom, he realized in shock—he was halfway through the gate before he noticed what lay on the walk at his feet. Two open suitcases had been set side by side right in the middle of the path. A leather Gladstone, also open, sat on the lawn beside them.

All three were half buried under an untidy pile of suits and shirts and gentlemen's unmentionables that had been flung out of that upper floor window, willy-nilly. It didn't need more than a pop-eyed glance for J.R. to identify both luggage and clothing as his.

As he watched, a dozen ties sailed out the window

to shower like confetti on the lawn and walkway. Only one landed anywhere near the open luggage. A moment later, his best dress tails, a suit handmade for him in London, followed the ties. The trousers landed on the gatepost. The tails caught on a lower branch of the elm to dangle there like some awkward black monkey.

The crowd laughed and shoved forward, craning for a better look.

Rage seized J. Randolph, a righteous rage that propelled him over the suitcases in one long-legged leap. He took the steps to the front door three at a time.

The rage flared hotter when he discovered his key no longer fit in the lock. He pounded on the door with his fist.

"Caroline? Caroline Rhodes Abbott! You let me in, do you hear?"

A cry from the crowd brought him around in time to see half a dozen of his good undershirts drift to the ground.

Swearing, J.R. charged back to the gate where he could get a better view of his bedroom window.

"Caroline Abbott!" he roared. "You stop this disgraceful behavior right this minute! Do you hear me? Right this minute!"

He ducked as one of a pair of his best wing tips came sailing toward him. It bounced off his shoulder and landed in the street. The second landed in the middle of a scraggly rose bush that had always produced more thorns than roses.

"Caroline!"

A pair of his best drawers, rolled and tied into a tight, hard bundle, smacked him in the face.

Three more pairs, unbundled, floated down to drape across the front gate and catch on the juniper bushes on either side of the walk. A pair of his long winter underwear followed.

Unfortunately, because the long johns were heavier, she got a bit more loft on the things.

An arching branch at the top of the big elm tree snagged them in midair, whereupon the breeze obligingly wrapped them even tighter around the branch, then teased them so both legs and one arm flared out like flags for all the world to see.

A cheer went up from the watching crowd.

Caroline stuck her head out the window for a moment. She smiled and waved at the crowd, then, without so much as a glance at him, ducked back inside and slammed the window shut.

Chapter Three

Four months later

She spotted him on the platform in Denver—too late
to do anything about it. One minute he was standing
there, tall, elegant, and incredibly handsome, idly sur-
veying the crowd and attracting the attention of every
woman within sight. The next, the conductor had
shouted, "Last call! All aboard!" and he'd picked up
the leather Gladstone bag at his feet and leapt aboard
as gracefully as a cat.

Caroline Abbott stuck her head out the window to
see which coach was his. Five cars up. First class.

She pulled her head back in, disgusted. Trust the
man to be riding first-class—at the *Tribune's* expense,
no doubt. As the powerful newspaper's star reporter,
J. Randolph Abbott, III was unlikely to be traveling
anything *but* first-class.

Not that she ought to hold it against him, she admitted, reluctantly settling back on the wooden third-
class seat. Until she'd locked J.R. out of her life,
she'd never traveled anything but first-class, either.

Too bad she hadn't appreciated the advantages when she had them. They hadn't left the station and already she missed the padded leather seats in first-class. Midsummer's heat seemed trapped inside the coach despite the jammed-open windows, a couple of the passengers could do with a bath, and the coach needed to be swept out, then scrubbed with lye. Worse yet, there'd been far too many male travelers— she refused to use the word gentlemen—who hadn't bothered with the spittoon at the back of the car. Not at all the sort of thing a person would put up with if they didn't have to.

As if to reinforce that assessment, the baby five rows up flung its pacifier away and started to wail. Caroline grimaced. Wailing babies sounded alike, no matter what class you were traveling. Fortunately, the drawn-out screech of the steam whistle, followed by a metallic clatter as the train jerked into motion drowned out the worst of the baby's screams.

She ought to look on the bright side. Third-class offered at least two advantages that first-class did not—it was cheap, and it did not contain her husband.

It might, in fact, be almost endurable if she got an article for the *Times* out of the experience. She studied her fellow passengers, hoping for inspiration.

The only thing that occurred to her was an editorial on the virtues of soap and regular baths.

She could probably wring a small piece on the state of business from the fussy little pharmaceuticals drummer two rows up, but she'd seen the label on his samples case guaranteeing that Dr. Rose's Digestive Powders would "relieve dyspepsia, indigestion, heartburn, constipation, belching, flatulence, and other digestive upsets or your money back.''

Just the thought of what J.R. would say about an article on digestive powders and flatulence made her shudder.

Well, to heck with J.R. and his notions of what a proper wife ought and ought not do! If reporting on this Cripple Creek murder trial worked out as she expected, she'd be traveling first-class from now on *and* at the *Times'* expense.

She couldn't have asked for a better story to start with. Any tale that included money, powerful men, beautiful women, illicit sex, and plenty of blood was bound to bring in the readers.

In its outlines, it was a common enough tale. Andrew ''Andy'' Osbald, dashingly handsome owner of Cripple Creek's most famous saloon and gambling house, was on trial for murder. Josiah Walker, the man he'd admitted killing, but only in self-defense, had been one of Cripple Creek's lucky ones. Unfortunately for Walker, his luck had gotten a bit tarnished of late.

He had already taken more than one and a half million dollars' worth of gold out of his Acme Mine when, not quite two years ago, he'd been sued for breach of promise by two different women, both of them prostitutes, in the same week that he married Boston society belle, Mary Dodge. In the end, he'd had to take his bride on an extended tour of the Continent until the flap died down a bit. His lawyers, or so it was said, had ended up paying the disappointed women the astounding sum of fifty thousand dollars each for their "loss."

The scandal had kept Denver readers entertained for weeks.

His death two months ago in what appeared to be a barroom brawl over an unmarried lady famous for her abundant charms and loose morals had made the papers in New York and Boston. The blast from Osbald's shotgun had hit Walker square in the face, making an open-casket funeral impossible.

Of course, the *Times* already had a reporter assigned to the case—a big, bluff man named Murray who was one of the paper's most popular reporters and who got most of his "news" across the beer-drenched bars of Denver's least respectable saloons. He'd already had several bylined pieces about the killing published, every one filled with as much scandal as could be crowded into two long columns, front page.

She'd convinced her editor, Cyrus Blackmun, to let her cover events by taking another tack entirely. Instead of making the trial the focus of her articles, she intended to tell Josiah Walker's story from the point of view of the women in the town…and in his life.

Women liked to read about other women, she'd told Blackmun, especially about women involved with the kind of man Josiah Walker must have been. Nobody else would try anything like it, she'd argued, because she was the only reporter who had a chance of getting both Walker's widow and his mistresses to talk. All it would take was one good article and the promise of more to sell papers. Lots of papers.

Blackmun had agreed, but not enough to offer her money up front.

"If you want to do it so badly," he'd said, "then do it. But don't expect the *Times* to pay your bills. Not until you've proven yourself and turned in work we can use."

Caroline's grip on her purse tightened. Blackmun hadn't made it easy for her, but she didn't care. She'd show him. She'd show *all* of them! To the devil with J.R. and his doubts!

Fighting against the sudden burning in her throat and the stinging heat in her eyes, she stared out at the stark Colorado mountains slipping past in the distance. The only thing she saw was the remembered image of a tall, handsome man who'd stood on that train platform looking as if he owned the world, and knew it.

"Aren't you J. Randolph Abbott, the reporter? You are, aren't you? I knew you were! I knew it! I said to Abby, here, I said, 'Abby, that's that famous reporter, J. Randolph Abbott, the one whose picture's always in the paper, remember? The one who went into that mine after that cave-in and helped rescue those poor men and then wrote all about it?' That's what I said. Isn't that what I said, Abby?"

Abby—plump, pretty, and with the sweet, slightly vacant gaze of a woman with more looks than sense—covered her Cupid's bow mouth with her gloved hand and nodded, giggling and blushing charmingly.

At least most men would have found it charming,

J.R. thought grimly. He found it damned annoying. He didn't like stupid women—never had. But he did like to keep his readership.

"Miss Abby," he said, nodding politely. "And you are…?" he added to the woman who gushed.

"Emma Jean Corcoran. *Miss* Emma Jean Corcoran." She simpered even worse than she gushed, but at least the introduction didn't come with question marks at the end of every breath.

"Miss Corcoran." J.R. tried not to grit his teeth as he smiled.

He would have stood, but the two women had him corralled. Miss Emma Jean was standing in the aisle with her knee pressed against the edge of his seat. All she'd have to do was move an inch closer and she'd tumble right into his lap—an approach that more than one enterprising young lady had tried to use before he'd learned to keep his Gladstone on the seat beside him. Miss Abby, less aggressive than her friend, was swaying over the top of the seat in front of him, oblivious to the stiff-backed disapproval of the old woman who'd claimed the place by the window.

Despite the breeze coming in the half-open window, J.R. could have sworn the air in the car had suddenly became uncomfortably thin of oxygen.

"Are you going to cover that trial in Cripple Creek?" Miss Corcoran inquired. "You are, aren't you?" she added before he could even nod. "I knew you were. I said to Abby, I said, 'He's going to cover that trial in Cripple Creek. You mark my words, he'll be right in that courtroom, getting all the details.'"

Regardless of the Gladstone, she swayed closer, her

expression avid. The faint mustache on her upper lip quivered. "I bet you'll be looking around for more information than what comes out in the trial, won't you Mr. Abbott? You always do. Isn't that right? I told Abby, I said, 'He'll be looking for more than what they say in the trial. That's what he does. He *always* tells us the *whole* story that no one else even knows about.' Isn't that what I said, Abby?"

Abby giggled.

J.R.'s smile was getting strained around the edges.

The old woman's spine had gone ramrod straight with contempt. Not everyone loved his articles, thank God. At least *she* would leave him in peace.

Be polite, he reminded himself sternly. It was because of people like Emma Jean Corcoran that he was able to cover the stories he wanted and command the outrageous salary he did. The salary wasn't that important, but the freedom to work on the stories that interested him for the most important newspaper in the West—now *that* was worth protecting. And according to his editor, the only crime worse than bad reporting was driving subscribers over to the rival *Times.*

"Yes, I'm headed to Cripple Creek," he said. "In fact, I was just working on my notes."

He held up a pocket notebook with scribbled writing clearly visible on the top page. The writing was a jotted reminder to buy a new can of tooth powder and to pick up his shirts from the laundry, but they didn't need to know that.

"Ohhhh!" said Miss Abby, pinkening. "How... *exciting!*"

Shaken by the effort of finding three words, especially a large word like *exciting,* she retired behind her glove, breathless.

"Really?" said Miss Corcoran, craning for a better look.

J.R. hastily shoved the notebook into the inner breast pocket of his jacket.

"Move along, ladies. Move along, please. You're blocking the aisle."

J.R. hadn't heard the conductor making his way through the car collecting tickets, but he would gladly have handed over twice the price of his ticket as thanks for the rescue. Miss Abby and Miss Emma Jean regretfully moved along, but not without many fluttering backward glances along the way.

"Sorry about that," J.R. muttered, digging for his ticket.

The conductor ignored the proffered bit of cardboard. "Say, aren't you that reporter fellow that always has his picture with his stories? The one from the *Tribune?*"

"Yes," said J.R. unhappily. "Yes, I am."

The other passengers were beginning to stare. Only the old lady in front of him pointedly ignored the exchange.

"You do good work," said the conductor. "Me'n the missus read you all the time. I especially liked that series you did on the last election. Never did trust that Smith fellow, but you were the only one who got the goods on him."

"Mmm," said J.R., pointedly waving his ticket.

The conductor punched it and handed it back. "Going to Cripple Creek, huh? Imagine! A millionaire mine owner shot down in a barroom brawl. Thing like that, who'd have thought? Me'n the missus'll be looking for you to give us the straight story on that situation, we surely will ''

When the conductor moved on at last, J.R. slumped back against the leather seat. When his editor first started running his picture with his regular articles, he'd thought it was a splendid idea, something that would set him apart from the rest of the pack. If he'd had any idea it would mean he'd be considered fair conversational game for anyone who'd ever had the price of a paper, he would have destroyed that engraver's plate, right at the start.

Scowling, J.R. looked up to find that Miss Corcoran had turned round in her seat. The instant she caught his eye, she smiled and waved and batted her eyes at him. He'd swear he could hear her companion's giggle from here.

Panicked, he grabbed the copy of the *Times* he'd picked up that morning and opened it with a loud rustle of paper. Even a spinster of Miss Emma Jean's stripe ought to know better than to bother a man when he was reading the paper.

He stared at the front page, unseeing, then flipped to an inner page at random. The society page. He grimaced and would have flipped back but a small piece near the bottom caught his eye. Ladies Organize To Vaccinate The Poor by C.A. He blindly flipped to another page, but all he saw there were two initials, seemingly floating in the air above the print.

C.A. Caroline Abbott. His wife.

Anger and longing surged through him in a confusing, inextricable mix. Caroline had never bothered him when he read his morning paper.

His fingers dug into the paper in an involuntary spasm, crumpling the edge. All right. Once. Not that he'd objected. It wasn't every morning a beautiful woman seduced him with strawberry jam. He still couldn't eat the stuff without suffering a troublesome stirring in his trousers.

Unfortunately, a troublesome stirring was all he'd managed in the almost four months since Caroline had kicked him out.

Logic, reasoning, rage, shouting, pleading—with the exception of going down on his knees and begging, which was asking *way* too much, he'd tried all of them. Nothing had worked. Nothing had convinced her to welcome him back into his house or the bed they'd once shared.

He was even prepared to admit he was, ultimately, the one at fault, but she'd started it with this ridiculous notion that she wanted to be a reporter. A reporter! His *wife!* Just the thought would have made him laugh if it weren't so appalling.

J.R. glared at a perfectly innocuous report on the price of wheat, but what he really saw was that damned article on the society pages.

If only she'd stick to society reporting it might not be so bad. But she'd made it clear she intended those pieces as a toe in the door of something bigger, more important. Something *meatier*. Meatier! Hah!

All right, sure, there were a few women fighting their way into the ranks of reporters for the dailies, but they were hard, experienced women, none of whom had come from the pampered background Caroline had.

She was too refined to fit in at a political convention. She'd never been confronted with the often rough habits and rougher talk of union organizers. She'd never had any dealings with the police at all. And wait until she confronted an angry cop who didn't know she was one of the upper crust who was supposed to be treated with kid gloves! He'd love to be there when she did—she'd change her tune quick enough.

Disgusted, J.R. tossed the *Times* aside and picked up the *Tribune*. The front page looked rather bare without his picture and article, he thought. But even he couldn't churn out enough work to keep the paper covered seven days a week, and he worked as hard if not harder than any man on the paper.

Why Caroline thought she should even try to compete with him was a mystery.

If only she'd listen to reason! He was willing to meet her halfway, but they couldn't work out anything when she refused to talk to him. She even sent his letters back unopened. Both the mailroom boys at the *Tribune* and the clerk at the hotel where he now lived had noticed. He'd ignored their sidelong glances and their sniggering, but with each returned letter, his anger had grown. When his last letter had come back ripped in two, envelope and all, with the pieces stuffed into the cheapest envelope available, he'd given up writing.

It was a wonder the *Times* hadn't written about his

woes. There was nothing they'd like better than to see him suffer.

He hated to think the lack of coverage might be due to his wife's influence. The last thing he wanted was to be beholden to her, even for that little service.

Still, the thought of his name appearing in a paper in any form other than a well-paid byline made him shudder.

With an angry snap, he folded up the *Tribune* and dumped it atop the *Times*.

The disapproving old lady in the seat in front of him had the right idea—keep your head up and your eyes straight ahead and don't ever waste time with fools, knaves, or newspaper reporters.

As if she'd read his mind, she suddenly turned round to face him.

"Would you mind autographing my newspaper?" Eyes wide and eager, she extended a pen and folded paper over the back of her seat. "My daughter will faint dead away when she hears I actually traveled on the same train as J. Randolph Abbott!"

At the stop in Colorado Springs, J.R. got off to stretch his long legs. Caroline spotted her husband the minute he stepped onto the platform—and so, she couldn't help noting sourly, did every other woman around. She shouldn't blame them. He was very easy to look at.

But watching him like this hurt, seeing the confident, familiar way he moved, the way he tilted his head or shoved his coat back to thrust his hands into his pockets. It hurt a lot. Worse, it reminded her she still loved him, no matter how often she'd tried to convince herself otherwise.

She watched as he smiled at the brash pestering of a newsboy, then casually flipped the boy a nickel and took the proffered paper. His laughter at something the boy said squeezed her heart. He had a beautiful laugh.

Caroline forced herself to look away. A long, raw gouge in the wooden seat in front of her caught her eye. She frowned, then, distracted, picked at the broken edges of wood with a finger.

Almost four months had passed since she'd locked J.R. out of the house, and it hadn't gotten any easier. No matter how hard she tried to convince herself otherwise, she missed him. It was going to be hell sitting in the same courtroom with him, day after day after day.

Well, she could handle hell, she told herself sternly, squaring her shoulders. She was going to be a reporter—a *great* reporter!—and great reporters handled hell in their sleep. J.R. had taught her that. He'd taught her a lot of things, whether he'd meant to or not.

"You have to be there first," he'd told her after dinner one night when they'd had nowhere to go and nothing to do but please themselves. Because the brandy was good and she was always curious about his work, he'd drifted into talking about the cutthroat newspaper business and the dirty tricks a reporter would play on another in the effort to "scoop" a story or to get an interview no one else had.

"Get there first and you get the story before anyone's had a chance to change the way they remember it, or to embroider their memories of what happened so it sounds a little bit bigger, a little bit better.

"But being there first doesn't count if you can't get the right story," he'd added, frowning into his brandy. "It's truth that counts in the long run, not being first. No matter what you read in the papers," he'd added, glancing up at her and grinning.

They'd talked for hours, she remembered, sitting there with only the width of a table between them and the world far, far away. Later, when she'd run out of questions and he'd run out of tales, she'd slid onto his lap and kissed him long and hard and hungrily. They'd discovered a rather creative use for the dining room table that night.

Caroline blushed, remembering, and tried to ignore the heat the memory provoked. Despite the heat and the blushes, she couldn't stop herself from glancing out the window at that familiar figure that was so close, and yet so very, very far away.

Get there first, he'd said. *Then get the truth.*

He was strolling down the platform, puffing on his favorite brand of panatela, oblivious to the travelers bustling past him. He wouldn't reboard the train until the last possible second, she knew. He never did, confident that no conductor would dare let the train leave without him.

And that gave her an idea.

After a quick check to be sure her bag was properly locked and out of sight, she laid her morning's papers and the book she'd brought with her on the seat, then quickly made her way up the train. In the confusion of passengers getting on and off, no one paid her any heed.

It wasn't hard to find J.R.'s Gladstone—she'd packed it often enough herself during their short married life to know it well. And if she'd had any doubt, there were his initials, JRA, three plain but elegant letters in gold-plated metal, clearly visible on one side.

With one eye cocked out the window to keep an eye on the bag's owner, she dragged it out from under the seat.

Just touching the smooth leather handles, both of them worn a little where his hand rubbed, sent a disconcerting tingling shooting through her hand and up her arm. She had to fight against the urge to open the bag and run her hands through the six starched white shirts he always carried, to savor the lingering scent of the shaving soap he always used.

A porter passed, following a fussy little gray-haired lady and carrying two out-sized cases. When he came back a couple minutes later, Caroline grabbed his sleeve.

"Excuse me, sir. Could you help me, please? My husband's gotten off here in Colorado Springs," she said, smiling and trying to look a little bit flustered and altogether helpless.

"Yes?" said the porter.

"He's left his bag. Could you please take it to him? I have a dollar," she added when he seemed uninterested. "A whole silver dollar...if you'll help."

A couple minutes later he was climbing off the train with J.R.'s Gladstone in his hand and his gaze fixed on a solidly prosperous looking gentleman of fifty who was bustling toward the exit and whom Caroline had thoughtfully identified as the owner of the bag.

"It's my bag, I tell you, and I am *not* getting off the train!" J. Randolph glared at the porter, who wrapped his hands even tighter around the handles of his Gladstone and glared right back.

"The lady said as how it was her husband's bag and he was gettin' off the train. Supposed to take it to him, I was, and that's just what I'm doin'. Takin' it to him."

"*What* lady? What are you talking about?"

"That good-lookin' lady there." The porter cocked his head in the direction of J.R.'s car, but no woman could be seen through the windows, good-looking or otherwise. "Paid me a whole dollar. Wouldn't do that if it wasn't her husband's now, would she?"

The man, jaw pugnaciously set, started to walk away. J.R. grabbed him before he'd gone two steps, dragging him back despite his squawk of protest.

Something in J.R.'s face, in the cruelty of his grip, killed the porter's protest before it was out. J.R. could feel the muscles of his face drawing back, pulling his lips away from his teeth in a feral snarl. He couldn't stop them. All the long weeks of baffled fury and empty nights had coalesced into the here and now and Caroline's deliberate taunt.

"Did she tell you her name?" he demanded, giving the man a shake, needing to know for sure. "What did she look like?"

"P-p-pretty," the man got out. "I told you. Real pretty. Black hair. Dressed real nice, too. Elegant, like."

"I asked you, did she tell you her name?" J.R. insisted through clenched teeth, and shook him again. Dimly, as if from a great distance, he heard the conductor shouting, "All aboard!"

The porter shook his head. He was sweating now, his pugnacious defiance gone. "Didn't give me no name. Just said she was the fellow's wife and he'd left his bag."

"*My* bag," J.R. said.

"Yeah. Okay. Your bag."

"She's *my* wife."

"Sure. Sure. Whatever you say. Here. Take it. It's yours."

J.R. snatched the bag out of the porter's hand, then let the man go before he hit him. He really wanted to hit something. Had been wanting to hit something for weeks, now, ever since Caroline had locked his own front door against him.

Fighting against the growl rumbling in his throat, he plunged his hand into his pocket and pulled out another dollar.

"Here. Thanks for your trouble."

"Sure. No problem." Muttering and rubbing his arm, the porter scuttled out of reach.

J.R.'s glare sent the gathered onlookers about their business quick enough. But not quick enough for him to come back to his senses. The train was already picking up speed by the time he'd turned.

He cursed and dashed for the last car. He might

have made it if he hadn't spotted the woman leaning out a window six cars up.

"Caroline! Damn you!"

His roar of rage was swallowed in the bellow of the engine and the clatter of iron wheels rolling over iron rails.

His wife smiled, a smile as bright as the sun, and waved, then ducked back inside as the train—*his* train!—pulled out of the station, leaving him standing there with murder in his heart and a longing ache deep in his belly just from the sight of her.

Chapter Four

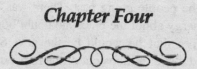

The main street of Cripple Creek ran downhill from the train station, shoving its way past fine brick buildings standing cheek-by-jowl with cruder wooden structures originally thrown up when the town began. The town, too unruly to confine itself to the streets that had been laid out with gridlike precision, spread out on either side, an untidy jumble of brick or clapboard houses, log cabins, and canvas-roofed shacks that sprawled up the hillsides and down the gulches when the streets no longer served.

In a couple of places, waste tips from the mines formed menacing walls of loose rock and dirt that loomed over the shanties built at their bases. Above the tips, like fine ladies too proud to see the dirt at their feet, stood the massive buildings that housed the hoists and ore crushers for the mines themselves.

The hills surrounding the town sprouted mines every hundred yards, or so it seemed. Rails for the electric trolley cars that ran to neighboring mining towns ran along the hills as naturally as if such things were commonplace.

Caroline stood on the station platform and stared and stared and stared, and had to remind herself to breathe.

Cripple Creek was nothing like Baltimore. It didn't even resemble Denver much except for the bustle and hurry of the people going past. There was an almost electric energy about the place, no doubt born of each man's hopes that he would be the next Stratton or Strong and make millions out of the rock he dug from the ground.

From this stew of hope and greed and hurry had come murder. Or what might be murder, Caroline reminded herself. Until the jury reached its verdict, Andrew "Andy" Osbald was only accused of murder, not convicted.

And she was going to be there to cover it.

J.R. didn't believe she could do it. Her father didn't believe she could do it. Even her editor didn't have much faith in her, but she'd show them. She'd show them all!

Her first real Adventure with a capital *A*.

Her heart pumped harder, just at the thought.

This was what she'd come west to find. Something different. Something challenging and rare. A chance to do things her way, with no servants to fetch and carry, and no man to open doors and carry her bags and treat her as if she couldn't lift a finger without his help. The first time in her life she'd ever been totally on her own, dependent on her own wits and resources, with no one to help her if those same wits and resources somehow came up lacking.

A chance to prove herself—to herself as well as to everyone else.

Before her suddenly wobbly knees gave out, Caroline collapsed on a trunk that had been abandoned on the platform. The sudden riot in her stomach and the pounding in her head blended perfectly with the battering racket around her.

She glanced at the schedule chalked on the blackboard hanging on the station wall, then at the small watch pinned to her purse. The next train back to Denver would be leaving in an hour and forty-seven minutes.

Her fingers curled around her purse, tight enough so she could feel the small lump of folded bills and the heavy coin purse in its depths. It was all the money she had in the world, the last bit left from the income from her trust fund before her father had stopped the payments. He'd refused to speak to her since. If J.R. hadn't still been paying for the house and Mrs. Priddy, she'd have been living on the street by now.

Caroline didn't have to count it; she knew to the penny how much was there—one hundred twenty-six dollars and seventy-three cents. A fortune to many, but a pittance compared to what she'd been used to having. There'd been a great deal more not long ago, but she'd spent most of it before she admitted that J.R. wasn't going to apologize and her father wasn't going to give in and that the only way she was going to get more was to earn it.

There was still more than enough to buy a ticket back to Denver if she wanted.

Right now, she wanted to go home about as badly as she'd ever wanted anything in her life.

What was she doing here? What in Heaven's name had possessed her to launch herself into a world where she didn't belong? She didn't know anything about reporting *real* events. All she'd ever covered were a few simpering ladies' teas. She had no credentials, no experience, and very nearly no money. What if she spent her small hoard and the *Times* refused to run her articles? Worse, what if she got things wrong? What if she made a fool of herself and got nothing at all?

That last thought made her sag. She'd already made a fool of herself when she raised that ill-bred stink about J.R.'s behavior. A lady would have ignored her husband's embarrassing little peccadilloes rather than make things worse by publicly kicking him out of the house. A lady would have dedicated her energies to ladylike good deeds rather than flinging herself into a dubious profession like newspaper reporting. A lady—

"*If* you don't mind?"

The angry query snapped Caroline out of her dark thoughts. She glanced up to find a stout, beetle-browed woman in brown glaring at her.

"I beg your pardon?"

"You're sitting on my trunk," said the woman. The very feathers on her hat trembled with indignation. Behind her, a porter rolled his eyes heavenward.

"Oh!" Caroline jumped up. "I'm sorry."

The porter immediately wheeled his hand cart up

beside the trunk, but the woman wasn't ready to call it quits.

"There are benches right over there," she said. "Perfectly good benches which you could have seen if you'd bothered to look."

"I didn't—"

"Sitting on a person's trunk, and without so much as a by-your-leave! Really! The manners of young people these days are simply appalling. I don't know what the world is coming to. Hoodlums in the streets and no respect for their elders and everyone here pushing and shoving and language that my dear father would have blushed to hear, and—"

"So, where do you want this, ma'am?" the porter asked, halting her tirade midrant.

The woman eyed him with as much dislike as she'd eyed Caroline. "This way."

The porter followed her without a word, but he threw Caroline a quick smile and a wink as he left.

The wink comforted her.

At the far end of the platform, the woman in brown was giving directions to the driver of a wagon while the porter loaded her trunk in the back. Caroline caught "Bonnard's Boardinghouse" and the sharp-toned murmur as the woman and driver haggled over the price.

Just the thought of having to haggle over the price of such basic transportation made Caroline's head ache more.

She'd have to arrange to have her trunk moved, but first she had to find a place to stay. And a place to eat, she silently added as her stomach grumbled in protest. She'd been too nervous to eat a proper breakfast, and she hadn't liked the looks of the sandwiches and dry rolls available to the third-class passengers on the train. Right now, a cup of hot tea sounded better than champagne.

Forcing down her doubts, she waved at a porter bustling past. He didn't even notice her.

"Sir?" she called to another, but a man with a family in tow snagged the fellow first.

"Pardon me?" The first porter, laden with luggage and headed in the opposite direction, zipped right on past.

The porter who'd winked at her was nowhere in sight. Not one of the men on the platform seemed to notice her plight, too engrossed in their own business to heed a stranger's problems.

The rude woman in brown hadn't had a problem getting someone to help, Caroline thought sourly as the first porter sailed by as if she were invisible. Whenever J.R. or her father snapped their fingers, obsequious servants poured out of the woodwork. Here, no one looked obsequious, and she might as well have been the woodwork for all the notice anyone took of her.

It wasn't at all what she was accustomed to.

Eventually she gave up and marched over to the ticket office. She couldn't think of anything else to do. Her head was pounding so hard it threatened to fall off.

"Sir?" she said. "Excuse me?"

The man behind the counter held up one finger but

didn't look up from counting a stack of shipping invoices. "Forty-eight, forty-nine, fifty, fifty-one." He slapped the last one down on the pile before glancing up. "Yes, ma'am? What can I do for you?"

"I need a porter and someplace to store my trunk and extra luggage for a few hours. I also need a cab—"

The fellow's eyebrows shot up. "A cab?"

"A hansom."

"Ain't none in Cripple."

"Then a buggy, or possibly a cart. *Something.*"

"Porter'll find yuh someone," he said, clearly losing interest. He turned back to his pile of papers.

"I can't find a porter." Caroline said, fighting to hold her temper.

"How can you miss 'em? Got a cap on, don't they? Just holler, they'll come."

Caroline stiffened. "I do not 'holler.'"

The man shrugged and would have turned away, but something in her expression stopped him. He eyed her for a moment, then sighed and, planting his palms on the counter, leaned forward and stuck his head out the opening.

"Ferdy!" he bellowed, making her jump.

The bustling porter—sans luggage this time—paused in his rush. "Yeah?"

The counterman cocked a thumb at Caroline. "Lady needs some help."

The porter's bristly mustache twitched. "I already got—"

"I have a trunk that needs storing," Caroline put in quickly, before he could run off. "And a valise.

And a bag. And I need a cab. A cart, I mean. Some- one to take me to a— To a boardinghouse.''

She'd almost said hotel, but her money wouldn't stretch that far.

Even to herself she sounded a little breathless. There was a tightness in her chest and her palms felt damp. If J.R. had been there right then, she would have thrown herself at his feet and begged for help and to hell with pride and independence.

She forced herself to take a steadying breath, then nodded toward a stack of luggage that had been dumped on one of the high-wheeled baggage carts, then abandoned at the far end of the platform.

''My trunk's the green one with the brass fittings,'' she added. ''The black valise is mine, as well, and the tapestry bag.''

The porter grumbled, but went to fetch a hand cart.

''Thank you,'' she said when he grudgingly slid her possessions off the cart and into a corner of the cramped station baggage room.

Instead of wheeling away, as she expected, he looked at her expectantly.

It took a moment for her brain to kick in. *He was waiting for his tip.*

She'd forgotten about the tipping.

Caroline swallowed. She'd never tipped anyone be- fore. Not so…so *openly.* Leaving a few extra coins by one's plate when one had tea in a proper restaurant wasn't the same sort of thing at all. The dollar she'd given to that porter in Colorado Springs had been payment for services rendered. It hadn't been a real *tip.*

The man pointedly stuck out his hand.

Blushing, she dug a quarter out of her purse and put it in his outstretched palm. Two bits, they called it out here. More than the cost of tea and toast in a good hotel in Baltimore.

He glared at it, then glared at her. A muscle at the side of his nose twitched, making his mustache jump.

Cheeks flaming hotter still, she dug into her purse again and pulled out a dime, then, after a glance at his face, another dime, then a nickel.

The mustache danced at a furious rate.

Throwing caution to the winds, she dropped two more quarters on that callused palm.

The porter grumbled, but his hand closed around the coins, then disappeared into his pocket. He didn't even bother to tip his cap respectfully as he walked away, still muttering.

Her face burning, Caroline watched him go. She was finding it hard to breathe. It was just her imagination that her purse seemed noticeably lighter, but a whole dollar for five minutes' surly service? At this rate, she'd be bankrupt in a week.

There was no cart or conveyance of any kind when she once more stepped out of the station. Fortunately, Cripple Creek wasn't so large she couldn't manage it on foot. The respectable parts, anyway. She wasn't going anywhere near those shanties unless she had to.

With her skirts delicately lifted out of the dust and a sharp eye peeled for the horse deposits—with all the wealth around here, you'd think the town could afford a couple more street sweepers—Caroline headed down Bennett Avenue.

Up close, Cripple Creek was a confusing mix of propriety and rugged boom town. Saloons were frequent, and well-frequented, yet the dry goods stores had the same merchandise in their front windows as similar stores in Denver and Baltimore. The grocers seemed to be doing a good business though the prices she saw when she peered in the window made her mouth drop open in shock. There were hotels, lawyers' offices, the telegraph office, banks, assay offices, and more hardware stores than she'd seen in one place in her life.

The people she passed looked like the sorts of folks she'd meet on the street in Denver any day of the week.

The town hadn't existed ten years ago and had endured two destructive fires a few years past, yet it had clearly settled in and looked as if it intended to stay. When she glanced down side streets she spotted neat houses with lace curtains in the windows, half a dozen churches, a school, and even a sign for a lending library.

Though she couldn't tell much difference between the two halves of the town, she'd been warned to keep to the streets on the north side of Bennett Avenue. South was Myers Avenue, a street infamous for its extensive selection of bordellos and seamier cribs. She wasn't exactly sure what a crib was if it didn't involve a baby, but she hadn't quite had the courage to ask.

Curious, Caroline studied the women she saw who'd ventured south of Bennett. A couple were overdressed and vulgarly loud, but most were respectably clothed and properly behaved—no doubt eminently respectable ladies going about their eminently respectable business. Many, she couldn't help noticing, were young, a few strikingly pretty.

It was the pretty ones who worried her.

Would J.R. see them? Want them? Would he buy their services if he did?

She didn't have anything to judge by except tales told by female friends who were probably as ignorant as she, but those four short months of married life had convinced her that her husband's appetite for sex was strong and varied.

"Call it sex, Caroline," he'd told her one night when they'd lain tangled together in the sheets. "It's fun that way. No pretenses, no lies. One of those gifts we took with us when we got kicked out of Eden. I *want* you to enjoy it."

He'd grinned, then, that devilishly tempting grin of his that always made her bones turn to water, and nipped at her exposed nipple. "God knows *I* do."

She wished she'd asked him where love was in all of it, but she'd forgotten in the heat.

Was it possible for a man like him to go without a woman for this long? Had he even tried?

They were questions she'd tried hard to suppress, just as she tried not to think of what, exactly, he'd been doing in that Denver brothel the night the police raided it.

It didn't help any that *she'd* been suffering the torments of the damned, wanting him. Everything she'd been taught said women weren't subject to the baser, animal needs that drove men, but four months of abstinence had proved that particular bit of "wisdom" was flat-out wrong.

A tall, dark-haired man strode past, catching her eye. He wasn't as handsome as J.R., and he didn't move with the same arrogant confidence, but the resemblance was there.

A stab of longing shot through her, so sharp and hot it made her stagger. Longing, and a twinge of guilt for the dirty trick she'd played on him this morning.

Caroline grimaced, shifted her grip on her purse, and forced herself to keep walking. Damn J.R., anyway! He'd survive the trick, but she wasn't sure she'd survive her need for him. If she ever gave in to his demands that she abandon this quest, it would be because she couldn't endure another minute of self-denial.

And if she gave in because of *that*, she'd never forgive either one of them.

The noise and bustle of Colorado Springs' busiest train station swirled around J.R. unnoticed. He was too engrossed in the dozen vivid, dangerous fantasies that were chasing each other through his head to care about the rest of the world.

They were really wonderful fantasies.

Caroline, anxious and eager to please, serving him his coffee in the morning and buttering his toast and jumping whenever he so much as looked her way.

Caroline, repentant and eager to please, demurely seated at his feet while he lectured her on the behavior appropriate to his wife and speaking not a word except "yes, dear," and "no, dear," and "whatever you say, dear," in the very meekest of voices.

No! Caroline, cringing and pathetically eager to please, down on her hands and knees polishing his boots while he stood over her with a whip in his hand, scowling fiercely.

He closed his eyes, savoring the feeling. He especially liked the touch of the whip.

Another image hit him, of Caroline, hungry and *very* eager to please, naked in his bed.

His gut clenched at the thought.

Cursing, he forced the fantasies away.

It was the abstinence that was doing him in. Which was all Caroline's fault, dammit! He'd tried—three separate times!—to ease the pain with visits to that luscious, cherry-lipped blonde in Lil's bawdy house on Larimer Street. Every time, he'd come up short. Or, rather, he hadn't come up at all.

The blonde had been soothing and sweet and understanding. She'd tried all the considerable tricks in her repertoire to remedy the problem. Nothing worked. She wasn't Caroline and that was all there was to it.

The whistle of the waiting train shattered his thoughts.

J.R. straightened, sudden determination stiffening his spine. Four hours of waiting for another train added to four months of waiting for his wife to come to her senses was too damn much. Caroline was going to pay for this, by God, she was!

Gladstone in hand, he leapt onto the train. The sooner he got to Cripple Creek, the sooner he could settle this. Enough was enough. It was long past time that he was back home and Caroline was naked in his bed where she belonged, and he was going to see that she was, or his name wasn't J. Randolph Abbott, III!

Chapter Five

Caroline took tea at the best hotel in town, the National—fifteen cents a cup, no toast included—and refused to admit, even to herself, that she was grateful for the familiar surroundings of a well-appointed, well-run establishment, even if she couldn't afford a room there.

Refortified, and with the throbbing in her head subdued to a dull ache, she pulled out the little black journal in which she'd made notes to herself and turned to the short list of respectable boardinghouses that people at the *Times* had recommended.

It was a very short list. She'd never in her life even thought about taking lodging in a boardinghouse, but this was all part of the Adventure. She'd visit the three establishments, inspect the rooms, and choose the one offering the best food, most comfortable accommodations, and the most congenial, well-bred company. How hard could it possibly be?

The first place on the list, Mrs. James's, was full. Uncomfortably aware of the landlady's curious stare, Caroline set off for the second. Just as well there'd been no space, she told herself. The place hadn't been at all prepossessing—the parlor was tiny and the smell of boiled cabbage pervaded everything. She detested boiled cabbage.

The second establishment was full, as well, and there the red-faced proprietress, Hilda Gooding, didn't even bother to apologize—she just slammed the door in her face. For a moment, Caroline stood on the step, mouth gaping at the appalling rudeness.

The five-block walk to the last place on her list seemed ten times longer. Her head throbbed, her corset pinched, and her high-heeled button shoes made her feet hurt. The energizing effects of the tea were rapidly wearing off.

With every aching step she took, she wondered what madness had made her think she could do this.

A two-year-old could manage better than she had. She was insulted by strangers and ignored by porters and ticket clerks. She couldn't afford tea in a decent hotel, couldn't get a cab or even a cart, and now she was being rejected by women whose manners would have gotten them fired as laundry maid in her mother's house. All that was left was to be run over in the street and her misery would be complete.

The red-faced woman running the last establishment on the list, Mrs. Grant, didn't even bother opening the front door of what the sign identified as Ida Grant's Boardinghouse for Respectable Ladies and Non-Smoking Gentlemen, First Week in Advance. She just flung open a window on the second floor and stuck her head out.

"No rooms, and it's no use you insisting or offering me more," she announced before Caroline could get a word out. "When there's no rooms there's no rooms, no matter how much you're willing to pay. Wish there was."

She was about to slam the window down when Caroline, desperate, called, "No! Wait! *Please.*"

The woman hesitated.

"Can you recommend another establishment, ma'am? My friends in Denver said this was the place to come"—she deliberately didn't mention the two boardinghouses she'd visited first—"but if you're full..." She drew in a steadying breath, fighting against the quaver she could hear at the edge of her voice. "Surely *you* can tell me what else might be available that's suitable for a lady?"

Not for nothing had she served on a dozen different charity and social committees, Caroline thought grimly, seeing the woman's stern expression soften.

"Well..." Mrs. Grant frowned. "Mrs. James is full up, too, so I guess that leaves Mrs. Bonnard. Not so fine as my house, mind, and she ain't the best cook around, but it's clean and decent and oughta serve. Three blocks up, two over," she added, pointing. "You can't miss it."

Bonnard's. The destination of the ill-tempered lady in brown. Caroline tried not to let her disappointment show. "Thank you. You're most kind."

She was turning away when Mrs. Grant flung open the window again and leaned out to add, "Don't let anyone talk you into trying Hilda Gooding's house!

With what she charges and the puny meals she serves, that woman'll rob you blind. And I wouldn't trust her cleaning three inches past the front door, neither!''

Caroline nodded and waved her thanks. The tiny triumph of having gotten around the woman's bad temper helped her navigate the three blocks up, two blocks over with a little more enthusiasm than she'd managed the previous ones.

Still, she was red-faced and panting by the time she spotted the clumsily painted sign posted on the picket fence—Bonnard's Boardinghouse, Good and Cheap. Caroline gratefully stopped to catch her breath and mop her brow, and wondered if Mrs. Bonnard knew that there was more than one way to interpret the message on her sign.

The house was two stories of weather-grayed wood shoehorned between two more prosperous-looking buildings. But if paint was lacking, at least the windows shone and the lace curtains looked properly starched and ironed. It was the bright pink geraniums in pots on the front porch that decided her.

Caroline tucked her now damp and rather dirty handkerchief back in her purse, patted her hair to make sure it was still decently tucked under her hat, and started up the crooked steps that led to the front porch.

At the sight of the short, stout lady who eventually answered her knock, Caroline almost backed right off the porch. Except that she was dressed all in green, not brown, the woman was the spitting image of the lady from the train station.

She fumbled at the latch, then swung the screen door wide, blinking vaguely at the light. "Yes, dear?"

"Mrs. Bonnard?"

"That's right. You've come about a room, I suppose?"

"Mrs. Grant thought you might have one available."

"Oh, dear. Sister's just come home and we're in a bit of a confusion at the moment, but..." The woman's words trailed off doubtfully. She glanced over her shoulder nervously, back into the shadowy depths of the house.

"You do have a room, then?" Caroline tried to keep the eagerness out of her voice. At this point, even the lingering smell of boiled cabbage would be preferable to more traipsing up and down Cripple Creek's hilly streets. Fortunately, what little she could see of the parlor behind Mrs. Bonnard looked clean, if spare and rather shabby.

"It's a very *small* room," said the woman, even more doubtfully, "and not at all fancy. I don't think... I'm not sure... Sister handles that sort of thing and..."

Did the woman ever finish more than one sentence in five?

"Georgianne?" someone called from the back of the house. A moment later, the lady from the train station marched into the parlor. At the sight of Caroline, she stopped dead. "You!"

Caroline winced. "Ma'am."

"*You* were rude."

Like a plump green wraith, Mrs. Bonnard shrank

into the shadows, leaving her sister in charge of guarding the portals.

Caroline straightened. "I was tired and...and a little overwhelmed," she admitted. "I did apologize."

"The lady is looking for a room, Elizabeth," Mrs. Bonnard said rather timidly. She gave Caroline a hesitant smile. "She seems very nice."

The grim woman in brown inspected Caroline from the top of her expensive hat to the toes of her very dusty, expensive shoes. Her gaze came to rest on the diamond ring on Caroline's left hand. Her eyes narrowed. "You're married? Where's your husband, then?"

She should have planned for this, Caroline thought. She should have known someone would ask and have had an answer ready. "He— He's not here."

"Walked out on you, did he?"

Caroline's chin came up at that. She drew herself up to her full five feet six inches in her stocking feet, which was more than enough to tower over the two sisters. "*I* locked *him* out of the house and haven't let him back in since."

For the first time, a smile brightened the dour features. "Did you?" She craned forward, avid for more. "Was it drink? Or did you catch him with a fancy woman?"

Caroline's back stiffened, adding another half inch to her height. "I don't discuss that sort of thing with strangers."

The woman's smile widened. "That's putting me in my place!" She shoved the screen door farther open and stepped aside. "Well, come in, then, and quit letting in the flies."

By the time he finally got into Cripple Creek—four hours later than he'd planned—J.R.'s temper had cooled from explosive to a mere simmering boil.

A man who knew his way around, he didn't waste time looking for a cab, just grabbed his Gladstone and strode off down Bennett Avenue toward the only hotel in town worthy of the name. The National, Cripple Creek's finest, was every bit as luxurious as Denver's best. He hadn't even considered staying anywhere else, and he was sure Caroline wouldn't, either. Knowing her and the fifteen trunks she'd come west with, she would have arrived in state.

But she hadn't. When he asked, the clerk at the front desk simply looked at him blankly.

"Mrs. Abbott, sir? Was she expected, too?" The fellow paled a little under his tan. The National wasn't supposed to lose a reservation, much less a wealthy guest's wife. He hastily checked the register. "I don't see her name here, sir."

J.R. wasn't quite sure how to answer that. It had been hard enough to ask in the first place. A man generally didn't have to stoop to asking hotel clerks for the whereabouts of his own wife.

Or could she have—? No, surely not. She wouldn't. Would she?

He gritted his teeth. "How about Caroline Rhodes? Has a lady of that name arrived?"

The clerk shook his head. "No, sir, Mr. Abbott. I'm sorry. But I'll certainly be on the lookout if we get a call from either lady and let you know first thing.''

Either lady. What a perfect summation of his situation, J.R. thought grimly, following the bellhop carrying his Gladstone. He'd fallen in love with one woman only to find himself married to another, entirely. And damned if he could figure out when the transformation had occurred or why.

Something of his thoughts must have shown on his face for the bellhop kept his eyes glued to the elevator controls as they slowly rose to the second floor, then scurried down the hall to fling open the door to his room.

''There's a telephone down the hall, sir,'' the fellow informed him proudly. ''We've an operator on duty till nine, when the night clerk takes over. Service bell's right here, case you want anything. Private bath's through that door there. Hot water, twenty-four hours a day, yessir. Electric lights is—er—''

The rest of his spiel died under J.R.'s withering glance.

J.R. flipped him a half dollar, then stalked over to the window and raised the curtain to look out at the street below. He didn't even notice when the man scuttled out of the room, drawing the door shut behind him.

Where was she? She had to have been headed here. Broxman from the *Times* had told him about the deal she'd worked out with her editor. It was a ludicrous notion, of course, reporting on the women's view of the case, but it was exactly the sort of harebrained idea that would have sent her off, hell-bent to prove him and every other male in the universe wrong.

As for tossing his luggage off the train… He could almost—almost—forgive her for it. That was the sort of under-handed trick that insecure, incompetent, greenhorn journalists used all the time to get a jump on their rivals. *He'd* never stooped that low, but he could understand if she'd felt she had to.

In a way, it even gave him an edge. Guilt, shame, insecurity—eventually they'd force her to her senses. *Something* had to!

But where in the hell *was* she? She should have been here long before now. There wasn't another hotel in town of this quality, certainly nothing that the pampered daughter of the Baltimore Rhodes would have found acceptable. So why hadn't she checked in?

Had she, perhaps, turned around and gone home? Had she finally realized that crime reporting wasn't the sort of thing a respectable married woman would ever consider doing?

J.R. let the curtain drop and turned back to the room with a curse. He wished he could believe Caroline had been stricken with a sudden attack of good sense, but he knew damned well that hadn't happened. Once his bullheaded wife got her teeth in something, she didn't let go until she'd chewed it up…or been chewed up by it.

Caroline Rhodes Abbott was here in Cripple Creek. But where?

Her first installment!
Caroline rubbed her gloved hands together in sat-

isfaction as she surveyed the street outside the telegraph office. It would have been nice if J.R. had been
lurking somewhere close so he could see her elation,
so he would know from her proud mien and the confident glint in her eye that she had begun.

Mr. Blackmun would accept the article she'd just
sent him. Bound to. He certainly wasn't going to get
anything like it from Murray, even assuming Murray
would emerge from whatever saloon he was patron-
izing for long enough to write anything at all.

Granted, it wasn't much. Just an overview of this
upcoming trial, taken from the women's point of
view. Well, her landlady and her landlady's sister's
point of view. Given the differences between meek
little Georgianne and bluff, opinionated Elizabeth, she
figured she'd gotten a pretty good general take on the
subject.

Not that she'd admitted she'd only interviewed two
ladies, of course. Not in print! No, she'd given a
rather sweeping tone to the piece, a majestic, almost
godlike view of what it meant when one man shot
another. The lady readers of the *Times* would love it.

Now the question was, when could she expect payment? She usually received payment for her society
pieces the Friday of the week after publication, which
usually meant at least two weeks from submission,
often longer. But Blackmun would use this right
away—he'd have to!—and he knew she was depending on prompt payment to cover her expenses. She'd
told him so, though she'd stressed it was business,
not need, that made her insist. She didn't know if he'd

believed her, but after much haggling, he'd finally agreed that for *this* story he'd send her a check as soon as he had a piece from her. Which would make it only a week later than she deserved, Caroline thought sourly.

Oblivious to the press of people going past and the protest of her much-abused feet, which weren't used to so much walking, she calculated her earnings. Halfpenny a word, four hundred fifty words, came to two dollars and twenty-five cents minus the telegram at one ninety-five—an outrageous charge!—which left... *thirty cents?*

Caroline blinked, then hastily recalculated, brow furrowing at the mental math. Thirty cents, and not a penny more.

Her shoulders drooped. Thirty cents was barely enough to buy a meal at a decent restaurant, let alone pay for her room or the train to get here.

She shifted uncomfortably. For the first time she wished she'd spent more time calculating her likely expenses and earnings and not so much figuring her strategy.

Not that she needed to worry! Halfpenny a word was her society pages rate. This article might not hit the front page of the *Times,* or even the second or third, but it would be published. It would not only be published, it would attract notice, which would lead to the second or third article, at the least, moving up to more exalted regions. By the time she got to the meat of the trial, she ought to be getting second page placement at the least, and *that* would earn her two, possibly even three cents a word or she'd know the reason why! A Rhodes did not settle for less than the best, regardless.

Something fierce must have shown in her face for a gentleman passing in the street before her nervously tipped his hat, then hastily put another three feet between himself and the boardwalk where she stood.

Caroline felt a little charge of power as she watched his rapidly departing back. *That's* what she wanted! To make people realize that she was a force to be reckoned with. To have them respect her and, maybe, be just a little bit afraid of what she could do.

J.R. might not understand, but once he saw that the rest of the world admired her work, he'd come round. He'd have to. She was his wife, after all, and he was her husband. They'd been joined together before God, their families, and Baltimore's snobbiest elite, which meant that neither his pride nor her ambitions could split them asunder. She wouldn't let them.

But first, she'd make sure she staked out her right to independence on the same firm ground where he'd staked his.

Taking a deep breath, she squared her shoulders, tugged her jacket into place, and stepped off the wooden walk.

Next stop, the courthouse, to secure her admission to the trial.

"Yes, Mr. Abbott, I'm fully aware of your reputation and your position with the *Tribune,* but neither is sufficient to guarantee you a front row seat at the trial. Best I can do is that press pass, there. So many of you folk in town, I'm not sure there'll even be enough of those to go around.''

J.R. counted to three. Then he counted to ten. Then he slowly let out the breath he'd been holding and gave the persnickety little clerk a curt nod. There were other ways to get what he wanted. ''All right. Thank you for your time.''

''Not at all, Mr. Abbott. Just doing my job.'' The little worm looked rather pleased with himself, which didn't help his mood any.

''I'll try to remember that,'' J.R. said dryly. He turned to leave, and almost ran over his wife.

''Of all the—!'' Caroline stopped dead. ''You!''

J.R. shut his eyes against the sight of her and gave a silent curse. It was that kind of day.

''What are *you* doing here?''

Even edged with anger and the tiniest touch of fear, her voice had the power to make his blood heat.

He swore again, with more feeling this time, then forced his eyes open. ''Caroline.'' He donned a smile that wouldn't fool her for a minute. ''So nice to see you.''

She eyed him warily.

A hot, bright burst of sexual hunger almost made him stagger. Damned if he'd let her see it, though.

Arrogantly, deliberately rude, he let his gaze skim down the length of her. Because he knew it would annoy her, he allowed himself a small smile of satisfaction.

To the casual observer, she looked neat, well-dressed, slightly dusty, and elegantly reserved. To his more familiar eye she looked tired, stressed, and he'd bet her feet were killing her. She'd always had a fondness for pretty, frivolous, high-heeled shoes. It wouldn't have occurred to her to choose more practical shoes for a tramp around a mountain mining town. Not until it was too late.

It would have been worse if she'd spent four extra hours standing on the platform in that damned train station in the Springs.

His smile widened. He owed her for that one.

Caroline retreated half a step. She could read the warning in that smile even if no one else could.

"I see you arrived safely," he purred.

Her throat worked as she swallowed down her nerves.

"I, on the other hand, ran into a little delay," he continued. Still purring, still smiling. "Problems with my luggage. A trifling matter but rather…ah…rather annoying."

"Really?" The word seemed to catch in her throat.

"Yes. A silly trick, the sort that ignorant neophytes resort to in the mistaken assumption that it helps their cause by delaying the competition."

That stung. She stiffened. Her mouth thinned into a prissy, disapproving line. "Indeed?"

His smile turned to one of satisfaction. "Oh, yes. Of course, they couldn't be more wrong. It only makes the experienced man all that much more determined to win."

"Bully for him."

"Indeed," he said, mimicking her as he leaned closer in the sort of friendly, intimate gesture a man could use with his wife, even in public.

She arched back and away, too stubborn to shift her feet but clearly unsettled by his nearness.

He couldn't decide whether that pleased him, or made him mad as hell. Reluctantly, he pulled back.

The blush stealing up her throat definitely pleased him until he looked up to find the clerk blinking owlishly back at them.

Glowering, J.R. backed away.

"If you'll excuse me," Caroline said, coolly slipping past him. She marched up to the clerk's desk. "Good afternoon, sir. I was wondering if you could help me."

The clerk shoved his spectacles up his nose and beamed at her. "I'll certainly do my best, ma'am."

J.R.'s glower darkened. He strolled over and, despite the clerk's pointed disapproval, propped his hip on the edge of the desk, determined to enjoy what followed.

Skin pricking at his nearness, Caroline tried to pretend he didn't exist. If she'd had a lick of sense, as Mrs. Priddy was forever telling her she hadn't, she'd have walked right back out the door the moment she'd spotted him. But she hadn't and now here she was, stuck.

She had the most horrifying urge to throw herself at him, to straddle that leg he'd propped on the edge of the desk and rub—

Face flaming, she forced herself to concentrate on the clerk.

"I'm Caroline Abbott and—"

"Abbott?" The clerk sat up a little straighter, his

sharp gaze flicking between the two of them. "*Mrs.* Abbott?"

"Well, yes, but I—"

"She's from the *Times*," J.R. offered helpfully.

Caroline frowned at him. He gave her a smile as blandly polite as it was annoying.

"You're a reporter?" Judging from the expression on the clerk's face, that lowered her a notch or two in his estimation.

She nodded. "That's right. I—"

"We don't get too many women reporters." Clearly a good thing in the clerk's opinion.

"There aren't many of us," Caroline said, bristling. "But I—"

"And you said you were with the *Tribune*," the clerk added, turning an accusing glare on J.R.

"I am."

"He doesn't have anything to do with this," Caroline snapped.

"His name's Abbott, isn't it?"

"Yes, but—"

"And your name's Abbott?"

"That's right, but—"

"She wants a front row seat, too," said J.R., ever helpful.

Caroline repressed the urge to kick him in the shins.

The clerk's mouth pinched into a disapproving frown. "No guarantees, front row or otherwise."

"But—"

"Not even for a pretty little lady like this?" J.R. asked.

"Will you stop that!"

He tried to look hurt. "Just trying to be helpful."

"Well don't. You aren't. And don't look at me like that. You don't fool me!"

"How do I look?"

Wonderful. "Like a puppy dog that's been kicked."

"You've nailed it! That's exactly how I feel. Like a puppy dog that's been kicked. A really nice, lovable puppy dog that didn't deserve to be kicked."

The clerk cleared his throat. They both ignored him.

"You've never felt that way in your life."

"Not before I met you, no, but afterwards…"

"Hah!"

"You see?" This appeal was directed at the clerk, who was watching them with a sort of befuddled horror. "This is what I have to contend with. Insults. Mockery. Lack of respect."

J.R. heaved a mournful sigh and turned a pleading look toward heaven. "It's enough to drive a man to drink."

The clerk nodded in shared masculine sympathy.

Caroline instinctively noted the simple gold band on the man's left ring finger, then wished she hadn't looked. J.R. had refused to wear a ring. His father hadn't worn one, he'd said, and neither had his grandfather. And he, he'd said, was sticking to family tradition. No ring. His refusal had never bothered Caroline…until now.

"Speaking of a drink…" J.R. slid off the desk. "I'm thinking it's about time to have one." He extended his hand to the clerk, who shook it without thinking. "You ever get free, just let me know. I'll buy you one myself."

"Well, I—uh—" the clerk faltered, blushing.

"I'll bet you've got a few good tales to tell," J.R. said heartily. "Man in your position's bound to know where all the bodies are buried."

"I can't talk about—that is—"

"Of course you can't! Doesn't stop you from sharing a drink and swapping lies, now, does it?"

The fellow relaxed, his professional scruples effectively scuttled by J.R.'s devious flattery. "That's mighty nice of you, Mr. Abbott. I just might take you up on the offer some day."

J.R. grinned, every man's best friend.

Caroline fumed and vowed revenge. She couldn't play the good-old-boy, buy-you-a-drink card, and J.R. knew it. Was rubbing her face in it, in fact.

"Guess we've taken up enough of your time," J.R. added, wrapping his arm around her shoulder. "Besides, the missus and I need to get going."

Her squawk of protest was stifled against the fine wool of his waistcoat.

He winked, making the clerk blush again, then adroitly steered her out the door and down the courthouse steps.

She was so befuddled at the feel of his body pressed against her, at the male heat and smell of him and the weight of his arm on her shoulders that she couldn't think, let alone speak. Four months without him was three months and thirty days too long.

Once out on the street, he set her free. Reluctantly?

Caroline couldn't tell. Flustered, she shook out her skirts and tugged her jacket into place. Her whole body ached for what she'd been denied so long. Her feet, she realized suddenly, were killing her.

He leaned closer, his eyes suddenly gone dark and soft with concern. "What's the matter?"

She pulled herself up straight and tall but couldn't quite bring herself to look him in the eye. Sharp-eyed devil that he was, he'd know exactly what she was feeling if she did, and she didn't dare risk that.

"Nothing's the matter. Absolutely nothing. What makes you think something's the matter?"

"Your mouth's gone all pinched and tight, as if something hurts and you don't want to admit it."

"Ridiculous."

"You want me, don't you?"

"Hah!"

"Of course you do. You can't help it." He studied her, smug as only a handsome man could be. "Are your stays too tight?"

"*What?*"

"Your shoes?"

She glared. If her feet hadn't hurt so much, she'd have kicked him.

For a moment he just stared at her with that sharp-eyed, assessing look that made her tremble. Then the corner of his mouth curled upward in a knowing smirk that made her hand itch to slap him and her mouth want to kiss him.

"It *is* the shoes, isn't it?" The smirk turned into a dangerous smile. "I thought so, right from the start." He laughed, then leaned closer.

"First thing a good reporter learns, Caroline," he said in a soft, intimate voice that should have been outlawed anyplace but the bedroom, "is to buy good, solid, comfortable shoes, and to hell with high fashion."

She eyed him with disdain. "Your advice, Mr. Abbott, is always so edifying."

It wasn't easy to restrain herself, but she pointedly didn't slap him. He grinned, then, a knowing grin that said he knew exactly what she really wanted to do, and dared her to try.

It took all the courage she had not to limp as she walked away.

She was halfway down the block before she realized he'd waltzed her out of that courthouse before she'd had a chance to get her press pass to the trial. She stopped, whirled back, and found the bastard leaning against the hitching rail in front of the courthouse, arms crossed over his chest, watching her.

Their eyes met and held for an instant. He grinned and mockingly doffed his hat.

He knew! He knew exactly what she'd forgotten. He'd deliberately distracted her so she *would* forget.

If the world were just and she had any say in the matter, he'd shrivel into a greasy spot on the road, right then and there.

Chapter Six

J.R. hit Johnny Nolon's famous saloon a quarter of an hour later. The whiskey there was always good, the conversation better, and this time of the afternoon there was a motley assortment of miners, traveling salesmen, businessmen, and hangers-on that made for lively discussion. As he'd expected, most of the talk ran to the trial that would start day after tomorrow.

"Guilty as hell," one elegantly-clad businessman opined. "Osbald and his friends had been arguing with Walker for months over that boundary between their claims, and just where that vein of gold started, and which way it ran."

"Longer'n that," a bearded fellow in a shabby suit objected. "Those two hated each other since before they got started here at Cripple. Walker swears Osbald cheated him in a business deal in Denver years ago."

"It was his temper did Walker in," the beard said. "That man in a rage would make a sore-footed grizzly look sweet natured, an' there's no denyin' he was in a rage that night. I saw 'im stompin' down the street toward Osbald's saloon. If Osbald hadn't shot 'im, it would've been Walker on trial for murder, not the other way around.''

"Woman trouble?" someone asked.

Several shrugs around the room.

"Could be," the bearded fellow admitted. "Them two were both eyein' that Dolly James down at Belle's.''

A murmur of appreciation rolled around the room. Miss James, it seemed, had been making a name for herself among the town's fallen angels.

"Walker always was a man for the ladies."

"And a nose for gold."

"You think he really blew up his own mine a couple years ago when he was havin' all that problem with the men workin' for him who wanted to go union?''

"Crazy."

"No way."

"Could have." The well-dressed businessman shrugged. "Sometimes you take a loss to make a bigger stake. And he came out of that smelling damned sweet, didn't he?''

"That's 'cause he grabbed that vein of gold that Osbald swore was his by rights.''

"Walker won in court on that one."

"Doesn't mean Osbald didn't keep on thinkin' it was his...and holdin' a grudge because of it.''

"So you think Osbald really did murder Walker? Used the fact that everyone knew Walker was mad as hell to say it was self-defense when it wasn't?''

No one could agree. As far as J.R. could tell, the

assemblage divided pretty evenly among those who thought Osbald was guilty, those who thought he was innocent, and those who couldn't decide, one way or the other.

But even as he listened and made mental notes, his thoughts insisted on straying.

No, not straying. They went straight as an arrow to the torment that had consumed him for months—his obstinate, wrong-headed, beautiful wife.

God, she'd looked good! Even tired, dusty, and footsore, she'd outshone every woman of his acquaintance. She was in way over her head here and clearly bound for trouble, but nothing he could say was going to convince her to give up and come home. Or, rather, to let him come home.

J.R. grimaced at the whiskey in his glass.

Maybe it was a good thing she'd launched herself into this. Maybe this would prove to her that being a newspaper reporter wasn't always as exciting or as satisfying as she thought it was. Maybe getting a few blisters on her feet and a few doors slammed in her face would make her realize that she deserved better, and that he'd gladly give it to her if only she'd let him.

Damned if he could figure why she wouldn't let him.

The scraping of a chair being pulled back from his table dragged J.R.'s attention back to the present. A burly, black-haired fellow plunked a half-full glass of whiskey on the table in front of the chair.

"Mind if I join you?" he said, and sat without waiting for an answer.

"Hell, yes, I mind," J.R. said genially. "No *Tribune* man would ever consort with one of you dregs from the *Times* if he didn't have to."

"Yeah, it's the devil, ain't it, havin' your nose rubbed in it, time after time. We got you boys licked ten ways to breakfast, but you're too dumb to know it."

"Tell me, Murray, were you born this way, or is it the years with that scandalmongering rag you call a newspaper that makes you so full of bull?"

Murray flashed him a toothy grin, then raised his glass in salute. "Here's to you."

"And you," J.R. said, lifting his glass in matching salute.

"So," Murray said at last, setting his empty glass down with a thump. "What do you make of the talk? Guilty? Or not?"

"Damned if I know," J.R. admitted. Truth to tell, he didn't really care. He'd taken the assignment because he wanted to get out of Denver and away from Caroline, and look how well that had served. "What do you think?"

Murray shrugged. "Two rich guys hate each other's guts. One ends up killing the other, but it could easily have gone the other way and nobody would've been surprised."

"Or cared."

Murray nodded. "Or cared." His gaze fell on his empty glass. "Still and all, this sort of thing keeps me in whiskey, so I'm not complaining. Much."

He caught the waiter's eye and held up his glass. Reassured a refill was on its way, he set the glass down and fixed J.R. with a sharp look. "I'm not too happy about your wife, though. Newspaper reporting—*real* newspaper reporting—is no work for a woman."

"Not the way you do it, no." J.R. sipped his whiskey, scanned the room. He didn't meet Murray's challenging gaze.

"Given the way those mine owners' bully boys beat the hell out of you that last time, I wouldn't think you'd let her."

J.R. grimaced and kept silent.

"Course, the way I heard it—" Murray grabbed the half-full whiskey bottle from the waiter who appeared at his elbow, then casually waved the man away. He poured a tot, squinted at the glass, then poured a little more.

"Way I heard it," he continued at last, setting the bottle down, "is you don't have much say these days. Not in what your wife does, at any rate."

J.R. snorted dismissively. "Does any man?"

Murray grinned. "Not so's you could notice. Not unless he keeps her barefoot and beats her regular."

"I've met your wife. She didn't strike me as much abused, or much inclined to take orders—from you or any man."

"No, my missus ain't one to take orders, but she hasn't locked me out of my own house or come harin' up to Cripple to do a man's job, either."

"What?" J.R. feigned astonishment. "Don't tell me you've taken to writing for the ladies' pages, Murray! Damn, man! I had no idea things had gotten so bad there at the *Times* that they'd have *you* covering society teas.''

''Hah, hah.'' Murray's expression hardened. His eyes narrowed to slits. ''I'm tellin' you, Abbott. Watch your wife. This ain't the place for her to be tryin' to wear your drawers.''

J.R. frowned at his glass, then picked it up, tossed back the rest of the whiskey, and gracefully got to his feet. He slapped a silver dollar down on the table, then, hand covering the coin, leaned forward so his face was only inches from the other reporter's.

''Just a friendly word of warning, Murray,'' he said, low, so no one else would hear. His smile had nothing friendly in it. ''Anything happens to my wife, I'll hold you personally responsible. Got that? *Anything.*''

He was halfway across the room when Murray called, ''Thanks for the whiskey, Abbott.'' The *Times* reporter mockingly flipped the silver dollar in the air, then pocketed it neatly.

J.R. touched the brim of his hat in a mocking salute, then turned and strode out of Nolon's.

Shifting uncomfortably on her weary feet, Caroline pulled out her little black book and checked her notes.

She'd tramped over half of Cripple Creek this afternoon, even venturing south of Bennett for a quick peep at Myers Avenue and the bordellos there. In the course of her wanderings, she'd learned a lot about the town and the people in it, but almost nothing that she could use for an article for the *Times*. Not that she'd expected to, of course, but still, it would have been nice to have a little extra for Mr. Blackmun. Something interesting that would catch a reader's eye and help build her name.

Not that it mattered. In a few hours she'd have all the story she needed. Mary Dodge Walker, Boston socialite and widow of the late Josiah Walker, had remained in Cripple Creek in the big brick house her mine-owning husband had built for her on their marriage.

Caroline frowned at the scribbled address, then at the street signs above her. No one had gotten in to talk to Mrs. Walker or get her thoughts on her husband's killing, but *she* would. Mary Walker might ignore the uncouth, prying busybodies who had approached her before, but she wouldn't ignore a lady who came from the same society background. The Dodges had been staunch pillars of Boston society, the Rhodes bred to Baltimore's upper crust, but a lady knew another lady when they met.

Mary Walker would talk to her. Caroline was sure of it. And when she did, she, Caroline, would have all the makings of a story that would make the people of Denver and the West sit up and take notice.

With one last check to get her bearings, Caroline tucked her little black book in her purse and set off up the hill to the Walker house.

J.R. caught up with his wife on one of the finer residential streets above Bennett Avenue. Or, rather, he spotted her hesitating in front of a tall, impressive brick house that stood on the hill above town. Because he was curious about her reason for being there, and because he wasn't sure what he'd say to her, he decided to keep back to see what she was up to.

The house, he had to admit, was impressive. Neatly tucked behind its wrought-iron fence and with its windows glinting in the light from the westering sun, the place looked as if it didn't quite belong in this upstart town, like a high-bred lady who didn't think much of her neighbors but was much too well-mannered to come right out and say it.

It looked like exactly the sort of place Caroline had grown up in, the sort of place half her friends in Baltimore and Denver owned. That is, if they didn't own something even grander. She should have felt right at home here, the last person he would have expected to be cowed by such elegance.

Yet something was holding her back. Twice she reached out to unlatch the gate, and twice she snatched her hand away as if the iron was too hot to touch. She didn't try a third time, just turned and walked quickly away.

Bemused, J.R. waited until he was sure she wouldn't look back, then stuck his hands in his pockets and sauntered after her.

Like her, he paused at the gate. His eyebrows rose at the small brass plaque mounted there. Walker, it said, each letter sharply etched in the gleaming brass.

J.R. glanced at the house, then down the street at the rapidly dwindling form of his wife, and smiled.

So Caroline Abbott was nervous, was she? Not quite ready to face her first big interview with a potentially hostile subject?

His smile widened. That was good. That was very good.

He was whistling as he set off down the hill after her.

Ninety-five cents for a large porterhouse steak with fresh asparagus, baked potato, and coffee. Dessert extra. A dollar ten for beef tips and mushrooms in a pastry crust, almond green beans, and coffee. Dessert extra. Seventy-five cents for pot roast and coffee. Dessert still extra.

Caroline stared at the bill of fare posted in the display case mounted to the left of the National's front door. The setting sun caught the glass at an angle, making her frown.

It *was* the glare and not the prices that were making her frown, she assured herself. The prices, while high, were well within the range of meals served at other fine restaurants. At least, she assumed they were. She'd never actually seen a menu with prices before—those were always handed to the gentlemen, never to the ladies. It never would have occurred to her to read a menu posted for the public.

Today was a day of firsts.

She wasn't sure she liked having quite so many firsts.

Mentally, she tallied the hoard in her purse and the dent that two dollars a day for board and room at Georgianne Bonnard's was going to make in it. At fourteen dollars a week, it wouldn't take long to go through her money, and there was no telling how long the trial would go on.

She glanced back at the framed bill of fare. Even the pot roast was too much. Forget the dessert. She'd be foolish to spend money here when she'd already paid for morning and evening meals at Bonnard's.

Granted, Georgianne Bonnard probably wasn't offering beef tips and mushrooms in pastry, but that wasn't really the point of this Adventure, was it? And though she'd never stooped to such informality in her life, she could sit down at Georgianne's table in a gown that didn't require she wear a corset and with slippers on her feet instead of the fashionable Iron Maidens she was wearing now.

Her feet were *killing* her.

Which was a tempting argument for dining here and not hiking up the hill to Georgianne's. And this afternoon's tea had been wonderful.

But afternoon tea was one thing, dinner quite another. She wasn't properly dressed for dinner at a place like the National. Her dress was a practical traveling dress, not an evening gown, and after hours spent tramping around the streets of Cripple Creek it was dusty and rumpled and inappropriate for the best restaurant in town. And even if her dress weren't so disreputable, her face was probably just as dirty, her hair untidy, and her shoes invisible beneath the dust they'd accumulated.

Yet with all that, she wanted to dine *here,* not at Georgianne's. She *needed* to dine here, needed to remind herself that she hadn't completely toppled out of the comfortable life she'd always known, that she still belonged, regardless. What had been merely refreshing this afternoon was fast coming to seem an utter necessity this evening.

It was stopping at the Walker house that had sapped the last of her confidence. She'd stood outside that house—a house not one whit larger or grander than her own very comfortable house in Denver—and found she couldn't even open the gate.

With her feet aching and her stays pinching and the sticky feel of dust and sweat under the wilting collar of her dress, she'd felt like an impostor, and a fool. What if Mary Walker refused to see her? What if she laughed or slammed the door in her face or, worse, treated her as though she'd come to clean the floors and scrub the steps?

For what seemed an eternity she'd argued with herself, but nothing worked against the insidious self-doubts that had taken hold of her. That's why dining here at the National seemed so important just now. Not tea and a chance to get her bearings, but a real meal to fill her empty stomach and a larger dose of confidence to fill the hollow that weariness and fear had carved inside her.

And still she couldn't convince herself that she could spend a dollar or two of her precious hoard on such foolishness. She was tired, that's all, and hungry. A meal—served at Georgianne Bonnard's table, not the National's—and a bath and a good night's sleep would solve the problem. She could face Mary Dodge Walker tomorrow and pretend this momentary madness had never happened.

And if all that didn't work, what then?

The silent arguments back and forth made her head

ache. When she'd dreamed of having an Adventure, back in the safety of her room in her father's house in Baltimore, she'd never once thought she'd have to give up so much to get it.

Her mother's warning came back to her like an echo. *Be careful what you ask for,* she'd said when she'd learned of her daughter's thirst for Adventure, *because you might just get it…and then what will you do?*

The thought of her mother's disapproval pricked Caroline into a decision. Bonnard's. Definitely Bonnard's. She didn't need an expensive meal and fancier surroundings to drag her confidence up out of the mud. She just needed a meal and a bath and a bed…and the courage tomorrow to make up for her failures today.

She turned away from the glass display case…and ran right into her husband.

J.R.'s arms came round her instinctively, solid, warm, and strong. The smell of him hit her like a fist. Sandalwood from the soap he always ordered from a pharmacist in New York. Fine linen, properly starched. A faint hint of the Cuban cigars he loved. And beneath it all, the indefinable, heart-stoppingly familiar scent of the man himself, dark and male and tormenting.

"Caroline?" His voice didn't sound quite right. Too tight, as though his throat was squeezing shut.

For an instant she wanted nothing so much as to lean into his hard body, to feel the fine wool of his waistcoat rubbing her cheek and his arms around her, strong and warm and secure. To hear his heart beating and feel his breath against her skin.

She wrenched away. "Mr. Abbott." She said it coolly, as any lady might to a gentleman she had encountered by chance on the street.

He stepped back and tipped his hat. Mockingly, as if he knew exactly what had gone round in her head. "Mrs. Abbott." He glanced at the display case. "Taken to reading menus, have you?"

Her chin came up at that. "I was curious about what might be offered in a rough mining town like this."

"And what was your conclusion?"

"The selection is…adequate."

"I'm relieved. I was hoping you would agree to share the evening's meal with me, and I would hate to have offered you anything less than the best."

How could a man look so damnably amused when not a muscle in his face had twitched?

"You make me sound like an insufferable, puffed-up prig."

"Impossible!"

She glared at him, daring him to push it further, but he was a great deal cleverer at this sort of give and take than she was. He smiled blandly back.

"If you'll excuse me." She moved to walk around him. His hand on her sleeve stopped her.

"Stay," he said. "Have dinner with me."

His eyes burned through her. His voice had dropped, taken on a faint pleading note that ought to have pleased her, but only made her ache, instead.

"I—"

"Please."

The single word shattered her defenses.

"All right," she said. "Thank you."

The smile she got in response was devastating.

"But I need to freshen up first," she added. "I—"

"You can use my room. I'll keep out," he added, before she could protest. "I'll even give you the key if you don't trust me."

"I don't."

His smile widened. "Smart woman."

Caroline wasn't so sure of that. As she rode up in the elevator with him, her arm laced with his, all she could think of was how good it felt to touch him and how long it had been since they'd last made love and what it had been like when they had. By the time they stepped off the elevator, her knees were going weak and she could feel the heat and wetness building up inside her.

The instant he stopped in front of a dark wood door she knew it was not only not smart to be here, it was absolutely insane. There was a bed on the other side of that door. Judging from the quality of the hotel, a big, soft, comfortable bed.

The expression on J.R.'s face when he straightened from unlocking the door said he was thinking the same thing.

She stuck out her hand, palm up. "The key, please."

The ache there, between her legs, was starting to affect her breathing. It had already affected her head. Had to have, because if she were thinking straight she'd be running for the nearest exit.

"Now, Caroline," he said in that smooth, talk-you-out-of-your-knickers voice of his. Just the sound of it was enough to send sparks shooting along her nerves.

"The key," she repeated firmly.

With a rueful smile, he dropped it in her palm. "Worth a try."

"And that's all it was worth." When he didn't move, she added, "If this is inconvenient, I can always use the ladies' powder room downstairs."

He stepped back. Not far, but enough that she could get past without brushing against him. The way she was feeling right now, she didn't dare touch him—they wouldn't even make it through the door let alone all the way to the bed if she did.

J.R., however, didn't believe in fighting fair. As she passed, he leaned down and whispered in her ear, "If you need any help, just holler."

And then he thrust his tongue into her ear.

It was just a quick flick, in and around and out, but it almost brought her to her knees. Caroline gasped and blindly grabbed for the door handle. If he tried it again, she'd probably have a screaming climax right here in the second floor hallway of the National.

The door swung away under her grasp, pulling her back to safety. She gulped, forced her knees to stiffen, and staggered out of reach.

"I do *not* holler," she said, and then she slammed the door in his face.

Chapter Seven

His plan was working brilliantly.

J.R., comfortably ensconced in a massive leather chair in a sitting area at the far end of the second floor hallway, pulled out a cheroot and lit it, then leaned back, propped his feet on the reading table in front of him, and blew a smoke ring at the ceiling.

Good smoke ring. Damn fine cigar.

Despite the lingering ache in his trousers, life was looking up. He grinned and blew another smoke ring.

It was a fine plan, an excellent plan, and it had all come to him as he'd followed Caroline down the hill to the National.

If he screwed his eyes half shut he could still see her standing on that sidewalk in front of the Walker house, so damned scared she couldn't open the gate, let alone knock on the front door and demand an interview.

She was almost ready to give up. Give her a few more days of reality, a little bigger taste of what being a newspaper reporter really involved, and she'd come round. Bound to.

That little trick with the tongue in the ear had almost done it. She'd always been sensitive there, and four months' abstinence had been as hard on her as it had been on him. A second thrust of his tongue and a little nibble or two would have driven her to her knees, had her begging for him to make love to her right there in the middle of the hall.

He smiled at the ceiling, pleased.

His wife was damn near turned inside out with wanting him.

A sudden urgent stirring in his trousers made him shift uncomfortably in his chair.

All right, he hadn't come out of that encounter unscathed, either. Just walking into the hotel with her on his arm had been enough to make him worry about the length of his jacket and the fit of his trousers. Opening that door, knowing there was a bed on the other side, had been hell.

Unfortunately, the suspicious little witch had not only demanded the key, she'd pocketed it once she'd locked the door from inside. Just because he'd once told her how you could open a lock when the key was still in it didn't mean he'd been going to try.

He frowned, then took a long, angry drag on the cheroot. All right, he *had* been thinking about picking the lock, but she still shouldn't have been so damned suspicious.

Didn't matter. He was tougher than she was. No matter what she thought, he wasn't ruled by what he kept tucked in his trousers. He didn't have to like it, but he could hang on longer than she could any day.

He hoped to hell he didn't have to try, though. He

wasn't sure he could survive too much more of a life without her in it.

He wanted his wife back, dammit!

And to nudge her in that direction, he'd do everything he could to make her see what she'd so blithely thrown away. Since rational argument hadn't won her over, more drastic measures were clearly called for.

J.R. smiled and took a drag on his cheroot, then tilted his head back and aimed another perfect smoke ring at the ceiling.

Dinner was only the first step.

Once she was sure she could stand, Caroline tucked the key in her pocket and shoved away from the door. Darn him for being a conniving sneak, and bless him for telling her about that trick with the key.

It wasn't easy ignoring the big, white bed...until she got a glimpse of herself in the dressing table mirror.

She stared, appalled, at the bedraggled creature that looked back at her. Hair falling out of its pins, dress inches deep in dust—it was a wonder he'd even recognized her beneath the dirt.

Fortunately, the room's luxurious private bathroom came supplied with towels, soap, and plenty of hot water. She cast a covetous glance at the big, claw-footed tub, then forced herself to concentrate on the possible.

Fifteen minutes later whatever parts of her stuck out of her sleeves and collar were properly washed. A little judicious tugging and brushing and tucking had restored respectability to her dress, and a little rubbing had taken the worst of the dirt off her shoes. But her hair was still a mess, and she had forgotten her comb.

Caroline frowned, thinking of J.R.'s silver-backed brush and comb lying on the dressing table in the bedroom. He *was* her husband, after all. Borrowing them wouldn't be the same as borrowing a stranger's.

Yet as she pulled out the pins, then combed out her hair, she couldn't help remembering the times he'd performed that office for her. When she looked in the mirror there was only her face, but her imagination insisted on seeing two heads, his dark head bent to hers as he plucked the pins out, one by one, then slowly unwound her hair.

He'd told her once he liked the weight and feel of it, liked the way it slid free when he pulled out the final pin. Sometimes, when it was still coiled like a rope, he twisted it around his hands and wrists, pulling her to him to claim a lingering kiss, then slowly letting her go, teasing her with the promise of more.

He'd loved combing her hair out, once it was free.

The rake of the comb through her hair, the look of his face in the mirror, so intent and beautiful, had never failed to rouse a slow, torturous heat in her that only he could cool.

Once, he'd undressed her, sitting there in front of the mirror. Slowly, one tiny button at a time, baring her to his gaze until her dressing gown was a drift of white spilling over his thighs and onto the floor; until she was naked, with only her unbound hair to cover her.

At the memory, Caroline's breath caught in her

throat. Their dressing table was different from this one. The mirror was wider, the table lower so that, seated as she had been at the end of the bench, she could see…everything, all the intimate parts of her she'd never dared look at before. He'd sat behind her, straddling the bench, his legs on either side of hers, his chest and belly pressed intimately close against her naked back and buttocks.

If she closed her eyes, she could feel the way the starched linen of his shirt had rubbed against her shoulder blades and ribs. She could remember how the button at the waist of his trousers had poked her spine when he'd leaned forward, remember the scrape of the fine wool of his trousers against the sensitive skin of her hips and thighs. She'd felt his need, hard and urgent between them, but he hadn't tried to ease it.

Instead, he'd made love to her with his eyes and his hands and his mouth. He'd demanded that she watch as he caressed her, as he kissed the side of her neck and cupped her breasts, as he let his hands roam up and down her body. He'd demanded that she open to him, and she had watched, aching and tormented and amazed, as he possessed her, and worshipped her body with his touch.

His eyes had been black diamonds, burning over her shoulder as he watched her in the mirror, watching him, watching herself.

She'd never felt so vulnerable…or known such exquisite power.

He'd brought her to climax three separate times that night, and just when she'd been sure she couldn't survive another moment's pleasure, he'd dragged her down onto the carpet and made fierce love to her until she'd shattered under his own explosive climax.

At the memory, a shudder racked her. The silver comb fell from her hand to clatter on the floor. The noise jolted her back to an awareness of where she was, and of the aching need that clenched her muscles and made her press herself against the dressing table chair in a futile effort at relief.

Fool! *Fool!*

Shaking, she retrieved the comb, then gathered up the scattered pins and retreated to the bathroom where the only mirror was over the sink, just large enough for her to see to pin up her hair and nothing more.

To her relief, the cold water from the National's taps was brutally cold. Almost cold enough to freeze the need burning inside her.

Almost.

When she finally stepped out into the hall and shut the door to J.R.'s room behind her, Caroline was praying that he'd grown tired of waiting.

He hadn't.

He was standing at the window in the little sitting alcove at the end of the hall, looking out at the street. In the gloom—the electric lights hadn't yet been turned on even though the day outside was fast disappearing—he was little more than a black silhouette against the fading light. It was enough to take her breath away. He was so…perfect. So tall and well-shaped and elegant. So…*desirable*.

What kind of fool was she to lock him out of her

life? What could possibly be worth denying herself the love of a man like this?

The *snick* of the key in the lock drew his attention. His head came up and he turned away from the window, watching her, waiting for her to come to him.

Trembling, Caroline pocketed the key. The walk down the hall toward him was one of the longest in her life. She wanted to run, but in which direction? Away? Or toward him? Flee, or fling herself into his arms and make sure he never, ever let her go again?

She forced herself to keep a decorous pace, head high, back straight, one foot in front of the other, all the way down the hall.

If he saw anything odd in her manner, he didn't show it. With the ease of a man used to charming the ladies, he smiled and took her hands in his as if he was going to kiss them.

At the first touch, his hold tightened. "God, Caroline. Your hands are like ice. What did you do? Bathe in the stuff?"

Caroline tugged, trying to get free. "Cold water's good for the complexion."

He laughed and let her go. "You don't need any help with your complexion, my love."

Lightly, soft as the brush of a leaf, he trailed the tip of one finger down the line of her cheek. She knotted her hands in front of her to keep from trapping his hand and holding it there.

"You have such beautiful skin, Caroline," he murmured. "Have I ever told you that? Like silk."

And then he bent and kissed her.

It was just a little kiss, a soft brush of his lips over hers, but it was enough to start a riot in her blood.

Because she wanted so badly to yield, she jerked away, instead. "J.R.! What are you thinking? Someone might see us."

His smile vanished. "Would that really be so terrible, Caroline? For someone to catch us kissing?"

"It's not…proper."

His eyes darkened as though clouds had crossed the sun. His gaze raked her, from her hastily repinned hairdo to the dusty hem of her skirt. "God forbid you ever indulge in anything improper, right, Caroline?"

She flushed. "Perhaps we should just forget din—"

"Oh, no. You already accepted my invitation…and muddied my towels with your dirt, I've no doubt. You *owe* me dinner."

The ride back down in the elevator was conducted in silence. Caroline was so aware of him that she quivered, little muscle spasms that shook her and forced her to clasp her hands together to hide the movement. The spicy-sweet smell of the expensive cigar he'd been smoking lingered in his clothes, and she could hear the rasp of his starched linen shirt with his every movement. The sound, faint as it was, was enough to make the muscles in her back tense with a remembered erotic thrill.

She wondered if it was possible to stop an elevator mid-descent and make mad, passionate love in the confining space. J.R. would know how to manage. All she had to do was ask.

Just the thought of asking was enough to make her sweat.

They stopped at the first floor with a jarring little bump. J.R. worked the lever to slide the rattling cage door back, then the solid steel door that opened to the lobby. She had to force her feet to move, her lungs to pump air. People would notice if she tripped her husband right there in front of the elevator and dragged him down to the floor with her.

"Caroline? Are you all right?"

The light touch of J.R.'s hand at her elbow pulled her back from the brink. "Fine. I'm fine. Really."

"You sure? You've turned pale and—" He eyed her worriedly. "It was the elevator, wasn't it?"

Panic struck her. He *knew*. Had she been that obvious, that—

"Those narrow, enclosed spaces get to a lot of people," he said. "Next time, we'll take the stairs."

Sex, on the stairs. She'd rip off his jacket and undo his tie and—

"That might be a good idea." Now it was her voice that sounded strained.

Or maybe they'd do it fully dressed. A little strategic rearrangement of clothing, a bit of—

"Shall we go in to dinner?" she said.

Chapter Eight

Once she was into her third glass of wine, things went a little better.

She could handle this. All of it—the job, her insecurities, her husband and her need for him. *All* of it. Really, it was no problem at all.

J.R. was pouring her fourth glass of wine—she was pretty sure it was the fourth—when the waiter arrived with their main courses. Beef tips and mushrooms in pastry crust, almond green beans, and coffee, all for the bargain price of a dollar ten each. Which J.R. would pay for, not she.

Dessert, of course, was extra.

She knew what she wanted for dessert, and it wasn't chocolate torte or melon compote or peach ice cream. Too bad she wasn't going to get it.

Fortunately, the wine was taking the edge off the worst of the need, leaving her feeling a little more mellow and relaxed, a little more accepting of the ache in her center that refused to go away.

"So, where are you staying?"

Caroline frowned as J.R. topped up her wineglass. Surely she hadn't drunk it *that* quickly.

"Caroline?"

The sound of her name on his tongue brought her attention back with a snap.

"Yes?"

"Where are you staying?"

He really *was* beautiful, in a very masculine sort of way. The light from the candles on the table accented the strong line of his cheek and jaw, the patrician arch of his nose, the tantalizing curve of his mouth. He had a beautiful mouth. An eminently kissable mouth.

Those beautiful, wine-damp lips curved in a smile. A smug little smile that irritated her for some reason, she wasn't quite sure why.

"Caroline?"

"Mmmm?"

"For the third time, where are you staying?" He enunciated each word carefully, as if he wasn't sure she understood them.

"Ahhh." She considered the question. "I have a room."

"That's good." His lips quivered, as though he was trying not to laugh. "Where is this room of yours?"

She thought about that some more. "Bonnard's Boardinghouse. It's good and cheap," she added with satisfaction. "That's what the sign says. Good and cheap." Her smile turned to a frown. "I'm not really sure it's either, but maybe it is. How would I know?"

"How indeed?"

Her frown deepened. "I'd know if you hadn't always arranged such things for me. You and my father."

"You want to know whether it's good and cheap?"

Answering that required a little thought. For some reason her brain wasn't quite as quick as it usually was. "I want to know how to rent a room. And tip a porter. And…and…"—she waved her hand as if that might blow the word she wanted back into her brain—"and whatnot."

She cocked her head and eyed him suspiciously. "Did you know I don't know about tips?"

"Was there some reason you wanted to?"

That took some thought, too. "Because." She weighed that answer, decided it needed a bit more explanation. "You do. Know about tips, I mean. And finding a room. And calling a cab and tipping a porter and…and…"

"And whatnot?"

She nodded. Her head seemed to bobble just a little when she did. "Pre*cis*ely."

"I'm sorry I've deprived you of such pleasures."

"You didn't know." She could be gracious, especially when he was the one apologizing.

J.R. smiled.

His smile was lovely. Absolutely lovely. She loved his smile, his mouth, his tongue—

No, better not think about his tongue.

Since the white-coated waiter had magically appeared at J.R.'s side, she didn't have a chance to.

"Dessert, madame?" the man asked as he whisked their plates away.

"That's extra." The waiter blinked. She touched J.R.'s hand and felt an almost electric jolt shoot up her fingers and through her veins. "Dessert's extra, J.R."

"Yes, it is." Really a *lovely* smile. "Would you like some?"

She frowned, considering. "I think I'd like some wine."

J.R. moved her half-full glass out of reach, then handed the bottle to the waiter. "You've had enough wine."

"It's a *very* good wine."

"Yes, it is, but there's a limit even to my perfidy."

It was her turn to blink. "There is?"

J.R.'s smile widened. "Yes, there is. Have some dessert, instead."

Her uncooperative brain groped for the meaning of the word *perfidy* and came up blank. It would come to her tomorrow. She had a feeling she wouldn't like it when it did.

The waiter, who had dispatched both wineglass and bottle under the keeping of a busboy, straightened disapprovingly. "We have an excellent chocolate torte— it's one of the chef's specialties—a melon compote, and freshly made strawberry ice cream."

"Peach."

The fellow frowned. "I beg your pardon?"

"Peach ice cream. Says so on the...the bill outside."

His nose pinched shut. He looked rather funny with his nose pinched shut. "It's strawberry, madame. *Definitely* strawberry."

"Madame will have the ice cream," J.R. said before she had a chance to reply. "And coffee. Black."

"At this time of the evening?"

"Brandy for me. The good stuff, not that swill from the bottle behind the bar."

"Very good, sir." The waiter was gone before she had a chance to protest.

It didn't matter, because J.R. had closed his hand over hers where it lay on the table. His skin was warm against hers, his palm rough. His fingers stroked up the inside of her wrist, then down, then up again.

A low purr rumbled in her throat.

The return of the waiter with the ice cream and coffee and J.R.'s brandy was like a dash of icy water straight in the face. Reluctantly, she pulled her hand free of her husband's.

The coffee was strong and rather bitter, but at least it cleared away a few of the fumes clogging her head. She took another sip, then another.

"You haven't touched the ice cream." J.R. nudged the dish closer to her.

Conscious of his gaze on her, Caroline picked up her spoon, then scooped up a bit of ice cream. She came away with a bit of strawberry, too.

The ice cream was exquisite, rich and creamy and sinfully sweet, the strawberry lusciously ripe.

With the taste came memory, of her and J.R. on a hot summer afternoon, sharing an ice cream cone he'd purchased from a vendor in the park. It had been chocolate, and almost as good as this. They'd eaten it turn and turn about at first, but then he licked it just when she was nibbling at the edge.

She could still remember the taste of ice cream taken straight off his tongue—sweet, with just a hint of male. She'd loved licking it from his lips, and almost melted in place when he'd licked it from hers.

He remembered, too. She could tell by the way he looked at her, by the hungry glint in his eyes.

Heat flooded her. Until tonight, she'd never realized how dangerous memory could be.

Abruptly, she put down her spoon and picked up her coffee cup, instead. After the ice cream, the coffee seemed even more bitter. She took another sip.

J.R. sipped his brandy, then swirled it in its glass, frowning. "So, how do you like this Bonnard's Boardinghouse? Comfortable?"

She remembered how brandy tasted on his lips, too.

The collar of her dress suddenly seemed too tight. "Fine. It's…fine."

He took another sip, but this time he held the brandy in his mouth, savoring the taste. Her gaze latched on the slight swelling of his throat when he swallowed. If he noticed her sudden attention, he gave no sign of it.

"I confess, I expected you to stay here. A boardinghouse doesn't seem quite your style."

It wasn't the words so much as the way he said them that made her realize she was being dragged into dangerous waters.

"I chose to stay in a boardinghouse," she said. It wasn't really a lie. Not quite. "I wanted to…to get to know the people of Cripple Creek better. For my story, you know. I thought it would be easier to…uh…to meet them that way." *That* was a lie.

He snorted in disbelief.

Her head came up at that. "It's true!" She waved a hand "Just look at this place! How could I possibly meet anyone from Cripple Creek if I'd stayed here?"

"Stratton keeps an apartment upstairs. Signed on for a fifty year lease when they built the place, or so I've been told."

Caroline sniffed disdainfully. "Stratton's a millionaire. He doesn't count."

"So was Walker. And what with his mine, his saloon, and his other investments, Osbald's worth at least half a million, if not more. Both of them ate here. Regularly." He set his brandy down and leaned across the table toward her. Again his hand claimed hers. "It's exactly the sort of place you ought to be if you want to meet the people who own the mines and run the town."

He was doing that thing with his fingers again, rubbing the inside of her wrist, the side of her hand. She had the sense that there was a trap somewhere, but her head was still too befogged by wine and lust to see it. It required an almost physical effort to wrench her thoughts away from what his fingers were doing and back to what he'd been saying.

"I like Bonnard's perfectly well, thank you." She tried to tug free, but he wouldn't let her go.

"You don't have to share my room if you don't want, Caroline. And if money's a problem, I'll pay for a separate room for you. The one next to me is vacant and—"

She wrenched free of his hold, but bumped the dish

of ice cream, sending the spoon clattering across the table.

"I don't need your money, thank you. I manage quite well on my own." The lies came out easily. She even managed to sound dignified, she thought, which was an advantage if you were lying. "Have you forgotten that I have a trust fund, too?"

"The income of which your father has cut off. You won't be able to touch the principal for another two years."

Caroline winced, then blinked back sudden tears.

"Look, I'm sorry about that. Your father told me."

"He would."

"He's worried."

"I can take care of myself."

For a moment he didn't say anything, then, softly, "Can you?"

"Of course!" That lie made her head spin. Or maybe it was just the wine catching up with her.

Still fighting against the tears that threatened, she tossed her napkin on the table, then pushed back her chair before J.R. could come around the table to help her. She staggered a little when she stood and had to clutch at his sleeve to steady herself.

"Are you all right?" Just the sound of his voice was enough to make her ache.

"Fine. I just want to go—" She drew in a deep, steadying breath. "I want to go back to Bonnard's."

She'd almost said home, but home—*her* home—was far away and, anyway, J.R. didn't live there any more.

Tears stung her eyes, but she didn't dare take refuge in the ladies' powder room—the way her head was spinning, she wasn't sure she could walk that far unaided. Instead, she stood there, fighting for control, while J.R. signed for the bill and called for a carriage. She couldn't help noticing the tip he left—five dollars. He tossed the money down as casually as if it were scrap paper.

The memory of the porter at the train station and the reluctant way she'd doled out the coins one at a time made her blush.

Resentment followed the shame. No matter what the price, she was *not* going to let him shove her into that neat little box labeled "wife" that he'd so blithely picked out for her. This rupture between them wasn't about money or his being caught in a brothel and not telling her about it. It was about independence and respect and the freedom to choose. It was about being an equal in this marriage and not just an adornment.

Easy enough to say, even in her blurry-minded state. Not so easy to live with.

Just watching J.R. scrawl his name to that bill with his typical flourish, or casually pull the five out of his money clip—simple tasks she'd seen him perform a hundred times—made her ache with loss and longing. She loved watching him. She always had. She loved the way he frowned when he was thinking or tilted his head back, just so, when he laughed. She loved the forceful confidence with which he always signed his name and the friendly nod he gave the waiter when the fellow, beaming, carried the bill and the tip away.

She missed all the little things—the scent of his soap on his skin, the rustle of his starched shirt when he moved, the way he held his fork—as much as she missed him and the life they'd shared. And she wanted it back. All of it. All of him. Everything they'd had.

Yet even with the ache of loneliness and longing, she wouldn't give in. She didn't dare. If she gave in now, she'd lose a part of herself forever.

Still, when he gallantly escorted her out the hotel and into the waiting carriage, she had to fight against the urge to demand that he take her upstairs, instead, and make love to her till dawn.

The short ride to the boardinghouse was conducted in silence. She sensed he was as aware of her as she was of him, despite the distance between them.

As formally as if he were courting her, he helped her down from the carriage, then slid her hand through the crook of his arm and escorted her to the front door. Still silent, he waited while she opened the door.

She hesitated in the open doorway, waiting, hoping he would kiss her. Instead, he took her hand and pressed a quick kiss on the back of it.

"Good night, Caroline," he said, setting her free, then stepping back. "I enjoyed our dinner tonight."

His smile was enough to make her dizzy all over again.

"So did I. I—"

She didn't get a chance to finish. He was already striding down the walk, hat tilted at a racy angle and with a cocky swing to his stride that made her hackles rise. There was nothing of the lonely lover in his walk, no sense that he was sorry to be leaving her.

He looked, in fact, exactly like a man who'd just won a risky bet and was congratulating himself on his victory.

Fury claimed her. He'd tormented her deliberately! He'd known *exactly* what he was doing and the effect he had on her. He'd rubbed her poverty in her face, then flaunted that ridiculous five-dollar tip to remind her of what she'd given up, and what she could have if only she'd throw away her pride and go crawling back to him.

Well, let him flaunt his money. She wasn't giving in. Hell would freeze before she so much as got down on her knees. The heavens would fall before she'd even think of crawling!

The walls of Bonnard's Boardinghouse shook when she slammed the front door behind her. She was half-way up the stairs before she remembered she was supposed to lock it, too, and hook the latch.

J.R. dismissed the carriage, but lingered on the street outside Bonnard's Boardinghouse, watching as, one by one, the lights went off downstairs, then came on in the curtained windows on the second floor.

Which room was hers? Though he could see an occasional shadowy image passing in front of the windows, the blinds and drapes distorted the outlines so that he couldn't be sure which one belonged to his wife.

Just the thought of Caroline undressing was enough to make his blood heat.

Tonight had been hell. Sitting across from her, chatting, arguing, laughing. Looking at her. He'd stared and stared and still he hadn't gotten enough.

Leaving her had damn near killed him.

His plan was working, though. She'd been stiff, at first, uncertain, but as the evening had worn on and the wine had worked its wonders, she'd relaxed, been more like the laughing, sharp-witted, loving woman he'd married.

Still, she'd been wary and annoyingly defensive, too. That nonsense about ''choosing'' this shabby little boardinghouse—J.R. snorted. She'd been desperate, that's what it was. Desperate and broke.

Not that he thought it was fair for her father to cut off her trust fund like that, but he had to admit it was convenient. Let her see what a journalist really earned. If the hardships and indignities of the job didn't slap her back to her senses, the economic realities would. Which wasn't much comfort. He'd rather have her come back because she wanted him as much as he wanted her than have her driven back by an empty purse.

He used to think he understood women, but he was damned if he understood his wife or what made her persist in this madness.

Above him, the lights in the windows of the boardinghouse went out, one by one.

He didn't know what would bring her back, either, but he was, by God, going to find out.

A bath. That's what she needed. A good hot bath. Caroline eased her aching, swollen feet out of her fashionable high-heeled shoes, then slipped off her stockings and wriggled her toes.

Reassured that they were still functional despite the day's abuse, she sank back on the lumpy bed, then, groaning, propped her feet on the painted iron bed frame. The pose was undignified and unbecoming a lady. It was also a wonderful relief.

She stretched, trying to work out the soreness in her muscles, then winced as her tightly-laced stays pinched her side. Her head felt as if it were going to pound right off her shoulders. Next time, two glasses of wine with dinner.

No, three, so she could throw the third in J.R.'s face.

When she'd stomped—*limped*—back down to lock the door, a worried Georgianne and indignant Elizabeth had emerged from the kitchen, agog to hear the details of her first afternoon on the job.

Since they'd provided all the gossip for the first article, she'd felt obligated to share at least a little of what she'd been up to. Over tea at the kitchen table, she'd told them, in carefully edited detail, about her small triumphs. She'd conveniently ignored the rest.

They'd preened and fluttered at the thought of being quoted in a big city paper, even if their names were never mentioned.

"It wouldn't be quite the thing, would it, dear, to have our names in the paper like that?" Georgianne had said, rather anxious at the thought.

"Nonsense. It's that no woman of sense wants her name associated with such a disgraceful affair," Elizabeth had snorted. "Except you, of course," she added with a gracious nod of the head in Caroline's direction. "If you're doing the reporting, that's perfectly all right."

"And the gentleman who saw you home?" Georgianne asked. "I couldn't help but notice with the door open and all," she added hastily, the tips of her ears pinkening. "He's really *very* handsome."

Elizabeth's nostrils flared at the mere mention of a male. "I trust there was nothing…improper about it all? I would not care to have Bonnard's reputation soiled by any hint of impropriety."

Caroline grimaced, remembering. She'd managed to reassure Elizabeth on the propriety of dining with her husband, but her own doubts persisted.

Was it just the wine and her burgeoning insecurities, or was J.R. really plotting something? And if so, what?

A dozen possibilities occurred to her, each one more lurid than the last.

With a groan, she forced herself back upright despite the spinning in her head. All that could wait until tomorrow. Right now, what she wanted most was a bath.

She spared one minute for longing thoughts of the *en suite* bath J.R. would be enjoying, another for troubling, lustful memories of the time she'd walked in on him in the bath at home and he had enticed her to share it with him.

Two minutes of self-indulgent longings couldn't possibly be enough to undermine her newfound independence.

Three minutes were downright subversive.

Wrenching her thoughts away from J.R.'s clever ways with soap, she stripped to her chemise and bloomers, then pulled on her dressing gown. The hike down the steep, unlighted stairs to the single bath was unpleasantly chilly. Even in slippers, her feet hurt. Every step jarred and set the hammers in her head pounding harder than before.

All part of the Adventure, Caroline reminded herself, punching the button for the electric light in the bathroom. The dim light glinted off the glorious porcelain bath that stood atop its clawed feet in radiant white splendor at the far end of the room.

A groan of anticipatory pleasure escaped her.

She set down her net bag with its sponge and little tin box of perfumed soap, then tottered over to turn on the tap for the bath. The tub was a quarter full before she realized no hot water was coming out. She fiddled with both taps. Right, cold water. *Really* cold water. Left, nothing. Not even a drip.

Puzzled, she peered over the edge at the pipes that ran from the faucet and into the floor. She didn't know anything about plumbing, but as far as she could tell, everything looked perfectly normal.

Abandoning the effort, she limped back upstairs to knock on her landlady's bedroom door.

"Yes, dear?" Georgianne Bonnard blinked sleepily up at her.

"I'm very sorry to disturb you, but there's no hot water for the bathtub."

"No." It didn't sound like a question.

"I want to take a bath," Caroline insisted. The

headache was getting worse. ''Tonight. Right now, in fact.''

Georgianne's mouth worked, but nothing came out. She blinked again, blindly, like a bird bothered by the light.

The sound of a door opening behind her drew Caroline around.

Elizabeth Carter, ready for bed, was a sight to frighten the bravest. Her round face was slathered in face cream so thick it formed a solid mask with openings for her eyes and mouth and nostrils. Dozens of tiny curls, carefully knotted around scraps of cloth that looked like the tails on a kite, stood up in all directions around her face. Her flannel nightgown billowed from the unexpected ruffles at her throat so that her head appeared to be sticking out of a drawstring sack.

''Is there a problem?'' she asked, making it clear there'd better not be.

''There's no hot water coming out of the faucet for the bath,'' Caroline informed her.

''Of course not. The hot water heater's not due to be installed till next year.''

It was Caroline's turn to blink. ''Next *year?* But I want to take a bath right *now!*''

''Baths are on Saturday, Mrs. Abbott, not before. As our guest, you'll get it first, which is more than you could count on any other place in town, let me tell you!''

''What do you mean, I'll get it first?''

''I mean, you won't have to make do with someone else's leftover bath water, of course. Stuff gets rather mucky after four or five people have bathed in it, you know. What did you think I meant?''

Caroline choked

The lack of a response didn't faze Elizabeth. ''For the rest of the week,'' she said sternly, ''you'll make do with a sponge bath, just like Sister and me. And most of the rest of the world, I might add.''

''That's ridiculous!''

A martial light ignited in Elizabeth Carter's eyes. ''That is the way we run this boardinghouse, Mrs. Abbott.''

Georgianne gave a little peep of distress. They both ignored her.

''If you absolutely must have a bath, then you may use the hot water in the kettle—assuming there's any left. In the meantime, Sister needs her beauty sleep, and so do I.''

With that, she shut her door in Caroline's face. The click of the latch was immediately followed by the *snick* of a lock as Georgianne made sure she wouldn't have to confront her demanding boarder again that night.

Torn between fury and frustration, Caroline glared at the closed doors, then, silently cursing, limped back downstairs to the bathroom.

In the end, she let the icy water run out unused. She brushed her teeth and washed her face, then, feeling considerably ill-used, limped upstairs to bed to dream of hot baths and properly respectful servants and J.R.'s hands gliding over her soap-slicked body with seductively nefarious intent.

Chapter Nine

Like the *Tribune*, the front page of the *Times* was devoted to the problems in the Philippines. In long-winded articles of excruciating prose peppered with more exclamation marks than the *Tribune* had in its entire print shop, it detailed what admiral had said what to whom and what the president said in response and who in Congress was calling for what and why they were blaming it all on someone else entirely. In other words, the business of politics was going on quite as usual.

Bored, J.R. turned the page, and froze.

The headline was in eye-catching 18-point bold type at the outside top of the second page—When It Comes To Murder, Ask The Ladies. Right beneath the headlines, in smaller but still clearly visible type, was the byline—"Exclusive to the *Times,* by C.A."

C.A. Caroline Abbott. On the top outside of the second page and under a screaming headline like that.

Coffee slopped as his cup slammed down on the saucer. He wouldn't have to ask the ladies about murder. If Caroline were here, he'd strangle her himself, witnesses be damned.

With a curse and an angry snap of newsprint, J.R. roughly folded the paper so he could read the piece more easily.

While the men of Cripple Creek talk about whether or not Andrew "Andy" Osbald acted in self defense or committed murder when he shot and killed wealthy mine owner Josiah Walker in a barroom in Cripple Creek this April past, the women of the town believe they're missing the forest for the trees.

"There's more to this killing than just a quarrel between old enemies," one knowledgeable lady told this reporter. "We may not spend all our time in the saloons gossiping like the attorneys and the judges and the men who'll be on the juries, but we hear what went on. We know what's what."

"All those fancy Denver papers like the *Tribune* are treating it as if it's just a 'boys will be boys' quarrel that ended in a shooting," another said. "That's ridiculous!"

This reporter, one of the intrepid breed of reporters who, with the support of the *Times,* are fighting to give a voice to the women of this country, agrees.

Caroline went on to repeat the known events of the killing, describe the stand the prosecuting attorney would take—how in hell had she found that out? He'd tried to run the man down and had drawn a blank—and explain the accused's plea of self-defense. Nothing unusual there except that she'd gotten hold of information no one else had.

No other paper, however, would have wasted so much as a column inch to claim that the men in Cripple Creek were blind jackasses not to realize there was more behind the killing than just hot tempers and old animosities. The *Times* had used ten inches, at least.

Not that Caroline or her paper had stooped to using the word ''jackass,'' of course, but the implication was clear—the women knew what was what and the men were just too dumb to see it.

That barb, J.R. thought sourly, was aimed at him as much as anyone.

When It Comes To Murder, Ask The Ladies.

The coffee in his belly curdled.

It was a horrible headline, a misleading, attention-grabbing, literary crime in the worst of bad taste, and he'd bet his entire fortune that Blackmun and the owners of the *Times* thought it was a humdinger. It fit right in with the paper's scandal-loving, pandering-to-the-masses brand of journalism.

That his wife had written the scandal-loving, pandering-to-the-masses article that followed was enough to make his bowels twist.

Furious, J.R. flung the paper aside. Enough was enough. He'd been fair. He'd been tolerant. He had, in fact, bent over backward to let Caroline have her way. No more.

As of now, he, J. Randolph Abbott, III, was putting his foot down.

If his wife didn't choose to see reason, there was only one thing left—all-out war.

"'When It Comes To Murder, Ask The Ladies.' What a *wonderful* title!" Georgianne Bonnard was so excited her fat pink cheeks quivered. "Look, Sister! Isn't that a wonderful title?"

"It's called a headline," said Elizabeth repressively, "and it sounds like one of those trashy dime novels rather than a respectable newspaper. But it *is* eye-catching," she added with a magnanimously condescending nod to Caroline.

Caroline smiled and bit her tongue. She'd fetched three copies of the early edition of the *Times* from the train station this morning, and she'd scarcely set foot back in the house when Elizabeth had snatched a copy and started hunting for the article.

She didn't feel like arguing. Top outside second page! And a nice, big bold headline, too. Not that the headline was her choice—that was the editor's job, not hers—but right below it was that marvelous line, "Exclusive to the *Times,* by C.A."

Her gaze fixed on those incredible words, that miraculous line. "By C.A." That's *me!*

She'd already pinched herself twice trying to convince herself it was all real. A byline, a prominent position on the second most important page in the whole newspaper, an article that was guaranteed to stir up attention—what more could a fledgling reporter ask for?

To have J.R. notice…and be proud.

She reached for her coffee cup and found she had to hold on with both hands so the tremor didn't show. He'd notice, but there wasn't a chance in Heaven he'd approve.

Little though she liked it, she wasn't sure she did, either. Not entirely. The basic article was hers, but some of the language wasn't. She hadn't written a word of the flamboyant, combative stuff for which the *Times* was famous. Infamous, J.R. would say.

None of J.R.'s business, she told herself, sipping the sweet, milky brew. She didn't have to have his approval. He'd come around eventually. What mattered now was getting the interviews she'd promised Blackmun, then writing stories that would grab readers' attention. Accurate, honest stories that offered a female perspective on things.

She sipped her coffee as she read her story. Hers and Blackmun's actually, since her editor had added all the touches typical of the *Times*.

Scandalmongering garbage, J.R. would say.

"You're looking very grim, my dear."

Elizabeth's words dragged Caroline back to the present.

"Thinking of what I have to do today," she lied, and folded up the paper.

The older woman frowned. "You know, I worry about you."

"Me?"

"There are people around here who aren't going to like what you've written. They're going to like it even less if you start digging up their secrets."

Caroline couldn't decide whether to laugh or be flattered by the belief that she was going to discover secrets no one else had.

"There's already one man dead in all this," Elizabeth reminded her.

"Oh, dear!" Georgianne breathed from behind the coffeepot. "You don't think she's in any *danger,* do you, Sister?"

Elizabeth sniffed and pursed up her mouth. "When you're dealing with *men,* Sister, anything's possible."

Caroline stifled a giggle and ended up choking, instead.

"Laugh if you like, Mrs. Abbott, but we have lived here and you have not. Cripple Creek is not your Denver high society and you'd do well to remember that."

"Yes, of course. But really—"

"After much careful thought last night, I decided it would be best if you had this." The gun she plunked down on the table was small, steely-gray, and deadly looking.

Caroline stared. Georgianne moaned.

Elizabeth smiled grimly. "It's a lady's pistol, of course, but quite adequate."

"For what?" She almost couldn't get the words past the sudden constriction in her throat.

"For whatever you might need it for. Like shooting any two-legged polecat that thinks that just because you're a woman, you're a fool and utterly defenseless."

"I don't need a gun."

"Of course you do."

"No," she said with a touch of desperation, "I don't. Besides, I've never shot one in my life. Never even handled one. I'd probably shoot my foot instead of a…er…whatever."

"Nonsense. Men have been carrying them for years, and they don't usually shoot their feet off."

"Usually," Caroline said faintly.

She groped in her pocket for the bottle of those new Aspirin tablets a friend had convinced her to try. The two tablets she'd taken that morning must be wearing off—she could feel the pounding headache, legacy of last night's wine, returning.

"What in the world are those?" Georgianne asked, diverted.

"Headache tablets. Something new. Aspirin, they're called." Caroline shook two pills out into her hand, then passed the bottle to Georgianne. She tried not to look at the gun, but the blue-black gleam of the metal against the white tablecloth was hard to ignore.

Georgianne shook out two tablets and popped them in her mouth. She grimaced at the bitter taste, then gulped some water. "Oh, my! If the taste's anything to go by, they must be *quite* effective."

Elizabeth sniffed her disapproval. "All those patent medicines will be the death of you yet, Sister."

"At least I won't end up shot to death!"

"Nor I!"

"How do you know? You're always quarreling with somebody and someday…"

Caroline was halfway out the door when Elizabeth

called after her, "I'll take you out for target practice this afternoon. Don't forget!"

J.R. was waiting for her on the walk outside the boardinghouse. He was leaning against a telephone pole, arms folded over his broad chest, legs crossed at the ankle. Elegantly clad, arrogantly confident, and so handsome the sight of him took her breath away.

Caroline stopped short. "What are you doing here?"

He casually shoved upright. "Waiting for you."

Despite the smile, there was a dangerous glint to his eye and a rock-hard set to his jaw that started alarms ringing in her head.

She tilted her chin defiantly upward. "Planning to follow me around to find out how this reporting thing's done, are you?"

"I'm planning on offering you breakfast," he said. Just when she started to thaw, he added, "and a few tips on what it means to be a reporter, if you want them."

"I don't," she snapped, and marched past him.

He fell into step beside her. "I notice you're wearing more sensible shoes today."

"How—? No, don't tell me. I don't want to know."

"You're a good two inches shorter than you usually are when dressed for the street. Good reporters notice that sort of thing, you know."

"Those who haven't anything better to do, anyway."

"Frankly," he said, ignoring her verbal jab, "I'm

surprised you even *had* sensible shoes. I could have sworn everything you owned had those silly heels."

"They're not silly. And you seemed to like them well enough before."

"I don't like anything that ends up crippling my wife."

My wife. On his lips, the simple words sounded dangerous and tempting and preciously sweet.

Since she was so tempted to give in, she gave a dismissive sniff, instead. "I don't need your advice on shoes."

"Then how about some sensible advice on the trouble you're going to run into if you persist in covering a trial like this?"

"I'm not going to run into trouble." She tried not to think of the gun lying on Georgianne Bonnard's breakfast table. "I can take care of myself."

"You sure about that?"

"Absolutely." Another lie. At the rate she was going, there'd be so many she wouldn't be able to keep them all straight.

They turned the corner onto Bennett Avenue. "Now if you'll excuse me, I have work to do."

"Caroline—"

"Good day, Mr. Abbott." She didn't look back. It was just her imagination that she could feel his eyes boring into her back as she walked off.

Three blocks away, under pretense of checking a street sign, she paused to glance over her shoulder. He was gone.

Not that she cared, she told herself sternly. She had far too much to do to worry about an arrogant, pigheaded husband. Still, it would have been nice if he'd been standing there, watching her. Nicer still if he'd looked at least a little bit forlorn.

Thank God she didn't care. Much.

Her first stop was the courthouse to collect her press pass for the trial.

"Not in," a gloomy-looking fellow said in response to her inquiry for the court clerk. "Gone to Colorado Springs. Back tomorrow."

Caroline clasped her hands to keep them from curling into fists. If J.R. knew about this yesterday, she'd kill him.

"Who's handling the press passes for the trial in the clerk's absence? The county clerk?"

"Nope."

"The prosecuting attorney?"

"Not here."

She was growing desperate. "The judge?"

"Nope."

"Then who?"

"Nobody."

Caroline gritted her teeth. Honey catches flies, she reminded herself, not vinegar. She smiled and batted her eyes, just the tiniest bit.

"Do you know what time the court clerk will be back tomorrow so I *can* get a pass?"

"Nope."

Her patience snapped. "Do you know any word that doesn't begin with 'no'?"

After a moment's mournful consideration, he spat at the spittoon, and missed. "Nope."

* * *

J.R. stifled the urge to fling his wife over his shoulder and haul her off, first to his room and his big bed at the National, then home to Denver where they both belonged.

No matter how much he wanted to, he couldn't do it. For one thing, Murray would be bound to hear of it, and there was nothing the *Times* would like better than to publicly mock the inability of the *Tribune*'s star reporter to get his wife to heed the "honor and obey" part of their wedding vows.

For another, he had a feeling Caroline would do him serious physical harm if he were crazy enough to try. She'd try to, anyway. His sweet little wife was proving to be a great deal tougher than he'd ever have imagined.

Since he couldn't kidnap his wife, he might as well go report on something. Caroline's nasty little trick with the luggage yesterday had set him behind. After that harebrained article in the *Times* this morning, it clearly behooved him to show her how a *real* reporter went about digging out the truth. And he knew right where to start.

Even this early in the morning, Osbald's Golden Diamond Saloon was doing good business. The saloon occupied a long, narrow, high-ceilinged brick building smack in the middle of town. Despite the red flocked wallpaper and the fancy beveled mirror behind the bar, it had the air of a place intended for serious drinking rather than the wild carousing common to some of the other establishments around town. Two large, round tables at the back of the room looked like good spots for a little high-stakes poker, though right now only the smaller tables nearer the bar were occupied.

J.R. casually propped his foot on the brass boot rail that ran the length of the bar. "Whiskey," he said. The bartender nodded and slid a glass his way.

Osbald himself was holding court from behind the bar and a bottle of whiskey.

"Damn foolishness," he growled to an apparently sympathetic audience of rough-looking miners and slickly dressed gamblers. He lifted his half-full glass as if in a toast. "Thousand dollars bail because I defended myself! Man's got a right to defend himself and his property!"

A half-dozen heads nodded agreement.

"That's right."

"Damn straight."

The saloon owner set his glass down with a snap. "Everybody knows Walker was a hot-tempered son of a bitch."

"Man was downright mean," agreed one fellow from behind a bush of a mustache.

"And that was when he was in a good mood," said another.

"If I hadn't shot him, he'd sure as hell've shot me." Osbald glanced around the room, clearly aggrieved.

His followers dutifully murmured agreement. Those who didn't agree wisely remained silent.

J.R. studied Osbald from behind his own glass of whiskey. The man was beefier than the drawings in the *Tribune* had indicated, ruddy-faced and with slightly protuberant eyes and a narrow mouth that didn't quite seem to fit the rest of his features. Not bad-looking, though he lacked the suave elegance of the man he'd killed.

Not the kind of man he'd want to have at his back in a dark alley, J.R. decided. Taking his glass, he worked his way down the bar, deliberately adding himself to the small crowd gathered to hear Osbald's grievances.

"Waste of time and the taxpayers' money having a trial like this," the saloon keeper growled.

More heads nodded.

"You and Walker had had disagreements before, hadn't you?" J.R. said, casually propping an elbow on the bar.

Osbald studied him with suspicion. "Don't think I know you, do I?"

"Abbott, from the *Tribune*."

Osbald's eyes narrowed. After a short, silent inspection, he turned his head and spat on the floor behind the bar. "Goddamned newspaper reporter."

J.R. nodded agreeably. "That's right."

"You here to write lies about me, too? Just like that goddamned C.A. from the *Times,* suggesting there's some sort of conspiracy going on here?"

At the mention of Caroline's article, J.R.'s hackles rose. Osbald's assembled court stirred uneasily.

"I told you, I'm a *Tribune* man," he said calmly. "The *Times* is nothing but a pack of liars and thieves."

Osbald blinked, then gave a sharp bark of laughter. He waved to the bartender. "Fill the man's glass."

He topped off his own much larger glass, then

picked it up and sauntered down the bar toward J.R. Wordlessly, his audience moved with him.

Osbald leaned over the expanse of polished wood, a move that could have been friendly, or subtly threatening, depending. J.R. watched him, and waited.

"You the Abbott who wrote those stories about the coal miners up north of Denver?"

"That's right."

"I'm by way of being a mine owner myself, you know," Osbald confided. "Mine owners don't much like union men."

"I'm a reporter," J.R. responded mildly. "That means I'm not necessarily on either side."

Osbald weighed that, decided to accept it. "I've been a miner, too."

J.R. took a sip of the whiskey. A cheap brand, but he'd tasted worse. "Way I heard it, you and Walker ended up in court a few years back over a mining dispute."

The saloon owner thumped the bar with his fist. "Goddamned thief was working my vein. Law says the vein belongs to the fellow whose land it surfaces on. That was *my* gold and the bastard was digging it out right from under my nose."

"Did the courts see it that way?"

"Hell, no! Idiots and liars, every one! Walker must've paid 'em, though I never could prove it." Osbald snarled, just thinking about it, then took another hefty swig of whiskey. His hand was so big it engulfed the glass.

J.R. grunted, took a sip from his own whiskey. It wasn't the first time he'd needed a good head for drink in his job. "When Walker's mine got blown up, what happened there?"

A couple of the men in the crowd went very still. J.R. glanced at them, then back to Osbald.

Osbald eyed him doubtfully, suddenly cautious. "What do you mean, what happened?"

J.R. shrugged. "I've heard so many stories of what happened, I'm not sure what to believe."

"That went to court, too," Osbald informed him. "He got off then, same as the other time."

"You think he blew it up himself? His own mine? Why would he do that?"

"Keep the striking miners from taking it over," Osbald said flatly.

"Seems pretty extreme to me."

"Yeah, well." The words were a dangerous rumble deep in the man's throat.

"I heard rumors it wasn't Walker *or* the miners, that it was someone else entirely."

Was it a trick of the dim light in the bar, or was that a flash of fury in Osbald's protuberant eyes? J.R. couldn't tell for sure. A moment later the man had buried his nose in his glass, hiding his expression.

"What do *you* think?" he asked the minute Osbald put the glass down.

The muscles at one corner of Osbald's narrow little mouth jumped.

"I think the bastard was a lying, cheating, thieving son of a bitch, and the world's better off without him."

J.R. grinned. "Yeah, but other than that?"

Nervous laughter swept their audience, and was immediately stifled.

"You reporter types always ask so many questions?"

"Always," J.R. said pleasantly. "Asking questions is our job."

"Hell of a job."

"Yes, it is."

Osbald laughed and raised his glass in a mocking salute. J.R. gave an answering salute and emptied his glass. There'd been three times as much whiskey in the other man's glass as in his own, but their empty glasses thumped down on the bar at the same time.

J.R. dug a dollar out of his pocket—five times what the whiskey should have cost—and tossed it on the bar.

"Thanks for your time. And the whiskey."

"You're going to be at the trial tomorrow?"

"That's right, along with every other reporter in town."

Osbald didn't seem overly bothered by the thought. "Blood sucking sons-a-bitches, every one of you."

J.R. grinned and touched the brim of his hat in acknowledgment, and turned away. He took two steps then, like a man who's just remembered something, turned back to the bar.

"Almost forgot. Another story I've heard going around is that you and Walker were fighting over the same woman. That true?"

"Dolly?"

"That's the name I heard."

Osbald shrugged. "We weren't fighting over her."

"Ugly, is she?"

"Dolly? Naw. She's all right. Great tits."

Someone in the crowd snickered.

The man grinned. It wasn't a pleasant grin. "She was Walker's fancy piece, not mine, but I had a hell of a good time screwing her, knowing it'd make him mad as hell when he found out."

"Mad enough to want to kill you?"

Osbald laughed. "Maybe. If I hadn't killed him first."

Long practice let J.R. keep the satisfaction from showing on his face. Not that the words were a confession to murder. The man was drunk and preening in front of his followers. Heavy drinking often led to loose tongues and wild boasts. It didn't always lead to the truth.

But sometimes, if you worked it right, it could get you close enough to the truth that you could grab hold by other means.

He was almost to the door when Osbald called his name.

"Abbott?"

J.R. glanced back. "Yeah?"

"One thing. You're a reporter. You see that C.A. bastard around, that fellow from the *Times?* You tell him to get his story straight or I'll wring his goddamned neck."

Chapter Ten

Caroline could have chewed nails. Her husband was a treacherous, conniving, unprincipled, low-down, no-good snake in the grass. He'd deliberately distracted her yesterday so that she forgot to claim her pass to the trial because he'd *known* the clerk was going to be gone today.

If she'd had the good sense to take Elizabeth's gun when it was offered, she could have marched right over to the National and shot him. Maybe she still would. No, better yet, she'd boil him in oil. She'd hang, draw, and quarter him. She'd...she'd...

Her imagination failed her. She couldn't think of anything awful enough to pay him back for his treachery, but somehow she'd get even if it was the last thing she did. And then she'd haunt him from the grave, just for the hell of it.

Her fury carried her up the hill and through Mary Walker's front gate before she had a chance to think about anything else, like being nervous or unsure of herself.

The sound of the gate clanging shut behind her

snapped her out of her temper long enough for her to remember where she was and what it was she wanted. She paused at the front steps for a hasty check to make sure her hair was neatly in place and her petticoat wasn't showing. Reassured, she quickly mounted the steps and pounded the massive brass door knocker until she could hear the echoes in the house.

The echoes were shortly followed by footsteps on hardwood floors, coming toward the door, then the sound of a latch being drawn back. The door swung open silently.

"Yes?" Mrs. Walker's maid would have qualified to serve in any upper-class Baltimore house—neat black uniform, white starched apron, and a nicely calculated, supercilious air that was always useful in discouraging unwanted visitors.

Caroline handed her one of her *Times* business cards that identified her as "Mrs. Caroline Abbott." She'd decided, right at the start, not to use her formal calling cards with the more socially correct "Mrs. J. Randolph Abbott, III" engraved on them in an elegant copperplate script. A friend, one of the few who approved of her venture into journalism, had urged her to defy convention even further by dropping the "Mrs.", but she hadn't been quite that brave...or that foolhardy. A married woman, after all, was often permitted where an unmarried woman was not.

"I'd like to speak with Mrs. Walker if she's available, please."

The maid started to refuse, then hesitated. She studied the expensive, engraved card, rubbing her thumb over the lettering as if to reassure herself of its quality, then eyed Caroline up and down. Her gaze latched onto the diamond stick pin in her collar. The diamond did the trick.

"May I tell Mrs. Walker what this is about?" she asked. The tone was polite, but it couldn't quite disguise her underlying suspicion.

The muscles in Caroline's shoulders tensed. She'd known this question was coming. Time and again J.R. had told her that the hardest part of an interview was getting through the door in the first place. He'd had wild tales of the stratagems to which he'd sometimes been reduced, but she had decided to try the simple truth. If that didn't work, she'd go for the "mutual acquaintances" angle and a prayer.

"Please tell Mrs. Walker that I am writing a series of articles on her husband's death and the upcoming trial, all told from the women's perspective. I'd like to talk to her about it if she's free."

The maid frowned. "I don't think—"

"She may have seen my first article in the *Times* this morning," Caroline hastily added.

The maid's mouth thinned in disapproval. "The one with the horrible headline?"

Caroline flinched. "I didn't write the headline."

"She saw it." After a moment's pinch-mouthed consideration, the woman grudgingly swung the door wide. "You can wait in the parlor, ma'am. I'll ask Mrs. Walker if she's receiving today."

The parlor was large and elegantly furnished, but there was a hollow feeling to the place, as if all the life had gone out of it. From the *Times'* files, Caroline knew that she and Mary Walker were close to the same age. Mary had been married a little bit longer, but now she was a widow, and childless, her world turned upside down in the time it took to shoot a gun and kill a man.

Just the thought of losing J.R. was enough to make her stomach churn.

The wait was beginning to get on her nerves when the maid finally reappeared.

"Madame will see you, but only for a few minutes. She hasn't been well these past few months, and social courtesies are often a strain on her. I'm sure you understand."

"Of course," Caroline murmured, frantically trying to figure out which questions were the most important in case she didn't get a chance to ask them all.

The maid led her up the stairs to a sitting room whose windows looked out over Cripple Creek and the hills beyond. Black swags over the drapes shut out half the light and gave a gloomy, claustrophobic feel to what would otherwise have been a very pleasant room.

A small, slender woman dressed all in black rose at her entrance.

Under better circumstances, Mary Walker would have been considered pretty, even beautiful. She had the kind of delicate, feminine features that were guaranteed to attract a man's attention. Right now, though, she looked tired and worn and far older than she really was.

"Mrs. Abbott?"

"Mrs. Walker. Thank you for seeing me."

Pale blue eyes, bruised looking and rimmed in red, fixed on her face. "That was a horrible headline."

Caroline flushed, grimaced. "My editor chose it."

It must have been the right response. Mary gestured to a chair by hers. "Please."

While the maid was dispatched to prepare tea, Caroline settled in the chair and desperately wished that she could drag out her little black notebook. Intuition and hundreds of hours spent enduring social visits warned her that Mary Walker would speak more freely without it.

Once the maid had departed, Mary knotted her hands together in her lap, then hesitantly turned to face her unexpected visitor.

Caroline smiled back. Take the initiative, J.R. had often said. Establish yourself as someone they can trust, then let them talk.

"I know this must all be very difficult for you," she said.

The woman flinched. "Yes." She hesitated, then, perhaps reassured by Caroline's very real sympathy, said, "I still have a hard time believing he's really dead."

"It hasn't been that long." That was, Caroline thought guiltily, exactly the sort of useless platitude she'd used before when friends and acquaintances had lost a family member.

Mary Walker seemed to find it comforting, though. She nodded eagerly. "I'll sit down to dinner and wonder why there's only one place set at table. Sometimes I'll read something in the paper and want to share it with him, then realize, too late, that he's not there any more. Or I'll wake up in the middle of the night thinking I hear his tread on the stairs." A sad little smile flitted over her face, then vanished. "I don't sleep very well."

"It must be especially difficult for you, being so far from your family."

Mary ducked her head to pick at a bit of black ribbon trimming her skirt. "They didn't really approve of the marriage, you know. Especially not after those two"—she hesitated, clearly choosing her words with care—"those two women sued him."

"But you loved him," Caroline said, remembering her own family's reservations about J.R.'s work as a reporter.

"He was very...strong. Very sure of himself. I...I liked that." She raised her head to meet Caroline's gaze. "It's so much easier when the man makes all the decisions, when all you have to worry about is the house and keeping things nice for him and...and things like that. Don't you agree?"

Caroline bit back the denial that jumped to her lips. "Many women feel that way," she said gently, and felt a little surge of pride at her cleverness.

The pride appalled her. She had the oddest feeling, suddenly, that she was really two people trying to stare out of the same pair of eyes. One was the woman who ached for another woman's pain. The other was a reporter who cold-bloodedly listened and analyzed, probing for more, relishing the game.

"A woman's place is in the home. I've always believed that." Again Mary hesitated—something she probably did a lot, Caroline thought—then, "He was good to me. Very generous. Very kind. I...I think he loved me, in spite of all the...all the other women."

I think he loved me. Caroline's heart squeezed. No matter how irritated she'd gotten at J.R., she'd never had any doubts about his love for her. "I'm sure he did."

"No matter what people say, he wasn't going to kill that awful man."

"Osbald?"

"That's right. He never would have killed him. Never!"

"Witnesses said he was very angry, though, and that he had a temper. Is that true?"

"That he had a temper? I suppose so." Mary seemed to weigh that. "Yes, yes of course he had a temper. He was a man, wasn't he? A very strong, determined man. He wouldn't have built his mine and his business up like he did if he hadn't been strong."

With each word, she seemed to get fiercer, more determined to protect her husband's memory.

"But anyone who says he would have killed someone, even that awful Osbald man, is lying. My Josiah never would have killed anyone."

"I'm sure you're right," Caroline murmured.

"Of course I'm right!" Mary Walker snapped. Those pale, red-rimmed eyes were beginning to flash real fire. "Everyone in town knows it, but they don't care. They didn't like my husband because he was successful and because he fought for what was his, so they're getting even by ignoring the truth. They don't care that Osbald blew up my husband's mine, then made it look as if Josiah had done it himself. They don't care that he was trying to sabotage Josiah's operations and steal his gold. They don't care about *any* of that. They're going to acquit him, and they're not even going to try to consider the truth when they do!''

Caroline listened to the tumbled, angry flood of words and tried to remember everything.

J.R. had been right. Being a good listener was just as important as knowing which questions to ask. Under the influence of a sympathetic ear, even one belonging to a newspaper reporter and a stranger, Mary Walker was letting down emotional barriers she'd probably been struggling to keep in place for a long, long time.

The reporter in her gloried in the revelations. The kinder, more womanly part of her shuddered, and was ashamed. The reporter won.

''So you're convinced there's a conspiracy to cover up the truth?'' she asked.

Mary's chin came up. ''Aren't you? Isn't that what you wrote in your story in the paper this morning?''

''That's certainly what some people think. But surely, when the prosecuting attorney starts asking questions—''

''He's not going to ask about anything except what happened at the Golden Diamond that night. He told me so.''

Caroline sat up straighter, startled. ''He said that? He really said he wouldn't investigate your husband's quarrel with Osbald and their legal wrangling and all that?''

Mary nodded. "Yes. He said everybody knew about the rest of it, that it didn't have any bearing on what happened."

"But—but that's outrageous! All those old quarrels must have had *something* to do with what happened that night. He can't just ignore them!"

"But that's what he's going to do." The fire in the woman flickered and went out. The angry color that had given life to her features bled away. Her shoulders slumped. "He's going to ignore all of it. Every little bit of it."

Caroline stared at her, desperately trying to bring some order to the wild thoughts and wilder speculations tumbling in her head.

"Doesn't that sound rather suspicious to you?" she asked at last.

"Suspicious?"

"Don't you think they ought to be considering all the…the quarrels and arguments that were already between Osbald and your husband? They had a history of quarreling. They'd gone to court over the issue of who owned a very profitable vein of gold. They'd even quarreled over the same woman."

That last popped out before Caroline realized it. The widow flinched, but made no protest.

"Don't you think they ought to consider *all* of that?" Caroline insisted.

Mary's gaze dropped to her hands and the bit of ribbon she'd been worrying. "Yes."

The single word sounded very small and timid.

Caroline suppressed a sudden urge to shake her, to shout at her that it was all right to not be meek and accepting, that she had every right to be angry, that she ought to scream and shout and throw things if she wanted. Instead, she said, "Did you ask him why?"

Mary shook her head but didn't take her gaze off the ribbon.

"Do you—" Caroline hesitated. It was one thing to write about vague accusations of conspiracy, quite another to confront them head-on. Then she thought of J.R. and what he would do, of what she would want if he were the one who'd been killed. "Mrs. Walker, do you think they're trying to hide the truth? That they're trying to protect Osbald?"

With a sharp ripping sound, the bit of ribbon tore free. Clearly agitated, Mary stared at it, then abruptly wadded it into a tiny ball and buried it in her lap.

Caroline leaned over to lay her hand on the woman's arm. "Mrs. Walker?"

"It wasn't that…that *whore*," she said. "My husband didn't care about her. He'd never, ever have gotten in a quarrel with Osbald over *her*."

"No?"

"No! He loved *me,* not her! She was just a…a diversion, that's all."

"Yes, of course," Caroline said soothingly.

"Men need that, you know," Mary informed her, struggling for calm. "They're not like us. That…that sort of thing…it's just… They just *do* it. It doesn't mean anything. It doesn't matter to them. *She* never mattered. Not to my husband. Not to my Josiah."

"No, of course not." That kind of hurt, at least, she could understand.

But did it mean that Mary Walker's doubts about

the trial tomorrow were really only a protective shell she'd drawn around her pride? That there was no reason for the prosecuting attorney to bring in all the old quarrels and hatreds because the cause of Josiah Walker's death really was just two men's jealous wrangling over the favors of a prostitute?

She didn't know. What bothered her more than not knowing was seeing how easy it was for a woman to lose her identity in her marriage. Mary Walker could be roused to hot-blooded anger in defense of her husband's reputation, but was reduced to cringing tears when his philandering threatened her heart, if not their marriage.

The maid's arrival with the tea tray gave Mary a chance to regain control of herself. Over tea they chatted about Cripple Creek and Denver and the differences between the West and the worlds they'd grown up in. Though Caroline wanted badly to return to the question of Walker's death and coming trial, she didn't say a word. One glance at the strain in the other woman's eyes was enough to silence her.

When she rose to take her leave a half hour later, she had a dozen new questions to carry with her and not one good answer.

J.R. shifted uncomfortably on a bench set near the front window of Cripple Creek's largest assay office. He'd been sitting there for a good half hour and the bench was getting harder by the minute. The assayer had a yen to talk and, apparently, absolutely nothing else to do.

"Both of 'em's mean as skunks," the fellow assured him for the fourth or fifth time. "Osbald and Walker, if they didn't have a good quarrel or two going, they'd start one just for the hell of it."

Bored, J.R. glanced out the window just in time to spot his wife crossing the street. There was an aggressive forward tilt to her body that said she was on a mission and no one had better get in her way. He craned forward to see where she was going.

"I knew Osbald'd be lookin' for an excuse to get back at Walker," the assayer continued, undeterred. "Have to say, though—"

She disappeared into the law offices of Matton, Lawrence & Snead, Osbald's lawyers.

"...that Walker smelled a bit better, him with his fancy clothes and city ways. But there're those'd say he was the one to watch just 'cause he'd fool you, lookin' like a gentleman an' all like he did. On the other hand—"

J.R. got to his feet, interrupting the man midsentence. "Excuse me, but I just saw someone I've been trying to run down all morning."

The assayer eyed him with amusement. "Wouldn't happen to be that good-lookin' lady that just went by here that's got your attention, now, would it?"

J.R. froze. "Why would you say that?"

The man grinned from behind his luxurious mustache. "Fellow hears things."

"Things? What things?"

The grin widened, encouraged by J.R.'s deepening scowl.

"Oh, things like how you checked in at the National yesterday, askin' for a Mrs. Abbott what weren't expected, and how there's a lady of the same name who just happens t'be boardin' with Georgianne Bonnard and her sister. An' that's not countin' your dinin' with that self-same lady in mighty high style last night. Leastwise," he added helpfully, "that's what I hear."

J.R. couldn't stop a wry grin of his own. That was the risk of dealing with gossips—they were as likely to be talking about you as they were to be talking about the people you were interested in. And some of the biggest gossips around were men who didn't have enough work to keep them busy.

"I appreciate the background on Osbald and Walker," he said.

The assayer good-naturedly waved away the proffered payment. "Any time." Again that knowing grin. "But you might tell the missus that Donnelly's carries good shoes at a good price. I couldn't help but notice there was just the tiniest bit of a hitch in her get-along, if y'know what I mean. All that walkin' around town can be mighty hard on the feet."

J.R. was halfway across the street when he decided not to beard her in the offices of Matton, Lawrence & Snead after all. He'd already called on Snead, who'd be representing Osbald at the trial tomorrow, and gotten exactly nothing for his pains. She'd be out soon enough.

When she hadn't emerged twenty minutes later he abandoned the lamppost he'd been holding up and stalked off, swearing under his breath.

At precisely a quarter to one, feet aching and head buzzing with all she'd learned that morning, Caroline emerged from the offices of Matton, Lawrence & Snead and hobbled off toward the National.

She could afford tea and a sandwich, she'd decided, even if a full lunch at the National wasn't in the budget. And while she sipped her tea and gave her feet a rest, she'd write up the interview with Mrs. Walker and all the other things she'd learned that morning.

She gave a little celebratory skip at the thought, despite her protesting feet.

The story would be good. She was sure of it. *Very* good. Murray couldn't dream of getting anything like this no matter how long he'd been writing for the *Times*. J.R., for all his vaunted charm, wouldn't have gotten past Mary Walker's front door.

She'd convinced other people to talk, too. The pieces were beginning to form a rather ugly picture whose outlines were fairly clear, though she lacked some of the details…and the proof.

The article was going to make people sit up and take notice. After this, C.A. was never going to be relegated to the society pages again. Not if she could help it!

The glowing electric Welcome sign over the National's front door, which yesterday she'd thought in such poor taste, today seemed a portent of the bright future that lay ahead for her.

C.A., world-famous lady reporter.

The words had a lovely ring to them, Caroline thought, and nodded cheerfully at the porter holding the door for her.

The table to which she was eventually escorted was too small and too near the doors to the kitchen, but she didn't protest, too eager to get to her writing to worry about petty details like that. While the waiter whisked off after her tea, she dragged out her little black notebook, then the new copybook with its crisp, lined pages that she'd just bought. The sight of it made her want to laugh with the sheer joy of it all. She'd bought another little black book, too, thicker this time, because she'd filled every last page of the old one with the notes of her interviews and questions for which she still needed answers.

There was something...*glorious* about those pristine pages just waiting for her pen. Something bright with promise, as if all she had to do was fill them with words to guarantee that everything she hoped for came true, and nothing of what she feared.

Filling them wasn't that easy, however. With every sentence she wrote, she saw more clearly just what she'd gotten into, and the price she might have to pay for it. And with every sentence, her determination to see it through to the end, regardless, became more fixed.

She was on her third cup of tea—she'd had to ask twice for the refill—and her fourth round of revisions when a shadow fell over the page. One glance confirmed her darkest suspicions.

"Mr. Abbott."

"Mrs. Abbott," J.R. said with exquisite courtesy.

She closed the copybook—ink-smudged now and with ripped out pages haphazardly sticking out the sides—then neatly capped her pen and set everything aside. The scent of him, of soap and expensive cigars and man, teased at her, jumbling her thoughts.

"May I offer you a cup of coffee?" she asked with the same exquisite, mocking courtesy.

His expression darkened. "Don't, Caroline."

The muscles in her jaw clenched. In the past hour she'd written her way to a clearer understanding of what she wanted, of what was important and what was not, but she wasn't ready to face J.R. with what she'd learned. Not yet.

He wasn't giving her a choice in the matter. Without asking permission he pulled out the chair opposite and, with a neat flick of his coattails, sat down. A waiter scurried over.

"Coffee."

"Yes, Mr. Abbott. Right away, sir."

Caroline scowled. J.R. ignored her and scanned the room, instead.

"Short of that table there behind the potted palm," he said cheerfully, "I don't think you could have chosen a more inconvenient, uncomfortable, out-of-the-way table if you'd tried."

"I didn't choose it. The waiter set me here," she snapped.

"Then you should have asked for another."

"Unlike you, I'm not accustomed to making ill-mannered scenes in public."

"Insisting on a good table is not ill-mannered, my dear. A good reporter would never allow himself to be stuck back here where he can neither see, nor be seen."

"A really good reporter doesn't require any pandering to his pride. Besides," she added sweetly, "we couldn't have quarreled nearly so comfortably at the big table at the front of the room."

Something hot flashed in his eyes. "True, but it's not a matter of pride. It's a matter of status and influence, two intangibles without which you'll find yourself scraping for dirt if you persist in writing."

"You're speaking from experience?"

"Observation," he snapped. "I've never lacked status or influence, and I've *never* scraped for dirt."

"Hah!"

The waiter's return with coffee and a fresh pot of tea stopped the conversation but did nothing to ease the hostility sparking between them.

"I hear you visited Mr. Snead today," she said when the waiter departed at last. She'd also heard that J.R. had scarcely gotten past the door before he'd been politely escorted out again.

"Indeed." He tried to put a good face on it, but she could tell it rankled. "And how did you find *your* visit?"

Snead had lied through his teeth, first to last, and smiled while he did it. "I found it…interesting," she said.

"He was helpful?"

She smiled. "Very."

"Informative?"

"That, too."

"Really?" He was starting to gloat, convinced she'd fallen for it.

"Really. Good, consistent lying is almost as useful

as the truth, don't you think? And *much* more entertaining.''

That shook him. His eyes narrowed. ''That sounds like something I would say.''

''It does, doesn't it?'' She gave him her most fluttering, my-aren't-you-clever look, a trick every female learned in her crib, and most men never caught on to. ''Too bad I said it first.''

The mockery vanished from his face, replaced by cold, hard anger. Anger and another emotion that was hidden beneath it, something darker and more unsettling that she couldn't quite read.

''This isn't a game, Caroline, and Osbald isn't one of your well-mannered society swells.''

''No, he's not.'' She met his gaze with a hard, direct stare of her own. If she was ever going to earn his respect as an equal, it would be now, with this. It *had* to be now, because she couldn't endure much more of a life without him in it. ''He's a murderer, and given what I've learned, I'd say he's got a good chance of getting away with it.''

He stared at her in shock. Whatever he'd expected from her, it hadn't been that.

The look on his face set the match to her anger, making it shoot hot and white through her veins, making it scald her throat.

''You think I'm playing at this, don't you?'' she snarled. ''You think that I don't understand what's going on here, that I'm just a naive little fool with no more sense than a—a *flea* or something. Don't you? *Don't you?*''

He flinched, clearly taken aback. "No, I don't think you're a fool."

"Incompetent, then."

"Out of your league," he amended. "This isn't a job for a woman. Certainly not for a woman like you."

"Like me? What do you mean, 'like me'? If I'm not a fool, or incompetent, then what *am* I, J.R.? When you look at me, what do you see? Tell me that. Tell me *exactly* what you see, because I swear it's not the same woman *I* see every time I look in the mirror!"

That shook him. He stared at her, clearly uncertain how to respond. The smooth-talking man of words was speechless.

"Well?"

"What do I see?" Now he was snarling, too. "I see a beautiful, intelligent, headstrong woman who's in too deep and won't admit it. I see the woman I love. I see my *wife,* dammit! But that seems to be something she won't admit to, either."

The woman I love.

Caroline drew a shaky breath. She'd always known he *wanted* her. Until now, she hadn't realized how much she needed the reassurance that he loved her, as well.

She forced herself to meet his angry, troubled gaze. "Do you want to know what I see when *I* look in the mirror?" She didn't wait for an answer.

"I see a woman who's just beginning to understand who she is and what she can do. I see a woman who loves her husband very, very much, but who doesn't want her life to be shaped by her mother's notions of what she's supposed to be. *Or* her husband's," she added, deliberately challenging.

His clenched into fists. "Surely there's some way you can do that besides tackling Osbald in your paper."

"No, there isn't. Not anymore."

"What the hell do you mean by that?"

She ignored the question. "I'm not giving up. Osbald murdered a man and there's a good chance he's going to get away with it because no one wants to look at what was between them...except me."

"Did you know he's threatened to wring your neck if you write any more stories like this morning's?"

"What?"

"You heard me. I talked to him this morning. Since I'm a reporter, he figured warning me was as good as warning you. He thought you were a man."

"Really?" She wasn't sure how she felt about that. "I assume by now he knows I'm not."

"I assume he does, but that just makes you more vulnerable, not less."

She couldn't argue with that, but she was damned if she was going to let him see her fear. "He wouldn't dare."

"A saloon full of witnesses didn't stop him from killing a man. A very powerful, influential man. What's to stop him from hurting you?"

He grabbed her wrist, pulling her to him.

"Caroline, please. Go home. Forget this...this job. This story. I can't protect you and do my job, too."

His voice was low, rough-edged and raw with emotion.

She started to protest, but something in his eyes, in the brutal way he gripped her wrist killed the words in her throat.

"*Please*. Go. Home."

It was fear she'd seen beneath the anger, she realized. Not for him, but for her.

"I can't, J.R. Not now."

"Caroline, dammit! If—"

"It's not the job. I'm not trying to prove anything, either. Not really. Not anymore."

"Then...why?"

Her gaze dropped to where his hand manacled her wrist. Carefully, deliberately, she pulled her hand free, then, because she wanted so much to hang on to him and never let go, she laced her hands together and buried them in her lap.

"This morning, when I was talking to people, asking questions, it was at the back of my mind—what if *you'd* been killed?" she said, picking her words with care. "What if you were dead and your killer went free because no one cared enough to act? I thought of Mary Walker, all alone in that big, empty house on the hill, sitting there staring out the window, waiting for justice that will never come. And then later, when I was writing my story"—she glanced at the closed copybook and the capped pen—"I kept thinking, no one else sees this. Or, worse, they don't *want* to see it."

"See what?"

"That Osbald deliberately provoked Walker, knowing Walker would lose his temper and storm the Golden Diamond.''

J.R. didn't even blink. Obviously, he'd thought of that possibility long ago.

He took a careful sip of coffee, then set his cup down. ''Go on.''

''You already know this.''

''Who cares what I know or don't? I want to know what *you* think.''

She glanced around to assure herself they wouldn't be overheard, then lowered her voice and leaned across the table toward J.R.

''I think he was very, very clever. If he'd shot Walker in some dark alley, people would have asked questions. But he shot him in front of witnesses, all of whom will swear that Walker was furious and threatening to kill him. A murder charge becomes, at most, manslaughter, and more probably self-defense. His target's dead and he's home free. Am I right?''

J.R. nodded slowly. ''I think so. But I can't prove it. Can you?''

''No.''

He cocked his chin at the copybook. ''Then what's that?''

''The facts I *do* know. A story that will start people talking about it.''

''And the talk will force others to dig out the proof of Osbald's guilt.''

''Yes. It worked for you when you were getting started on that story of the coal miners' working conditions, didn't it? I think it will work here.''

''And if Osbald's innocent?''

"Then they'll find that, too. But he's not. I'm sure of it."

Something dangerous flickered in J.R.'s eyes. "He won't stand idly by and let you undermine him with your stories."

"I'll be careful."

"Careful? Since when do you know anything about *careful?* Since when do you know *anything* about men like Osbald?" He slammed his fist on the table, making the dishes jump and drawing curious, wary stares from the few guests left in the dining room. "No. Dammit, *no!* I can't let you do this, Caroline. It's too dangerous."

Caroline was sitting up so stiff and straight her spine hurt. Without thinking, she laid a protective hand atop her copybook. "You don't have any say in the matter, Mr. Abbott."

"Yes I do. I'm your husband, remember?"

"All too well."

"As your husband, I have a responsibility to protect you, keep you safe."

"Really? And how do you propose to do that without my cooperation?"

"I—" That was all he said. His mouth opened, closed. A look of exquisite frustration claimed his handsome features.

"Exactly," she said, ruthlessly squelching the sudden stab of doubt.

Chapter Eleven

J.R. signed the bill in silence while Caroline, equally silent, tucked her pen and her copybook in her purse. She offered a small, prim "thank you" when he held her chair, but that was it.

They were halfway across the National's lobby when he pulled her to one side.

"You're really going to file that story?" he asked, nodding at her purse where the copybook was.

She stopped herself an instant before she clutched the purse to her chest. "Yes."

"How?"

That wasn't what she'd expected. "I'll send a telegram. Or maybe I'll telephone." She cocked her head in suspicion. "Why do you ask?"

"You can call from here, if you like. There's a phone on the second floor. It's very private." He said it casually, as if he'd just thought of it.

Her suspicions deepened. "I'm not a guest here."

"Charge it to my room. I'll make sure you pay me back," he added, before she could object.

Caroline weighed the offer, mentally turning it around and shaking it, trying to see the hidden trick.

"You're going to spy on me, lurk around the corner and listen to every word I have to say."

He put on a wounded look. "I won't lurk around any corner."

"Hide behind a door, then."

"Me?" He almost quivered with wounded innocence. "I would never stoop that low. Besides, there aren't any doors near the telephone."

He was definitely up to something, but what? She didn't know much about phones, but there had to be a trick, some secret he was privy to and she was not.

When she didn't respond, J.R. shrugged. "All right, don't use the phone. I'm sure all the hangers-on at the phone company offices will be very interested to hear what you have to say."

He would have walked away if she hadn't grabbed his sleeve and dragged him back.

"All right," she snapped, exasperated. "Thank you. I'd like to use the phone. It's very kind of you to offer."

"That's very kind of you to say so."

The mockery in his voice made her teeth grate.

"I'll just alert the gentleman at the front desk that you'll be calling, shall I?"

Caroline let out a little huff of exasperation. She'd trounced him in the dining room, but he was getting the better of her now and the devil of it was, she didn't know how. "Thank you."

"Don't mention it."

He was at the front desk, chatting with the clerk,

when she shut the elevator door. As she walked down the second-floor hallway to the sitting area and the little alcove with the telephone, she looked for places he could hide, ways he could sneak up on her unheard. There weren't any.

Still, she waited, taking a few minutes to reread what she'd written, then stalked up the hall and back again, just to be sure she was alone.

Alone.

The word made her shiver. She moved so that her back was to the wall and she could see the elevator and the stairs and the empty hall, and thanked Heaven that the door to his room was around the far corner, safely out of sight. She wasn't sure what she was more afraid of—Osbald, or the uncertain future, or J.R. and her own desperate need for him.

The operator came on the line, her voice tinny and distant. ''What number please?''

Caroline could hear the clicks and hums as her call was put through, then the even more distant, mechanically distorted voice of the male receptionist at the *Times*. It seemed forever before her editor answered. Even blurred by the miles of metal wires between them, the raspy bark of his voice was surprisingly familiar, almost comforting.

''Hello? Mrs. Abbott? Hello?''

''Mr. Blackmun. I have a new story for you. A *great* story.''

As she spoke—almost shouted, really, compensating for the static—the doubts receded and the excitement of earlier came bubbling back. Her grip on the copybook tightened. She could feel the grain of the paperboard cover, the brush of the ripped-out sheets that stuck out on the edges in untidy confusion.

It wasn't much, but it was something solid to hold on to. And inside that paperboard cover was her future. Part of it, anyway, and all of it of her own making.

A penny and a half a word.

Caroline's hand was trembling so that she had a hard time settling the receiver back in its cradle. Mr. Blackmun had promised her a penny and a half a word for her story.

She wanted to scream and dance. She wanted to run down the stairs and find J.R. She wanted—

She forced herself to breathe, then carefully closed the copybook and tucked it into her purse. J.R. wasn't waiting, and he wouldn't much approve if he were. And dancing down the hallway didn't seem so appealing when she didn't have anyone to dance with. Worse, when she remembered that all this was built on the body of a dead man, the excitement dimmed, making her triumph seem rather sordid.

Had J.R. ever doubted his choice of work, she wondered? He'd always seemed so sure of himself and where he was going, but had he ever, deep inside, wondered if he'd chosen the right path after all? She wished she could ask him and knew she wouldn't, and that he probably wouldn't answer even if she did.

And he loved her. *Still* loved her.

That was some comfort. He might not have granted her the respect she craved, but he loved her. She had to believe they'd work it out somehow. Had to, because she couldn't bear anything else.

Life would have been a great deal less complicated if she'd just stayed in Baltimore and married George Davies like her parents had wanted. A lot more boring, a lot less satisfying, but a whole heck of a lot less complicated.

And thinking of Baltimore...

The telephone operator's voice sounded just as tinny and distant as it had the first time. "What number please?"

Caroline gave her the number.

The wait was interminable. Her impatience was rewarded when her father answered the phone instead of the butler. She hadn't dared hope he would.

"Papa! I hoped I'd be lucky enough to catch you at home."

"Caroline? Good God, girl! What are you doing spending the money on a long-distance telephone call? Are you all right?"

"I'm fine, Papa. Really."

"And J. Randolph? He's all right?"

"He's fine, Papa. Never better."

For a moment there was only static, then, "You're back together again, right? That's why you're calling, to tell me you've come to your senses and gone back to your husband."

Her mouth seemed very dry, suddenly. "No, Papa. I called to tell you that my first real story was published in the *Times* today. Second page on the top! And I'll have the next one in tomorrow's paper. A really *good* story, Papa. An *important* one."

"What about your husband, girl? *That's* what's important! All this foolishness about being a reporter and getting your stories in the paper—absurd! Your mother can't sleep nights for worrying, did you know that? Can't sleep! And you call me about some fool *newspaper* story?"

Bright, hot tears stung her eyes. Caroline angrily blinked them back. Why did the two men she loved most want so badly to force her into a mold of their making, not hers?

"Where's J.R., anyway? Can't for the life of me understand why he allows you to continue with this foolishness."

"He doesn't have any say in the matter."

"Of course he does! He's your husband, isn't he? He has every right. I thought he had more sense than to let this mess go on so long."

"I was the one who locked him out, remember, Papa?"

"Of course I remember!" The angry roar carried clearly despite the hundreds of miles between them. "I thought *you* had more sense, too!"

"He was caught in a brothel. A whorehouse, Papa! And he didn't once apologize, didn't try to explain."

She could feel her father's shudder of distaste all the way from Baltimore.

"A lady shouldn't use such language, ever."

"I wouldn't have had to if J.R. had stayed decently at home, where he belonged." No use trying to explain everything that had gone before. Her father would *never* understand that!

Resentment pinched her—J.R. in a whorehouse

didn't trouble her father half as much as her with a job and no husband. At the thought, anger sparked, white and fierce. Anger and a sudden decisiveness.

"Papa?" she said. She didn't wait for him to answer. "I want you to release my trust fund."

"What?"

Even though she knew he couldn't see her, she set her chin and squared her shoulders. It made her feel better when she did. It made her feel stronger.

"You heard me. I want you to release my trust fund. That's *my* money, Papa. Not yours. Not J.R.'s. *Mine.* And I want it. You had no right to stop my quarterly payments."

"I had every right! That fund's not yours until you turn twenty-five, and I won't—"

"Yes, you will."

The steely determination in her voice stopped them both cold. She'd never talked to her father like that. Not once.

Caroline licked lips suddenly gone dry.

"Papa," she said, coaxing now. "The money is mine. More important, this work is mine. Until this morning, I didn't realize how much that mattered."

"J.R.—"

"I love him. I love him with all my heart and soul. But I can't be what he wants me to be any more than I can be the kind of wife you think I should be."

"But—"

"We'll work it out somehow, Papa, J.R. and I. But we'll work it out between us because we want to, because we love each other, not because you bullied and coerced me into it. Can you understand that?"

The only answer she got was the static of the still open line.

Her heart squeezed, but her shoulders remained square, her chin firm. "Tell the bank to send the payment to my bank in Denver. They have all the necessary information."

Something that might have been a growl of agreement—or of outright refusal—came over the static, but not one word.

"I love you, Papa," she said. And then she hung up the receiver.

In a tiny, airless room tucked behind the National Hotel's front offices, J.R. carefully set down the receiver through which he'd been eavesdropping on Caroline's calls. He had to force a smile of thanks for the prim little woman who ran the hotel's switchboard in between keeping its books, doing its billing, and typing up all its official letters.

She smiled back, rather flustered, and nervously pushed her wire-rimmed spectacles back up her nose.

For the first time it occurred to him to wonder what she and other women like her were paid for the work, and whether she liked it.

"You must keep very busy," he said, gesturing to the modern typewriter that occupied pride of place on the battered desk, and to the heavy ledgers stacked beside it.

"I do, yes. But I don't mind!" she added quickly. "I don't know what I would have done if Mr. Rawlings—the manager, you know—hadn't given me the job."

"These your sons?" He picked up a framed picture of two sturdy boys who bore the stoic expressions common to all small boys who have been washed and brushed and crammed into their Sunday best, then told not to wiggle or get dirty. "They're handsome little fellows."

The woman's cheeks turned pink with pleasure. "They look like their father, bless them. They're good boys, and they've been such a comfort these past couple of years."

A shadow passed over her face, draining away the color as quickly as it had come. "Their father died in a coal mine cave-in. You'll understand where that left us, Mr. Abbott. I read those articles of yours in the *Tribune*. Everything you said was true. When my Martin—"

She stopped, then abruptly ducked her head, picked up a stack of papers on the desk, and shuffled them into tidier order. "I shouldn't keep you, sir. Chattering away like that. I don't know what I was thinking."

Feeling as awkward and uncomfortable as she obviously did, J.R. fished a five out of his pocket and discreetly slipped it part way under the bottom ledger. "And I shouldn't be keeping you, ma'am. Much more of this and Mr. Rawlings will double my room rate. But I do thank you for your help."

He stepped through the open doorway, then glanced back. She was already hunched over her papers, industriously jotting numbers in an open ledger as if her life depended on it.

* * *

Myers Avenue looked pretty much like any other city street, broad, dusty, and lined with two-storied houses of varying pretensions to grandeur that marched, shoulder to shoulder, along both sides. The houses eventually gave way to tiny little places that weren't much more than one-roomed shacks at the far end.

An open carriage bearing four well-dressed women and driven by a liveried Negro passed at a sedate trot. Another woman, not so well dressed but sporting an enormous feathered hat hurried along the other side of the street. Lace curtains or what looked, in some cases, like heavy velvet drapes, cloaked the windows, hiding whatever lay behind the neat clapboard exteriors.

Caroline suppressed a stab of disappointment. She wasn't sure what she'd expected of the state's most notorious red-light district, but it was something a little more scandalous than this.

No doubt things livened up at night and on the weekends, when the mines were closed and the men were on their own. Right now, everything looked depressingly respectable.

Reassured, Caroline, head high, crossed to the third house on the left, a large, blindingly white house with both lace curtains and velvet drapes at the windows and a fine brass knocker on the front door.

The maid who answered her knock was not, however, the sort who might have been accepted in her mother's house. The woman was dressed in a rose-colored gown trimmed in a rather startling shade of fuschia, and she eyed Caroline with insolent directness.

"Madame ain't hiring, if that's what you came about," she announced after a sharp assessment of Caroline's dress, jewelry, and person.

Caroline braced her hand against the door before the woman could close it. With her other hand she extended the business card plucked from her pocket.

"I'm not here about a...er...job. My name's Caroline Abbott and I'd like to talk with Miss Lola Spears about the Josiah Walker killing, if she's available." When the maid moved to close the door, she added hastily, "She may have seen my article in this morning's edition of the *Denver Times*."

The woman's face lit up. "The one that says you want to know about murder, you gotta ask the ladies?"

Caroline winced. That headline was going to haunt her for the rest of her life. "Yes."

"The girls liked it lots. Fact is, they're talking about it over breakfast right now."

"Are they?" Caroline said weakly. *Breakfast?* It was already well past noon.

If J.R. ever learned that her stories were appreciated in some of Cripple Creek's best brothels, she'd never hear the end of it.

The woman swung the door wide. "You can wait in there." She waved to a parlor decorated with entirely too much red velvet for Caroline's taste. "I'll go tell Miss Spears you're here."

The sound of her footsteps disappeared down the

hall. Caroline, scarcely breathing, stood listening to the silence after she was gone.

She was in a *brothel*.

The thought hit her like a runaway steam engine. Rubber kneed, heart pounding, she sank onto a velvet upholstered chair.

When she'd proposed these articles to her editor, including this particular interview, she'd expected to hire a man to carry messages for her, arrange a meeting in a respectable, public place. She'd never actually planned on marching up to the front door and demanding entry. After that confrontation with her father, though, she'd been so buoyed by pride at having stood up to him that she hadn't stopped to think, just charged full steam ahead. And now, here she was.

Dazed, she stared at the room, drinking in every detail and wondering how it compared to the fancy house where J.R. had been visiting when he was arrested and hauled off to jail. If he ever learned she'd been in a whorehouse, he'd lock *her* out of the house.

She was in an honest-to-goodness whorehouse.

"Mrs. Abbott?"

The woman standing in the open doorway was strikingly handsome, lushly endowed, and dressed in the prettiest, most outrageously daring morning wrapper Caroline had ever seen. For a moment, she wondered where she could find a gown like that, and what J.R. would say if she ever got the nerve to wear it, then she was on her feet and stammering an introduction.

Lola Spears smiled, clearly amused by her embarrassment. "Please, sit down, Mrs. Abbott. I've told

Delia to ignore the door for awhile and keep the girls out. We won't be disturbed.''

Caroline breathed out and tried not to let the sudden wash of relief show on her face. "Thank you.''

She sank back into the chair while the madam, who didn't look much older than she was, gracefully sank onto a chaise opposite. "And thank you for agreeing to see me.''

Lola cocked her head to one side, studying her. "After I read that article this morning, I wondered if you'd talk to me. I have to admit, I didn't expect you to show up on my front doorstep.''

Caroline laughed. She couldn't help it. There was something about the woman's brash confidence that was very appealing.

"I didn't expect to, either. But I had a rather... challenging conversation with my husband over lunch, then an even more difficult conversation by phone with my father, and I guess I thought, after all that, that I could tackle anything.''

It was the madam's turn to laugh. "Good for you! It's never a good idea to let a man get too full of himself, hon. Especially not a husband.''

Lazily, she twirled one of the trailing ribbons from her wrapper around her finger, then, just as lazily, undid it again. Caroline could almost see the wheels turning in her head.

"You want to know about Josiah Walker.''

Caroline nodded. "You sued him for breach of promise and won. I figured that meant you...er... knew him pretty well.''

"Beyond the biblical sense, you mean?''

"Yes." She couldn't stop the blush. The woman was clearly enjoying her discomfort.

"Why do you want to know?" That question was sharper, the look behind it more piercing than Caroline had expected.

She decided to be just as direct. "I wondered if he would really have cared enough about his new…ah… girlfriend—"

"Dolly."

"That's right. Dolly James. I wondered if he would have cared enough about Miss James to get into a fight with Osbald over her."

The ribbon curled around the carefully manicured finger, then spiraled off.

"No."

The bald response made her blink. "You're sure about that?"

"Honey, Josiah loved women, but he loved life a whole lot more. Knowing Osbald was screwing his private little fancy piece would have made him mad as hell, but it wouldn't have made him stupid."

"I see." Caroline had never heard the word "screwing" used in quite this context, but she was pretty sure she knew what it meant, anyway. She wasn't about to ask.

The maid who'd opened the door returned bearing a tray with coffeepot, cups, sugar and creamer.

"Thanks," Lola said carelessly, waving the woman away. "Want some, Mrs. Abbott?"

"No, thank you."

"I have to have my coffee first thing. I'm not worth a damn until I do."

"First thing?"

The woman's laugh brought the color rushing back to her face.

"Honey, we're up all night working. This is the top of the morning in a whorehouse."

Caroline wondered if it was possible for human flesh to spontaneously combust. Her cheeks felt hot enough for it. "I didn't realize— That is, I didn't mean—"

"That's all right. You'll learn. You stay in this newspaper business very long, you'll have to." Lola clinked her silver spoon against the edge of the fine china cup, then carelessly tossed it back on the tray. "You mentioned a husband. He wouldn't happen to be J. Randolph Abbott, would he? From the *Tribune?*"

"You know him?"

"Not to say *know* him, if you know what I mean." Caroline would have sworn the woman winked at her. "But I know *of* him. He as handsome as that picture of his in the paper?"

"Handsomer."

"Little prickly, aren't you? Does he have a habit of running around on you?"

"No. Unless you know something I don't." The instant the words were out, she regretted them. What if she got an answer she didn't want to hear?

Lola took a sip of coffee, savoring it while Caroline's heart tried to pound its way out of her chest.

"No," Lola said at last. "Never heard of him visiting on Myers Avenue, and a man like that"—she smiled—"I would have heard."

The sudden rush of relief left Caroline shaking.

"A woman always wonders, doesn't she?"

Caroline chose to ignore the barb. "Do you think Mrs. Walker knew?"

"About Dolly?"

"Yes. After all the publicity, she would have had to know about you."

Another laugh. There were no blushes to go with it. "Mary Walker knows about all of us even if she does keep herself locked up in that big house on the hill, pretending we don't exist."

"Whatever happened to the other lady who brought suit against him when you did? Miss LaCoste?"

"Maggie?" Lola shrugged. "Disappeared. Probably bought herself a husband and a new name and is busy right now praying no one ever finds out what she was before."

She stared at the coffee in her cup, considering. When she looked up again, the look of tolerant, slightly ironic amusement was gone, replaced by a hard, assessing stare.

"Just what do you hope to accomplish with all this, Mrs. Abbott? Dredge up old scandals so your editor can sell a few extra papers this week? Get some attention for yourself? What?"

Yesterday, that would have been an easy question to answer. Today, it wasn't that simple.

"I talked to Mrs. Walker this morning, Miss Spears. She doesn't believe her husband's death was an accident or that it was the result of a quarrel over the favors of a...of Miss James."

"A fancy woman, you mean." The madam set her

coffee cup down with an angry clink of china. "Around here, we don't hide behind nice words, Mrs. Abbott. Dolly's a whore, just like me."

"Is she as rude?"

That brought a laugh. "Good for you. No, she's not as rude as I am."

"Would Osbald have killed a man over her?"

"Sure, if he thought he could get away with it. Andrew Osbald's even meaner and more ambitious than Josiah was, and that's saying a mouthful. Those two have hated each other for years."

"Enough to commit murder?"

"More than enough."

"What else was between them besides old hates and a whore?"

"My, you do learn quick!"

Caroline wasn't sure she liked what she was learning, but she didn't have time to think about that now. "In your position here, you must hear things—business talk, rumors, plans. Did you ever hear that either one of them was up to something sneaky?"

"Honey, they were *men*. Men are always sneaking around after something. You can count on it."

Caroline's chin took on a mulish cast.

Lola shrugged, making the silken wrap shift in ways that would have done serious damage to a man's concentration.

"I did hear a little here and there. I think Osbald was planning to go after Josiah's mine. He never forgave him for winning that court case a few years ago...or for making a hell of a lot more money than he had."

"How did he plan to go about it?"

"I don't know. As I said, I just caught bits and pieces."

Caroline's shoulders slumped.

Silently, Lola studied her, winding that ribbon on her finger, then unwinding it, then slowly winding it up again. Caroline was on the point of making her excuses when Lola let go the ribbon and sat up.

"Mrs. Abbott," she said in the crisp, efficient tones of someone accustomed to making decisions, "if you're really looking for proof, the place to find it will be in stock transactions and land records, not here, digging for bits of gossip someone let fall by chance."

"Stock transactions? Land records?" Caroline's head spun in dismay. "It would take days to dig through all that."

"Weeks. But unless Osbald does something stupid to incriminate himself first, it's the only way. He wants Josiah's mine. He's always wanted it."

"The trial will be over by then."

They both went silent, contemplating the awful truth of it. If Osbald was acquitted, he could never again be tried for the murder of Josiah Walker, not even if the court had a signed confession in their hands.

"Josiah deserves a fair shake," Lola said at last with conviction. "He was bullheaded and arrogant, and when it came to business he could be downright mean, but he wasn't a bad man. Except for promising to marry me, then marrying that prissy little Boston miss, instead, he always treated me decently."

"Do you think Osbald killed him deliberately?"

"Murdered him?" Lola hesitated. "I don't know how, but I think he did. And since it doesn't look like the men in this town are going to do much to see justice done, I don't mind seeing the ladies raising a bit of a stink, instead."

With a graceful sway, she rose to her feet, then gave a little tug on the sash of her wrapper to make sure it was decently closed. "I'll walk you to the door, make sure there's no one on the street to see you when you leave."

"Thank you." Caroline hoped her relief didn't show on her face. She'd been so determined to get here, she hadn't thought about how to get away. "That's very kind of you."

Lola didn't move. "Why haven't you asked?"

"Asked?"

"Why I'm here." The woman raised her hands to indicate the room around them. "Why, when I got so much money from Josiah in that settlement, I came back to a place like this. Haven't you wondered?"

"I've wondered, but there are limits to how rude even I can be, Miss Spears."

Lola smiled, but there wasn't much humor in it. "You ever try to support yourself, hon? I mean, earn every single penny that puts a roof over your head and a meal in your belly?"

Caroline thought of her painful calculations yesterday comparing what she'd earn on that first article versus what she'd spent to get it. She hadn't even tried to figure out what it would take to really live on. "No."

"Pray God you never have to." The woman's eyes glittered in the lace-filtered light, hard and angry. "You get a respectable job, they work you twice as hard as a man and pay you half as much. Most women end up getting married, and then they have to hope he doesn't drink it all or piss it away gambling or chasing after women like me."

Caroline winced. Clearly, Lola knew the difficulties firsthand.

"I was married once," Lola continued. "Probably still would be if the bastard hadn't up and died on me one winter. With him, life was hard. Without him..."

She shrugged and looked away. Her gaze fixed on the far wall of the room, but Caroline could tell she wasn't looking at the red flocked wallpaper or the framed prints of dying children and repentant maidens that hung there, but at old memories that still had the power to hurt.

Reluctantly, she dragged her gaze off the past. "Josiah paid me fifty thousand dollars. Seems like a fortune when you say it like that, but, honey, fifty thousand dollars'll slip out of your hands so fast it'll make your head spin right off your shoulders. So I thought about it some and decided the best thing I could do was invest it in what I knew best."

"This house."

"That's right. I've done well, too. Lately, I've been investing in stocks, bonds, a couple of gold mines here and there. A few years, I'll be a rich woman. Rich enough I can retire."

"And do what?"

The lazy, teasing look of amusement was back on

her face, hiding the anger. "Why, take a lover, I suppose. A young, good-looking one."

Satisfied at the intense red in Caroline's cheeks, she opened the front door and leaned out. "All clear," she said. "You want to leave, now would be a good time."

Chapter Twelve

Caroline took a late afternoon tea at a little eatery off Bennett Avenue—on the respectable north side of the street rather than the disreputable south. While she sipped the tea, she wrote up her interview with Lola Spears, adding bits she'd gleaned from other people she'd talked to over the afternoon. She wasn't anywhere near as direct as that outspoken madam, but readers would be able to read between the lines. If that story didn't increase the *Times'* sales by five percent, she'd eat her hat.

While she wrote, Lola's words echoed in her head. *You get a respectable job, they work you twice as hard as a man and pay you half as much.*

Well, not for her! C.A. was going to be the *Times'* star reporter, but it was going to be on her terms, not the *Times'*.

To her relief, the telephone company offices were empty except for the clerk at the front desk, who directed her to a phone half-hidden behind a wooden screen. It seemed to take forever for the call to go through.

"Back already, are you, Mrs. Abbott?" Blackmun said jovially. The noise on the line made his voice crackle and hiss. "I hope that means you have another good story for me."

Caroline drew in a deep breath, then slowly let it out on a prayer.

"I have it right here, ready to dictate."

"Great, great! I'll—"

"I want five cents a word for it."

Stony silence.

"Mr. Blackmun? Did you hear me?"

"Absolutely not! That's ridiculous! That's highway robbery! That's—that's—"

"The absolute minimum before you get a word."

"No!"

"The interview's with Lola Spears, one of the prostitutes who sued Walker for breach of promise a couple years back."

More silence. She could almost hear the wheels going round in his head.

"Lola used the money she won to start her own... aah...house of business here in Cripple Creek. It's called Della's, after the previous owner."

"Della's? *That* Della's?"

Caroline smiled at the screen in front of her. "It sounds as if you know it, Mr. Blackmun."

"Know *of* it, Mrs. Abbott, that's all," Blackmun huffed, offended. The protest didn't sound quite as innocent as he'd intended. "Any newspaper reporter worth his salt knows...er...things like that."

"Exactly. But how many not only have an interview with the lady, but also a couple of rather interesting leads into what might really be behind Walker's murder?''

"You have that?'' She could hear his ears pricking all the way from Denver.

"I do. But it will cost you five cents a word to get it.''

Something that wasn't quite a growl, and wasn't quite agreement, grated in her ear.

Her stomach was turning somersaults inside her. "Five cents, a bonus if sales increase when my articles are running, and a promise that you won't ever again rewrite a story of mine like you did the story this morning.''

"What?"

"You heard me.''

"That's...that's *outrageous!* You're a new writer, no experience. Five cents a word! Bonuses! And now you want to write whatever you please? No! Absolutely not. *No!''*

Caroline set her jaw and ignored the riot in her stomach. "I don't much like what you did with my article this morning, Mr. Blackmun.''

"*You* don't like it! My editing's the only thing that made that piece work. I *had* to change it, jazz it up!'' Blackmun sputtered. "You don't think you got that top of page two position because of the brilliance of your stuff, do you?''

She straightened her back, squared her shoulders. "Yes, as a matter of fact, I do, Mr. Blackmun.''

The momentary silence on the line was deafening. "You been talking to that swell-headed husband of yours?''

"No. Not about that."

"Well, don't. What does a *Tribune* guy know, anyway? We outsell 'em two to one, and you want to know why? I'll tell you why. Because we give the people what they want."

"The owners of the *Tribune* claim they outsell the *Times* two to one, Mr. Blackmun."

"What do they know?" She could almost see him, shouting and pacing at the end of the telephone line, hands waving angrily, a forgotten cigar burning between his fingers. "Anyway, that's not the point. The point is that we aren't the *Tribune* and we don't intend to be. We write for the people of Denver, the ones that want a good story and a little scandal to go with their bacon and eggs in the morning, and that's what you're giving 'em. A good story and a scandal. And a murder, which helps to liven things up a bit."

"I'm giving them the truth!" Caroline snapped, irritated.

"Yeah. That, too." Blackmun's dismissive tone said that item was a fortuitous addition, not an essential. "But you're still not gettin' five cents a word."

"Five. And a bonus. And no editing except what's absolutely essential."

"Three. I'll give you three. That's double what I gave you this morning and a hell of a lot more than most writers like you will ever make."

"Five, or I'll go to the *Tribune*."

"You wouldn't." Horror choked his words.

Caroline's stays suddenly felt tighter than they'd been a moment ago. She was going to win this one. She could feel it. "I would."

"They won't buy it."

"They will."

"Hell and damnation."

"Mr. Blackmun!"

In the end, he gave in, just as she'd known he would. She got the five cents a word and the bonus and a mealymouthed promise not to edit her that she knew he wouldn't abide by. At least, not yet. But it was a start, and the day would come when her work would run as she wrote it. She was sure of it.

When she finally hung up after dictating the story, she was almost floating from the excitement. Only the outrageously expensive bill the clerk presented her the moment she stepped from behind the screen managed to bring her back down to earth. But even that spurred her off, renewed, in search of Miss Dolly James, the woman who'd caught Josiah Walker's attentions and unwittingly served as the means for his enemies to murder him.

At a quarter to five, having finagled a front-row pass to the trial from a judge who'd proven susceptible to feminine charm and a little judicious flattery, Caroline abandoned her fruitless attempts to track down Dolly James and turned her steps up the hill toward Bonnard's Boardinghouse.

Her head ached and her feet hurt. Her stomach had been complaining of its empty state for hours even though she knew that Georgianne's supper wasn't going to be up to the National's elegantly exacting standards. There'd be no hot water for a bath, no cozy feather bed, and no husband to warm the bed there was.

None of it mattered because she'd gotten a *great* story out of her day's work and five cents a word!

She wasn't going to stop there, either. If her quarterly trust fund payment didn't show up at her bank by the end of next week, then she'd tackle her father again, and this time she wouldn't give him any peace until he gave in.

The boldness of it all made her dizzy. Her father would never approve of such unladylike demands. Her mother would probably take to the sofa and moan.

J.R. would laugh and cheer her on.

At least he hadn't laughed at her over lunch. They'd talked, argued, and traded information and insights like equals. Just thinking of it was enough to make her dizzy with the promise of what might lie ahead for them, working together as equals, true partners in marriage and in life.

And then he'd ruined it all by ordering her to quit because he "couldn't protect her."

Frustrated, she kicked a rock in her path, then watched as it bounced and skittered away, raising dust as it went. She glared at the rock, then looked up to find J.R. coming toward her on the opposite side of the street.

Her heart skipped a beat before she realized her eyes were playing tricks. The man was close to J.R.'s height and build, but he lacked her husband's elegance and his confident swagger. Caroline turned to watch him anyway, uncomfortably conscious of a wistful longing prickling somewhere under her breast-bone.

To her relief, the stranger disappeared around the next corner, still unaware of her scrutiny.

Just as well he'd been a stranger, and oblivious. She wouldn't have known what to say if he *had* been J.R.

There had to be a happy medium for her some-where, a point midway between her mother's unques-tioning acceptance of the role her husband and society had assigned her, and Lola Spears' angry indepen-dence. She was changing, growing, and J.R. was go-ing to have to accept it whether he liked it or not.

She felt like a crab must feel when it discarded its shell for something bigger, something that fit a little better than the old shell that had always been home. The trouble was, between the time it abandoned the old shell and the new shell hardened, the creature was terribly vulnerable. She came from Baltimore. She knew what happened to soft-shell crabs—they got eaten.

So caught up in her musings was she, she didn't notice the burly man angrily bearing down on her until it was too late.

Murray waved his rolled and crushed copy of the *Times* in her face. "Just what in the hell did you think you were doing when you wrote this…this…this *gar-bage?*"

A week ago, she might have yelped and run for cover. Now, she swallowed her fear and stood her ground.

"I do not write 'garbage,' Mr. Murray, and I'll

thank you not to swear and shout when in my presence. Such behavior is not becoming of a gentleman.''

"I'm not a goddamned gentleman,'' Murray roared, "I'm a reporter! If you want to play the fine lady, then you can just get your sweet little ass back to Denver and quit poking in things that are none of your goddamned business!''

Spittle flecked his lips. His face, the tips of his ears, and his throat all the way down to his shirt collar flared bright red.

Caroline fought the urge to scuttle back, out of reach. "A public trial is as much my business as it is yours. If you bothered to get out and do some real investigative reporting instead of relying on whatever gossip you can pick up in the saloons, you'd realize that.''

That made him sneer. "Feisty one, are you?''

"Honest. And not about to be intimidated by a rude bully even if he does work for my paper.''

"*Your* paper! If that don't beat all!'' He leaned closer, close enough that she could smell the beer on his breath. "You write a couple of froufrou pieces for the society section and suddenly it's *your* paper? Well, let me tell you something lady—it's *my* goddamned paper! Got that? Mine! And I'll see Hell freeze over before I give you an inch of it!''

"Then I hope you're prepared for a lot of frost around the edges, Mr. Murray, because I'm taking over yards of it, not just inches!''

With that, she stepped around him and continued

up the street, head high, back straight and stiff, and with her heart pounding like a mad thing in her chest.

Her nerves were still twitching when she finally shut the front screen door of Bonnard's Boardinghouse behind her. She found her landladies gathered at the dining room table, waiting for her. Three glasses, a sweating pitcher of iced lemonade, a plate of sugar cookies, and a gun sat atop the table between them.

"I made some lemonade and cookies, dear," said Georgianne, pinkening delicately. "I thought you might be thirsty, tramping around town all day the way you have."

"Er...thank you." Caroline couldn't take her eyes off the gun. The cold gray metal seemed to be affecting her brain, making it difficult to put one intelligent thought with another. "That was very...uh... thoughtful of you."

Elizabeth cleared her throat and looked stern. "We've heard all about where you've been today and whom you've talked to."

"Do you think that was wise, my dear?" Georgianne's round little face grew pinched with worry.

"What with the talk you stirred up today and the talk you'll stir up tomorrow, we decided you really do need to be prepared," Elizabeth added.

Caroline pushed aside the mental image of Murray, shouting at her, the paper crushed in his massive fist. "I don't *want* a gun."

Elizabeth gave a dismissive little snort. "You just have a little of that lemonade and a couple of those cookies Georgianne made, and when you're rested, we'll go out and shoot up a few tin cans.''

She rubbed her hands together with anticipatory relish, eyes sparkling. ''You'll like it. Nothing's more entertaining than shooting cans, unless you'd rather shoot a few pea-brained men, instead.''

By the time Caroline wearily trudged back into town in Elizabeth's wake two hours later, lamps were being lit in the houses they passed. She patted the pocket where the gun now lay, a hard, threatening weight that thumped against her thigh with every step she took. Maybe she wouldn't notice it so much if she stashed it in her purse.

She wouldn't notice it at all if she left it in the boardinghouse.

The smell of pot roast emanating from the open boardinghouse windows made her stomach growl and reminded her that it had been a long time since lunch at the National. A foot inside the front door, she stopped dead as J.R. rose from Georgianne's best upholstered chair.

''Mr. Abbott is joining us for supper.'' Georgianne gave her sister a nervous little smile. ''I hope you don't mind.''

Elizabeth frowned at her sister, then she frowned at J.R. And then she plucked a wicked looking hatpin out of her hat. ''I don't mind if Mrs. Abbott doesn't.'' She studied the sharp tip of the pin, then plucked out a second, even more deadly-looking pin.

''No, of course not,'' Caroline said. She couldn't take her eyes off him.

He looked...wonderful. They'd parted only a few hours before, yet still she drank in all the details—the sleek golden hair turned honey-colored in the lamplight, the angular line of cheek and jaw, the starched collar, neat tie, superbly tailored coat. The long, long legs in their equally well-tailored trousers. The spotless, well-shined shoes. His eyes gleamed.

She had to fight against the urge to polish the toes of her shoes on the hem of her petticoat. He hadn't deliberately tried to catch her at a disadvantage. She refused to give him the satisfaction of admitting he had.

"I came to see how your day had gone," he said. "Miss Bonnard very kindly invited me to join you ladies for supper."

His voice, so low and rich, set her heart pounding. Even Elizabeth wasn't immune.

"We generally eat at seven sharp, Mr. Abbott," she said, graciously unbending, "and it's five to now. But we can set that back a bit. I imagine Mrs. Abbott would like a moment to wash up, first." She stuck the pins into her hat and set the hat aside. "Would you care for a drink while we wait?"

J.R. brightened at the offer. "Yes. Yes, thank you very much, I would."

"Excellent." Elizabeth beamed, the very picture of feminine charity. "We have some really lovely elderberry wine that our sister sent us. Nice and sweet, just the thing to whet an appetite."

Caroline took one look at the stricken expression on her husband's face, then muttered a hasty excuse and darted out of the room before she could explode from laughter. Poor man. Elderberry wine!

The face in the bathroom mirror shocked her out of her amusement. She couldn't let J.R. keep seeing her this way, dusty and disheveled as a rag picker. And that slight touch of red on the tip of her nose couldn't be sunburn, could it?

She angled her head a little, frowning in the mirror. Of course it wasn't sunburn. She never burned. She was far too sensible for that.

It was still there when she washed the dust off though, and redder than before. Groaning, Caroline patted on some powder to soften the glow, then hurriedly tidied her hair. It was only when she tried to shake the dust out of her skirts that she remembered the gun.

It was solid in her hand, with just enough weight to remind her of its serious purpose. Just seeing it was a shock, and a reminder of how much had changed in just two days. The woman who'd climbed on that train in Denver yesterday morning would never have touched a gun, or worn blisters on her heels, or walked into a brothel. The woman who stared at her from the mirror wide-eyed had done all that and more.

Shoving the gun back in her pocket, she peeped around the door to make sure no one saw her, then silently darted up the stairs to her room. A little touch of perfume, a pretty locket round her throat, one he'd given her when they were courting, and she was ready.

She gave herself one last, swift check in the narrow little mirror above the dresser, then slid the gun beneath her pillow and hurried back downstairs to supper and J.R.

Chapter Thirteen

The elderberry wine had been horrible, but the pot roast wasn't bad. The company was deliciously distracting.

While Miss Elizabeth Carter animadverted on the shortcomings of the governor and the fools an even more foolish electorate had put into office, J.R. drank in the vision of his wife, seated across the table and demurely working her way through an astonishingly large helping of meat and potatoes.

She really was gorgeous, and there was a new fire in her that he found irresistible. He even liked the red-tipped nose. It gave her a hoydenish look that was dangerously appealing.

He ached to have her back in his arms, and in his bed.

Tomorrow. She was weakening. He could see it in her eyes and in the smiles she bestowed on him every now and then when she thought her landladies weren't looking.

Though he'd never admit it, certainly not to her, he

was finding this newfound independence of hers surprisingly erotic.

He *would* admit that she'd done first-rate work on this story so far. Her analysis of what had really happened and how and why was spot on the money as far as he could see. The way she'd gone about it was certainly unorthodox, but it had gotten results. It would also get readers.

He still didn't like the idea of his wife involved in such sordid horror, even at secondhand, but he was slowly, and grudgingly, coming to realize that she was changing, and that if he wanted to keep her, he would have to change, too. That didn't mean he liked it, but he was a practical man, after all, and he loved her.

His little surprise ought to be the final proof of just how much he loved her, and how far he was willing to go to keep her.

That surprise was foremost on his mind when he finally had Caroline to himself. He'd paid his compliments, given his thanks, then charmed his wife into bidding him good-bye on the front porch where they'd be safe from her landladies' prying eyes.

Because he couldn't help himself, he drew her into his arms and kissed her. He didn't care if the rest of the world was watching.

She flowed into the kiss like water into his hand. She tasted of pot roast and sweet coffee, and, for a moment, he wondered if his head would spin off his shoulders from the sheer pleasure of it.

He wasn't sure if the sigh when they eventually broke apart was hers...or his.

"I do miss you, you know," she said, so softly he almost didn't catch it.

His hold on her tightened. "Not half as much as I miss you." He brushed a kiss on the curve of her ear. The delicate scent of her perfume teased him with memories of other, more intimate caresses. His pulse pounded.

"Let me come home, Caroline. I don't think I can take much more of this. I swear I've learned my lesson. You've proved me wrong with a vengeance."

The smile she gave him was blinding.

Reassured, he rushed on, eager to capitalize on the moment by sharing his surprise. "I called your father today."

"My father?"

"That's right." He smiled, pleased with himself. He'd been picturing her delight all afternoon, fantasizing about exactly how she'd reward him for his support and understanding. "I told him I thought he was wrong to have cut off the payments from your trust fund."

"What?"

He could feel his smile widening, the hot-blooded quickening low in his belly. Maybe she'd just come back to the hotel with him tonight and to hell with this boardinghouse and its fussy landladies. By the end of the week they'd be back in Denver and everything would be right again between them.

"I said you were doing an impressive job covering this story, as good as a man could do, and that he should release your money immediately."

"You *what?*"

Instead of flinging herself at him, eyes shining with gratitude, she wrenched away, spitting fire. "Who gave you the right to interfere in my private business like that?"

J.R.'s jaw dropped. His brain scrambled to understand...and went nowhere. "Caroline, I—"

"Did you expect me to be *grateful?* Did you really think I was so incapable of dealing with my own affairs, my own *father,* that I needed *you* to do it for me?"

"I just—"

"When I need your help with something, Mr. J. Randolph Abbott, I'll ask for it. Until then, keep your nose out of my business. Do you hear? Out"—she poked a stiff finger into his breastbone, making him grunt and take a step back—"of"—another poke, another step—"my"—poke, step—"business!" Poke, poke. He slammed into the house. "Got that?"

"Ah—"

"Good! Next time, remember it!"

She wrenched the screen door open. He lunged for it and missed.

For the second time in as many days, the front door to Bonnard's Boardinghouse slammed shut in his face.

What in hell had he said that could have set her off like that?

J.R. glared at the whiskey in the tumbler he held, then set the glass down on the table with a snap.

Her father had been unfair and refused to listen to her side of the story. He'd stepped in and supported her, convinced her father to release the quarterly funds that were her just due. What was so wrong in all that?

The questions had spun around in his head for hours and still he hadn't found a reasonable answer. He just didn't understand why she so resented his trying to defend her against her father's bullying.

Even the National's best whiskey hadn't managed to make the muddle any clearer…or drown the memory of her lush body pressed against his, her mouth open and hungry for his kisses.

J.R. gritted his teeth against the groan that threatened to escape him. A man could take only so much of that kind of torment before he snapped, and he was this close to snapping. With an angry flick of his wrist, he drained his glass, then shoved his chair back.

The moon was down, but the saloons were still well lit and heavily patronized when he stepped into the street. From somewhere down the street he caught the rattling of a player piano and a chorus of out-of-tune voices merrily, and rather drunkenly, shouting about a bicycle built for two. He waited on the sidewalk, letting his eyes adjust to the dark and listening to the night's own music, softer beneath the rowdy racket from the saloons.

Once, he would have found the racket inviting, sweet with promises of good company and, perhaps, a sweaty, satisfying bout of mindless, no-strings sex to round out the evening. No longer. Now, all he wanted was a home to go to and a wife waiting there to welcome him back into her arms…and her bed.

Frowning, he tossed the still-glowing stub of his

cigar into the dirt of the street, then stepped off the sidewalk and deliberately ground the butt under his heel. A few long, swift strides had him off Bennett and onto the quieter residential streets beyond.

His footsteps seemed to echo from the houses around him. The saloons might be busy, but the rest of Cripple Creek had gone to bed long since. Only an occasional light shining from behind drawn curtains hinted at the houses on either side with their silent, sleeping inhabitants.

By the time he reached Bonnard's his eyes had adjusted to the dark enough so that he could see the sign on the front fence. Only a little groping in the dark was needed to find the ladder he'd spotted earlier, leaning against the house two doors down.

The darkness was thick and enveloping when a muffled thump against the side of the house brought Caroline jerking upright in bed, heart pounding. Again that image of Murray, spitting mad, crushing the paper in his massive paw, flashed before her eyes.

She slid her hand beneath the pillow. The gun was there. Her fingers closed around it.

The ladder hit the side of the building with a soft thump.

J.R. waited, heart pounding. Not a sound from the house or from the street beyond.

When he'd found the boardinghouse's windows dark, he'd almost given up and gone back to the National. But the thought of Caroline, peacefully asleep in a bed that he wasn't sharing, had stopped him. She was his *wife,* dammit! Enough of this nonsense!

He was pretty sure he knew which room was hers because he'd distracted himself from the horrors of elderberry wine that afternoon by listening to her footsteps as she'd moved about overhead. And Caroline had always liked sleeping with the window opened a crack to draw in fresh air.

Cursing softly at the demeaning stratagems to which his wife had reduced him, he started up the ladder, cautiously feeling for each rung in the dark.

His head came over the windowsill. He smiled in satisfaction: He hadn't been mistaken. The window was open. Just a crack, but that would be enough.

He moved a rung higher. The ladder groaned and wobbled, but held fast. Almost there.

One rung more, the next to the last. He slid his fingers under the window and shoved it higher.

A shadow loomed in her window, broad-shouldered and menacing.

Slowly, heart pounding, Caroline slid out of bed. The gun in her hand seemed comfortingly solid. When the intruder shoved the window farther open, she almost shot him right then and there.

"Caroline? Ssst! Caroline! Are you awake?"

The sudden flood of relief at the familiar voice was immediately replaced by an even hotter, almost overwhelming flood of anger. Scare her, would he? As if treating her like a helpless child wasn't enough?

When he hooked an elbow over the sill, she fired.

* * *

J.R. was half in the window, precariously balanced on the top rung of the ladder, when a gun went off in front of him. A bullet whistled past his head.

He ducked. The wobbly ladder swayed, scraped along the side of the house, then toppled.

J.R. had time for one heartfelt curse before he lost his grip on the windowsill and went tumbling.

The fall seemed interminable. The ground felt like solid rock.

With a clattering thump, the ladder landed on top of him, knocking the last of the air out of him. Shooting lights and dizzying flashes of color drowned out the night's stars.

J.R. groaned, blinked, and fought for breath, then heaved the ladder off himself. Above him, he could see a head poking out of the open window.

"Goddammit, Caroline," he growled, wincing at the pain. "It's me."

"I know," she said in a voice that cut like knives. "And I think it's only fair to warn you—next time I won't miss."

She drew in her head, then firmly slid the window shut just as lights began coming on in the other windows and the buildings all around.

Chapter Fourteen

Caroline awoke before dawn. Her head hurt and her body ached, the legacy of a restless night plagued by dreams of J.R. Lying there in the tangled sheets, she wondered if she shouldn't have let him in after all.

The thought of what Elizabeth would have said if she had made her giggle.

The thought of what might have happened if she had made her ache for lost opportunities.

With a growl of disgust, she threw back the covers and awkwardly rolled out of the narrow, lumpy bed. Cramped muscles protested as she stretched, shivering a little in the cold morning air. This high in the Colorado mountains, even mid-summer mornings had a nip to them.

That bed in the National would be broad and soft and welcoming. With J.R. to keep her warm, she wouldn't have to worry about working out any early morning kinks or—

Don't even think about it! she scolded herself.

Trying to climb in her window like that had been stupid. She could picture the headlines if he'd been caught—Top Tribune Reporter Caught Climbing In Married Woman's Bedroom Window. The *Times* would love it.

Not that *she* would ever write anything as scurrilous as that! She wouldn't have to. She had *real* stories now. *Important* stories.

The thought of the two stories she'd written yesterday made her smile. That would show him! Once J.R. read those stories, he would never again be able to say she wasn't a real reporter.

Shivering—with excitement this time, not cold—Caroline slipped on her dressing gown, then grabbed her comb, soap and bath sponge. If she hurried, she could get the early copies of the *Times* to savor with her breakfast.

This time the headline was smack in the middle of the front page. "Townspeople Ignoring the Truth." Below it, in slightly smaller type. "Widow Suspects Conspiracy Against Her Husband."

And below that, "Exclusive to the *Times*, by C.A."

J.R. winced and wiggled his shoulder a bit, trying to ease the pain and stiffness.

Pale, yet beautiful in her grief, Mrs. Josiah Walker, widow of the murdered—

He gave a low growl. Caroline had a lot to learn about the meaning of the word *alleged*.

...widow of the murdered mine owner, received this reporter in her elegantly furnished private sitting room with its sweeping view of the town of Cripple Creek—the town her husband helped build and the town where he died, shot down in a barroom quarrel.

"Josiah was a good husband and a fine, upstanding man," Mrs. Walker said, fighting back the tears. "He wasn't killed because of a quarrel over some fancy woman, as some folks are saying. He was killed because his enemies saw a chance to get him out of the way without any risk to themselves."

The article filled two columns with the widow's claims and accusations—all cleverly interspersed with lines like that "fighting back the tears" that were blatant, and successful, attempts at grabbing the readers' sympathies.

All that was bad enough. Worse was the article immediately below the first, which also carried the C.A. byline. Spurned Lover Defends Murdered Man—Caroline was going to chew nails when she saw *that* headline!—and Truth Of Killing Will Be Found In Land Records And Stock Transactions.

Miss Lola Spears, a Cripple Creek businesswoman who successfully sued murdered mine owner Josiah Walker for breach of promise two years ago, admits he was a hot-tempered man but says he was far too sensible to let a quarrel over a woman lead to gunplay.

"Josiah was a good man," Miss Spears avers. "Except for that breach of promise, he was always good to me. I know he wouldn't have risked his life in a senseless quarrel over a woman.''

According to Miss Spears, the killing was about business, not love, an opinion that coincides with the opinions of many of the Cripple Creek residents to whom this reporter has spoken in the last two days. Those business affairs were often hidden and sometimes convoluted. Unfortunately, the prosecution seems to be making little or no effort to untangle them before the trial tomorrow.

It was a good article—certainly far more attention-grabbing than his own straightforward recounting of Osbald's and Walker's often stormy business relations. Only the headlines retained the lurid flare of yesterday's article. Either Blackmun had decided the stories didn't need any dressing up to meet the *Times'* low standards, or she'd somehow bullied him into leaving it alone.

If he were a betting man, J.R. thought, grinning, he'd bet on the latter.

His grin vanished as another thought hit. Without ever coming right out and accusing him of murder, Caroline had managed to sketch in the details of Osbald's plot to kill Walker.

Alleged plot, J.R. reminded himself grimly.

Osbald was going to explode when he read this. In two short days, Caroline, brashly determined to make a name for herself and oblivious to the danger, had exposed his underhanded dealings for the world to see.

His own article had far more concrete information, but Caroline, with unerring instinct, had nailed the people and the issues that were most likely to attract public attention…and start public speculation. Carefully expressionless, J.R. folded the paper and set it aside. Fear squeezed him, making it hard for him to breathe.

Osbald wasn't going to sit passively by while she conducted an open trial on the front page of the *Times*. The man had killed before. There was absolutely nothing to stop him from killing again.

"Spurned Lover Defends Murdered Man!"

Caroline growled and gave the paper a good shake, then scanned the article that followed, oblivious to the newsboy on the street corner behind her, shouting out the headline. *Her* headline.

As she read, her teeth gradually unclenched and the tension in her shoulders eased. Other than the outrageous headlines, Blackmun had pretty much left her stories alone.

She held the paper out at arm's length, studying the effect. It looked good. Two substantial articles, right there in the middle of the front page. She'd even squeezed out the president of the United States, whose opinion on the situation in Manila had been relegated to a short item at the top of the page with a continuation on page two. Not bad for a fledgling reporter. Not bad at all.

"Admiring your handiwork?"

Caroline jumped, crushing the paper, and spun to confront her husband. A still-raw scrape on his cheek and a purpling bruise along his jaw marred his golden looks, giving him a dangerously piratical air.

"Don't scare me like that!"

"Spurned Lover Defends Murdered Man!" the newsboy cried. "Townspeople Ignoring The Truth." He shoved a paper under J.R.'s nose. "Buy a paper, mister?"

J.R. impatiently waved him aside. "Be grateful I'm the one who scared you," he growled, "and not some others I could think of."

The urge to soothe his wounds vanished. "What others?"

"Murray, for one. Don't tell me you don't know he's mad as hell about you horning in on his territory."

"I can handle Murray."

His eyebrows arched in mocking query. "You sure about that?"

She shifted uncomfortably. "Absolutely."

"Liar."

"Sticks and stones."

His expression hardened. "Sticks and stones might not hurt you, Caroline, but Osbald sure as hell can."

"Townspeople Ignoring The Truth!"

They both turned to glare at the newsboy, but he was too busy selling papers to pay them any heed. Business was brisk.

"Spurned Lover Defends Murdered Man!" Two more papers vanished off the stack at the boy's feet.

Caroline grabbed J.R.'s sleeve and pulled him

away from the corner, far enough so the boy couldn't overhear them.

"Osbald wouldn't dare attack me. Not with the trial starting today."

"You don't sound all that sure of it."

She wasn't, but she wasn't about to admit it. "At least he won't be climbing in my window in the middle of the night and scaring me half out of my wits!"

J.R. dragged her to him. His eyes burned with a dangerous blue fire. "Goddammit, Caroline! Do you have any idea what you've started?"

Beneath the anger, she could hear real concern in his voice. If she didn't know her husband better, she would have called it fear. It almost made her want to call Blackmun and retract the short piece she'd sent him that morning. Almost. She still owed him one for frightening the spit out of her, as Elizabeth had put it last night.

"I have plenty of ideas, Mr. Abbott. I also have a trial to attend, so if you'll kindly unhand me..."

Their gazes locked in a silent duel. J.R. gave in first.

"Fine." He let go her arm as if it burned him. "But if you get into trouble, don't come running to me for help."

"I won't."

She pointedly ignored the rude noise he made. Instead, she folded her newspaper so her headlines showed, then tucked it under her arm.

"I'm headed to the courthouse," she said. "I managed to get a front-row pass yesterday despite your underhanded attempt to keep me away."

"I didn't try to keep you away."

"No?" She sniffed disdainfully, then stifled a wince as she stepped off the walk into the street. If she had to do much more traipsing around in these shoes, she'd be crippled for life. She wasn't about to let J.R. know that, though.

J.R. angrily fell into step beside her. "Why in hell don't you at least buy yourself a decent pair of shoes?" he snarled. "Another few days of this and you're going to be crippled for life."

Though they were early, the courtroom had already begun to fill with reporters and townsfolk eager for the best entertainment Cripple Creek had seen in ages. J.R. had pointedly abandoned her at the front steps of the courthouse so Caroline, heart pounding, had to force her way through the crowd alone.

From conversations that suddenly went silent at her approach, then started up lower and more insistently after she'd passed, she could tell her morning's stories had set tongues wagging. The sight of more than one copy of the *Times* folded to her headlines made her want to give a celebratory little skip. Instead, she kept her head high and her eyes sharp. J.R.'s warnings weren't as easy to ignore as she'd pretended.

To her relief, Murray had been stuck with a seat five rows back from hers. Unfortunately, the large gentleman on her left from the Chicago *Daily Journal* was several days overdue for a weekly bath, and the fastidious little fellow on her right from the Boston *Herald* had been way too generous with the cologne. She tried, discreetly, to breathe through her mouth and prayed her sense of smell would eventually give up under the combined onslaught. At least she needn't worry about any deficiencies of the quick wash with icy water that had been all she'd had the courage for these past two days.

The Boston man, a chatty fellow given to catty asides about his colleagues, said he'd read her stories in that morning's paper.

"The piece about the widow was quite nice," he said, delicately crossing his legs at the knee, then adjusting the crease of his trousers.

Caroline glowed, and decided his cologne was rather pleasant now that her nose had numbed a little.

"Not up to Boston standards, of course," he added once he was assured of the crease's perfection, "but quite good. I'm sure a number of the less particular newspapers will be picking it up. *Our* readers, of course, wouldn't stand for the second piece. Not at all the sort of thing one puts in a family paper, you know."

"But I didn't mention the exact nature of Mrs. Spears' business," Caroline objected, stung.

"Any fool could guess what you meant," the Chicago man interjected. "Did a good job of gettin' your point across, though. I already sent it on to my editor. Piece like that's worth two cents a word if I get it to him before the services pick it up."

Caroline took a deep, indignant breath, then choked on the smell of stale masculine sweat. "You *stole* my piece?"

"Sure," said the Chicago man, grinning. "Why

not? By the time my editor got it officially, it'd be old hat.''

"But you're giving me credit, right? C.A. Exclusive to the *Times?*''

"Nah. Why bother? Nobody'll've heard of you, anyway.''

"Why, you—''

"Now, now, dear lady.'' The Boston fellow grabbed her sleeve and dragged her back to her seat. "No sense in bristling up like that. That's the way the game's played, you see.''

"But *you* wouldn't steal my article like that, would you?''

"Of *course* not.''

She beamed.

"I always take the trouble to rewrite them first. That way you get full pay.''

"Waste of time,'' Chicago said with a snort.

"It doesn't take that much time if you know how to write in the first place,'' Boston sniffed.

"You saying I don't know how to write?''

"Implying, dear fellow. You really need to get the concept straight. If I were *saying* it, I'd just come right out and *say* it, wouldn't I?''

Before Chicago could reply, he leaned toward Caroline and confided, "Never settle for pennies a word, my dear, not even for someone else's story. Piece like that in Boston would get you a hundred and fifty, easily.''

"*Dollars?*''

He blinked. "Of course. Why, what did they pay you?''

Her fingers curled into fists, crushing her copy of the *Times*. "Not two cents a word."

It was his turn to beam. "Good, good. I'd heard you were new to the business, but you're obviously learning."

"Yes, indeed. I'm learning by the minute."

Two cents a word to steal an article for which she'd only gotten a penny and a half? Another round of negotiations with Mr. Blackmun was clearly in order.

Out of the corner of her eye she caught J.R. settling into his seat on the opposite side of the aisle. She quickly looked away and found Andrew Osbald standing in the aisle, glaring at her. His eyes glittered menacingly from beneath puffy lids. Muscles at either side of his jaw worked as if he were gnawing on a bone. A raw and very bloody bone. In his right hand he held a crushed and torn copy of this morning's *Times*.

"You C.A.?" he snarled, leaning across Boston to wave the crumpled newspaper in her face. His fist looked the size of a boulder. "You this goddamned reporter who's been writing all these lies about me?"

J.R. would have slammed his fist into the fellow's face, but he wasn't beside her. Boston shrank back in his chair, as far out of Osbald's reach as he could get. Chicago shifted in his seat to get a better view. She was on her own.

Caroline knotted her hands around her own copy of the paper to hide their sudden trembling and lifted her chin in what she hoped looked like cool defiance.

"I'm Caroline Abbott," she said, grateful for the

steadiness in her voice, "and I don't lie. Everything I wrote was the truth."

"The hell it was! Lies! Every single word of it! If I get—"

"Andy!" Augustus Snead, Osbald's attorney, dragged him back. "Not here."

"That bi—"

"Not. Here." The cold, emphatic way he pronounced each word cut through Osbald's anger. Snead shoved him through the gate in the low railing that corralled the spectators. "Ma'am," he said, granting her a curt nod as he followed his client to the table set aside for the defendant.

Caroline gave an involuntary shiver. When they'd met hers, the attorney's eyes had been cold and hard as black glass.

Osbald reluctantly settled into his chair. His murderous glare was like a dagger, pinning her to her seat. Caroline held his stare for as long as she could take it, then looked away to find J.R. watching her, his eyes hooded, his expression coldly unreadable. She tilted her chin up, daring him to say something. He turned aside, pointedly ignoring her.

The message was unmistakable. If she wanted to prove she could take care of herself, he was going to let her.

Casually, as if she didn't care what he did, she shifted to survey the packed courtroom behind her and caught Murray staring at her, a nasty little smile on his face. Caroline wrenched back around in her seat.

Chicago tried to hide his laughter under a cough.

"Awfully rough looking fellow, that Osbald," said Boston. "I don't think he likes you much."

"I don't care." Caroline defiantly squared her shoulders. "I'm not afraid of him."

"No?" said Boston. "Well, all I can say is, better you than me, my dear lady. *Much* better you than me."

Proud. Unreasonable. Bullheaded. Stubborn as a mule. Damned, pigheaded fool.

As he listened to the prosecutor's opening statement, J.R. mentally cataloged his wife's less endearing qualities.

Willful. Contrary. Perverse. Unruly. Opinionated. Independent. Bullheaded. Had he already said that? *Flat-out, no two ways about it, downright cussed difficult.*

And that was putting it mildly.

Intelligent. Perceptive. Resourceful. Brave.

Beautiful.

Utterly desirable.

J.R. stifled a groan. Caroline was driving him crazy.

He was damned proud of the way she'd stared down Osbald and his threats...and she was scaring the hell out of him. Facing a man like Osbald in the middle of a crowded courtroom was one thing. Facing him when there was no one around to restrain that murderous bastard...

J.R. could feel the sweat stand out on his brow, just at the thought.

She'd been right about the prosecution's plans.

Hargreave was treating the killing as an isolated incident, not the culmination of years of hostile rivalry between two powerful, hot-tempered men. It might get Osbald cleared on the murder charge, but it made for deadly dull listening and would make even duller reading. Not that Caroline and the *Times* wouldn't try to spice it up, of course.

Just the thought of what new mischief she might get into over this had his heart pounding.

Irritated and deeply worried, when the noon recess was called J.R. flipped his notebook closed and rose with the rest. Out of the corner of his eye he caught his wife, jaw set with dangerous intent, sweeping into the aisle. That runty little fellow from the Boston *Herald* wisely kept out of her way, but Osbald, eyes narrowed, face twisted in a scowl, watched her all the way down the aisle and out the door.

Caroline paused on the courthouse steps and anxiously scanned the crowd. She was sure she'd seen Dolly James at the back of the courtroom, and she didn't want to lose her in the crowd. It couldn't be anyone else. The woman fit every description Caroline had been given of her—incredibly beautiful and incredibly badly dressed, a blond goddess with an eye-popping taste for flashy clothes.

Even in the confusion, Dolly wasn't hard to spot. Despite her protesting feet, Caroline caught up with her half a block from the courthouse.

"Miss James? Miss James!"

Dolly hesitated, but a critical perusal of Caroline's hat and dress and shoes seemed to reassure her. Her expression brightened. "You're that newspaper lady, ain'tcha?"

"That's right. Caroline Abbott." Caroline held out her hand. "How do you do?"

Like royalty, Dolly gave her the tips of her fingers to squeeze, then regally pulled her hand back. "Lola said you was lookin' for me. Said I'd know you right off 'cause you was tall and dressed like money."

"Did she? Yes...well..." Caroline felt more flustered in the presence of this brash, confident, ill-bred woman than she'd felt in Lola Spear's whorehouse. "I was hoping I could ask you a few questions, Miss James. About Mr. Walker. And Mr. Osbald."

Dolly shrugged. "Sure. But I got things to do. You wanna buy me lunch while we talk?"

Dolly's notion of the proper place for lunch was a saloon and gambling hall that served meals as well as liquor. At reasonable prices, Caroline was relieved to note, nervously studying the chalkboard where the day's menu was posted. The air was so thick with cigar smoke that her eyes watered. The smell of cheap whiskey permeated everything.

If her mother ever found out she'd been in a place like this, she'd take to her bed for a month.

As they walked to the table Dolly had chosen, the hairs at the back of Caroline's neck pricked from all the attention they drew. Dolly reveled in it.

"Josh usta bring me here," she confided, happily settling into her chair. "He was real generous. Bought me these earrings, see?"

She flicked back the carefully arranged curls so

Caroline could get a better look at the pearl drops she wore.

"Very nice. Did Mr. Osbald ever object?"

"Andy?" She laughed. "Sure. Which was fine with me, 'cause every time one of 'em gave me somethin', the other gave me somethin' better. Those two hated each other so much, neither one could think straight."

"So you didn't love Mr. Walker?"

"Josh? You're kiddin', right? He was near old enough to be my *father*."

"Mr. Osbald's older."

Again that careless shrug. "It's mostly the older ones got the money. That don't mean I'm countin' on 'em marryin' me. 'Specially not if they already got a wife."

She studied Caroline, a speculative glint in her eye. "You married?"

"Yes. Didn't you notice the ring on my left hand?"

"Sure, but lotsa girls wear those. 'Specially when they go out in public like this."

"Really?" said Caroline faintly. Before she could think of anything else to say, J.R. walked in the door.

He pretended not to notice her, but he chose a table not far from theirs, then sat with his back to the wall so he had a clear view of the room, and of them. Caroline deliberately scooted her chair around so that her back was to him. It didn't help. She was still as intensely aware of him as if he were leaning over her shoulder whispering sweet nothings in her ear.

She pushed aside the fantasy and concentrated on reality. Trying to pry any useful information out of

Dolly James proved a daunting task. The woman was far more interested in the men around her than past lovers, especially dead ones.

"There's a fellow at a table behind you keeps eyein' me somethin' fierce," she informed Caroline with satisfaction. "Dressed real fine and good looking, too. *Real* good-lookin'. I—"

"*That,*" said Caroline repressively, "is my husband."

"Your *husband?*" Dolly eyed her with blatant curiosity. "What're you doin' here when you got a man looks like that at home?"

"I'm a newspaper reporter. I have to be here."

"What about him?"

"He's a newspaper reporter, too."

"Really?" Dolly's eyes narrowed as she studied him. Her scrutiny must have drawn his attention because she smiled suddenly, and tossed her curls, then gave a tiny little wave in his direction. "He don't look like any newpaper reporter *I've* ever seen."

"You've known many?"

The sarcasm went right over Dolly's head. She gave that characteristic little shrug of hers. "A few. Not many. We don't often see 'em in the house where I work."

"Why is that?"

"They never have any money." Dolly's gaze was still fixed on J.R. "None worth speakin' of, anyway. Can't hardly afford an hour, let alone anything else, so they generally end up with the girls in the cribs. They're *lots* cheaper than a girl like me," she added confidingly. "But then, I'm the best!"

Caroline choked, gasped, then spat out a mouthful of steak.

"He looks like he could afford all night, easy," Dolly continued, oblivious. "Dresses expensive, just like you. He really is *awfully* good lookin.'"

"And he is *awfully* married."

Dolly laughed. "That ain't never stopped 'em yet! It don't even slow 'em down much."

An image formed, of J.R. in a room hung in red velvet with half a dozen Dollys languidly draped around him, cooing sweet nothings in his ear.

Caroline's jaw hardened. She'd come to believe him when he said he hadn't indulged that night he'd been caught in Denver, but he still hadn't apologized, either. Hadn't been the least bit contrite, even. *He* could do anything he wanted, including whiling away his evenings in the company of fallen women or scaring her half to death, but he still thought *she* ought to go home...and stay there.

J.R. ordered steak and a whiskey. If he had to spend his time playing bodyguard, he might as well make the best of it. While he waited, he scowled at the back of Caroline's neck and tried to ignore Dolly's coquettish overtures.

A damned gambling hall! And in the company of a prostitute! What more could his wife possibly do to ruin her reputation? Run naked through the streets?

At the thought of Caroline, naked, his pulse jumped.

Chapter Fifteen

Dolly worked her way through the steak and fried potatoes with impressive efficiency, then patted her lips with her napkin, plumped her curls, and pushed back from the table.

"You ain't hardly touched your food," she said by way of apology, "but I gotta run. Got some errands, you know, and then there's the trial. I promised Andy I'd be there for him." She giggled. "He ain't naturally as generous as Josh, but he's better in bed, you know what I mean? Way I figure it, a girl's entitled to a little fun, too. Right?"

Caroline couldn't think of a single answer that wouldn't make her blush worse than she already was. She pushed her plate away, then blindly threw a couple dollars on the table. "I'll walk out with you."

She had to escape. A headache was starting to pound in her temples. From the smoke and the smell of the whiskey, she tried to assure herself, knowing she lied.

When she rose, J.R. rose, too. He didn't look at her. She tried to pretend she wasn't looking at him as she followed Dolly out of the saloon, but she'd swear she could hear his every step.

"Had a spat, did you?" Dolly said, amused. "You be careful. That sort of thing's what gets 'em visitin' girls like me."

"I'll remember that." Caroline held out her hand. "Thank you for your time, Miss James." The woman hadn't said much that was useful, but there was still a good story there. And it wasn't going to go for five cents a word, either. Not even if she had to wear out the phone lines between here and Denver making sure it didn't.

Dolly giggled. "You gonna write about me like you wrote about Lola?"

"Probably." Caroline stifled a wince as she stepped off the walk into the street. Sitting all morning had made her feet swell, which only added to the agony of the blisters she'd earned over the past two days

"I liked that headline," Dolly confided, following her. "Spurned Lover Defends Murdered Man. Had a real nice ring to it. Only I ain't spurned. And Andy wouldn't like it if I defended Josh. But I'd like it just fine if you could get me somethin' good like you got Lola."

"That's up to my editor," Caroline said, gritting her teeth against the pain of her throbbing feet and the almost overwhelming urge to snap at the silly twit.

"You know," said Dolly cheerfully, "you might wanta visit Donnelly's. They got some real nice shoes there."

"Donnelly's?"

"That's right. Best place in town for shoes. And, say! If you buy a new pair, can I have those? Never seen nothin' anywhere near that fancy around here. I bet Andy'd like 'em just fine."

The afternoon's proceedings were, if possible, even more boring than the morning's. The witnesses all sounded as if they'd memorized their testimony off the same crib sheet. Walker had been an enraged and jealous lover, irrational and dangerous. Osbald, the epitome of an upright, law-abiding businessman, had shot in self-defense.

If the prosecutor, Hargreave, really was trying to get Osbald off, he was doing a darned good job of it.

Caroline had to fight to keep from squirming in her seat. Though she tried to follow what was being said, her intense awareness of J.R. across the aisle made it impossible to concentrate. She knew every time he scratched his chin or flipped a page in his notebook. She could almost feel the soreness in his shoulder with every move he made.

Her own body throbbed with a different, more unsettling ache.

He didn't once glance her way.

Had a spat, did you? Dolly had said.

Did it matter, if he was the one in the wrong?

That sort of thing's what gets 'em visitin' girls like me.

The words kept spinning round in her head. The words, and the way the woman's face lit up at the sight of J.R.

It was her feet that were making her so cross, Caroline told herself. She'd buy herself a pair of comfortable, sensible shoes and everything would be all right.

To distract herself, she wrote up her interview with Dolly in a small, cramped hand that Boston couldn't possibly decipher, no matter how much he strained to read it. She'd write up the report of the trial's first day later, when J.R. wasn't close enough to distract her.

A collective groan of relief went round the room when the judge called the afternoon recess. As Caroline made her way through the milling crowd, she had to force herself not to look back to see if J.R. noticed her departure. She didn't want him following her, yet she found half a dozen excuses to glance in the store windows she passed, hoping to catch a glimpse of him behind her.

At the front door of Donnelly's Dry Goods Emporium, she paused to scan the street behind her. J.R. was nowhere in sight.

Stupid to be so disappointed.

Donnelly's shoe department consisted of a few dozen shoe boxes stacked behind a narrow, crowded display shelf, but it had just enough pretension to grandeur to have a chair to sit in and a clerk to help her with her selection. Caroline couldn't stifle a sigh of relief when the fussy little man eased her right shoe off her foot and reverently set it aside. She wiggled her toes and tried to ignore the lumpy, thick-soled brown shoes he held up for her inspection.

"These shoes are designed to provide comfort, support, and years of wear," he said, politely ignoring her grimace of distaste. "Made of the finest leather and double stitched on all seams. And see the sole? Good and thick. Very practical and only a dollar fifteen the pair."

"No, thank you." Very firmly. The shoes she was wearing had cost nine and a half.

He put the first pair down and held up another. "These, perhaps?"

Caroline shuddered. "My cook wears shoes just like that."

He scanned the display where ladies' party slippers and button-top shoes where crammed in with men's dress lace-ups and sturdy miners' boots. The lack of choice would have made her mother weep.

"Perhaps there's something in the back," he said doubtfully.

"Wonderful. *Anything* but those." She cast a look of loathing at the two pairs he'd set on the floor beside his stool.

While he went to look, she closed her eyes, stretched out her right leg, and waggled her foot back and forth. It felt so *good*. If she took off the other shoe…

As if in answer to her prayers, hands closed around her left foot. She heard the scrape of the clerk's stool over the floor, then the easing of pressure as her shoe was unbuttoned. She didn't open her eyes. It felt so good, she didn't want to spoil the moment by looking at the clerk's chinless, pointy-nosed face.

The hands gently slid her shoe off.

Eyes tight shut, Caroline smiled and wiggled her

foot, savoring the release. Maybe she'd just go barefoot.

Strong fingers dug into her arch, kneading the weary muscles.

Caroline's eyes flew open. Her indignant protest died in a gasp. "J.R.! What—?"

He glanced up from under sinfully thick lashes. Caroline curled her hands into fists against the temptation of running her fingers through his hair. He was…beautiful. Beautiful and dangerously male.

"You need to take better care of your feet." Even his voice caressed her, sparking fire. "A reporter's not much good if he's too crippled to walk."

Slowly, sensuously, he stroked his thumbs from heel to ball and back again. Her breath caught as heat flooded her.

She tried to pull her foot free. He held fast.

"I'm not too crippled to walk." The words came out thick and rough, squeezed passed the constriction in her throat.

"Not yet."

"I—" The rest died unspoken, strangled by another surge of heat as he lightly trailed his fingers across the sensitive curve of her arch.

He laid her left foot in his lap and bent to pick up her right. She made a feeble effort to resist, but his hold was firm and exquisitely sensual. Utterly irresistible. It had been so *long!*

"You should wear socks."

For an instant, she thought he'd said *sex.*

The hard *thunk* of shoes hitting the floor brought them both around with a start.

"Sir! *What* are you doing?" The clerk's eyes were almost popping out of his head. "You can't— It's not proper— I—"

J.R. glanced up at him, amused. "I'm lecturing my wife on the need for socks."

"No socks." Again Caroline tried, and failed, to pull her feet free.

"*Socks,*" said J.R. firmly. "Big, thick ones."

Caroline shuddered.

The clerk dithered.

J.R.'s eyebrows arched. "Wool, if you have them. Very fine." He waved the little man away with the arrogance of a gentleman born.

Caroline just sat there staring, torn between embarrassment and the mad urge to make love to her husband right in the middle of the shoe department of Donnelly's Dry Goods Emporium.

J.R.'s hands curled over her battered feet, gently soothing, dangerously erotic. The thin layer of her silk stockings only made the gesture that much more sensual. A hungry, demanding ache started in her belly.

"This is outrageous!" she hissed.

He nodded. "It is. No man should be forced to seduce his wife between the corset department and the rubber boots."

"J.R.—"

"Don't, Caroline." His long, elegant fingers kept digging into her foot, easing the pain and tightness. He seemed not to notice the stout matron at the end of the aisle who gasped and stopped short at the sight of them, then turned and stalked off, her fat chins quivering with indignation.

"Socks." The clerk, mouth pursed in disapproval, held a pair out at arm's length.

"Thank you," said J.R. "Those will do fine." He waved the man away. "We'll call if we need you."

The clerk retreated in high dudgeon, muttering to himself.

"That's better," said J.R. in satisfaction. "Now, where were we?"

He gave her a wicked grin and dug the heel of his hand along her arch, drawing a stifled moan.

"J.R...."

"Say it softer." He massaged her toes with the tips of his fingers, then worked his way back to her heels. "Slower. As if you mean it."

She ought to run and keep on running, but with both feet inelegantly propped in his lap and every bone in her body threatening to turn liquid at his touch, she wouldn't get five feet.

They could hear the indignant gabbling of the offended customer even here at the back of the store.

Caroline clamped her hand around the chair arms, fighting against the dangerous tug on her senses. "Put my feet down."

"I will...as soon as I'm sure my wife won't end up a cripple." He held up a sock. "In case you didn't know, this is a *sock.* You wear it. Thus." He slid it over her right foot and up over her ankle, smoothing it as he went.

"I wear stockings," she snapped. "I do *not* wear socks."

"Your stockings have holes in the heels."

"They do not!" He let go of her right foot and

grabbed her sockless left before she could pull it out of his lap.

"Big holes." He slid a finger through the hole and tickled the sensitive spot just behind her ankle bone.

"J.R.!" It came out half gasp, half plea. His every touch sent fire licking up her legs.

He slid the second sock on. "You'll need some garters to hold these things up."

"I already have some garters, thank you," she snapped.

Again that wicked grin and a glance from under those thick lashes. "I know."

Caroline thought of all the times he'd unfastened her garters, of the slow, teasing way he'd rolled her stockings down her legs. She thought of what had always followed, and whimpered, ever so softly.

His knowing wink made her squirm in her chair. He retrieved the shoes the clerk had dropped and held them up for inspection. "Not quite your style, but *very* practical."

Deftly, he slid the right shoe on her foot and laced it up. She wiggled her toes in surprise. She hadn't worn anything this comfortable since she was a schoolgirl.

"Like it?"

"It's ugly." She tugged her foot free just as a grim-faced contingent rounded a display of men's long underwear, headed in their direction. At their head marched a gimlet-eyed gentleman in three-piece suit and painfully stiff collar. The indignant lady harried his right flank, still sputtering, while the shoe clerk followed eagerly in their wake.

Caroline stared in dismay. If she rammed the woman and trampled the clerk, she might make it to the door, but—

J.R.'s hold on her ankle tightened.

Gimlet-eyes came to a smart halt. His troops straggled to a stop behind him.

"May I help you?" Frost coated every word.

"Sure," said J.R. and slipped on the other shoe. "Go away."

"If the lady is looking for shoes, Mr. Warburg, here, would be happy to assist."

The woman glared. Mr. Warburg gave a disdainful sniff.

Caroline abandoned thoughts of escape and started hoping she could die right there on the spot. J.R. gave her an encouraging smile, then tied the laces with a flourish and scooted back.

"There you go, my love. Try that."

She scrambled to her feet. J.R. languidly got to his, then bent and lifted the hem of her dress, which now brushed the floor. "How do those fit?"

"J.R.!" She snatched her skirts away, blushing furiously. Without the extra couple of inches her high-heeled shoes provided, she felt at even more of a disadvantage. "They're too big."

"Just right for when your feet swell," her husband said, beaming.

The stout woman turned even redder. "This is outrageous!"

"No it's not," J.R. assured her. "A reporter needs good, comfortable shoes." He grinned at Caroline.

"You'll like them just fine once you get used to them."

"Reporter?" The woman eyes widened. "Did you say *reporter?*" She elbowed the gimlet-eyed gentleman out of her way. "Are you that lady reporter who's caused so much uproar over this trial?" she demanded, peering up at Caroline. "The one Elizabeth Carter's been talking about?"

Caroline nodded.

"Really? You're C.A.?"

"Yes, I am." She batted away J.R.'s hand as he reached for her skirt again. "I'm Caroline Abbott."

The woman's frown disappeared in a wide, approving smile. "Well, why didn't you *say* so? Good for you! It's about time someone told these men what's what! *When It Comes To Murder, Ask The Ladies.*" She cackled in satisfaction. "That was a *fine* headline."

The clerk and the gimlet-eyed gentleman gaped. J.R.'s face tightened. It wasn't quite a scowl, but there was a dangerous glint behind the polite facade.

Caroline looked away. Her muscles still felt weak from the heat he'd stirred. Her body ached. She was furious with herself for giving in so easily, and she wanted revenge for the easy way he'd played her. But first, she had to pay for these blasted ugly shoes. *And* pacify her unwelcome audience. She forced herself to ignore J.R. and concentrate on the matter at hand.

"I'm a friend of Mary Walker's," the stout woman was saying. "I didn't think much of the way he ran around on her, but she deserves justice, and she's not getting it. But *you're* doing something, Mrs. Abbott.

The decent women of Cripple Creek are grateful for that.''

''Why, thank you.''

The approving smile tipped into a disapproving frown. ''We don't approve of some of your sources, however!'' She turned her attention on J.R. ''You, I assume, are Mr. Abbott.'' She gave a scornful snort. ''I've heard about you. You and your ladders.''

Beneath the scrapes and bruises, J.R.'s face turned a delicate pink.

The gimlet-eyed gentleman was not so easily distracted. ''Do you want those shoes, madame, or don't you?''

''Yes. Yes, of course.'' Caroline said briskly. She'd deal with J.R. later.

While the stout lady rattled on about Walker and Osbald and society's declining morals, she paid for the shoes and socks, and tried to ignore a frowning J.R. hovering over her right shoulder. At least the frosty gentleman had retreated once he was assured the shoes would be paid for and that there would be no further hanky-panky in his store.

Mr. Warburg, gratified to have served a famous reporter, boxed up her old shoes, then tied the box with string.

''Triple-knotted,'' he assured her, handing her both box and change.

J.R. watched in grim silence, then followed her out the door. The instant they were out of sight of the store, she turned on him.

''How *dare* you humiliate me like that?'' she demanded. "What got into you? Did you really think I'd enjoy being made a public spectacle? *Did* you?"

J.R.'s face went white. The hotter her temper got, the stiller he grew until he might have been one of those Greek statues she'd seen in museums, cold and hard and perfect. His lack of response only made her angrier.

"What? Not even a word of apology? Not so much as—"

The rest was swallowed in a brutal kiss. His arms closed around her, trapping her against him. His mouth crushed down on hers, hot and demanding. Her hands were pinned between them, but instead of trying to push him away, she found herself grabbing hold of his suit so he couldn't escape if he let her go.

He didn't let go.

He held her so close and tight she couldn't breathe or think or move.

She didn't care. All she wanted was for him to keep on kissing her. The taste of him, the heat and scent of him were driving her wild. The fire he'd started flared hotter than before, racing from the soles of her feet all the way up until it fired her heart and brain, burning away the anger and leaving blinding, bone-melting need, instead.

What could they possibly have found to quarrel about?

When he abruptly shoved her away, the world spun. She gasped, staggered. "J.R.? What...?"

J.R. tugged his coat into place, then smoothed the lapels her fingers had crushed. "Nice to see you haven't lost your flair for that sort of thing, Caroline."

"What?" Dimly, she was aware of people stopped dead in the street, staring, but right at the moment, she didn't give a damn. "What did you think you were doing?" she demanded hotly.

"Kissing you. It's been so long, I'd wondered if you'd forgotten how." He stooped to retrieve the shoe box she'd dropped. "Your shoes."

She flung it back, barely missing his head. He didn't try to follow when she stalked off.

Two men on the walk abruptly stopped snickering and scrambled to get out of her way. She was almost to the corner when Murray suddenly appeared.

"I want to talk to you," he said, belligerently parking his bulk in her path.

She didn't break stride. "I don't want to talk to you."

"Listen—"

"Out of my way, Murray," she growled, thrusting out her arm to fend him off.

"If you think "

The rest vanished in a loud *oof!* when her open palm connected with the middle of his chest. Caught off balance, Murray staggered, then toppled backward off the boardwalk into the dirt and the horse droppings.

Caroline didn't stop, and she didn't look back.

Chapter Sixteen

J.R. passed a restless night in dreams of Caroline, tormenting dreams of making love to her that eventually brought him awake, sweating and aching with lust.

A cold bath at one in the morning did nothing to ease his suffering. Frustrated, he sought distraction in a book he'd picked at random from the collection the National maintained for guests, then fell asleep again in the gray hours of early dawn and dreamed of Caroline and a man with angry eyes and fists the size of boulders who stalked her through his dreams.

The face that looked back at him from his mirror shortly after eight was strangely unfamiliar, hollow-eyed and hard. When he went down to breakfast, the waiter's usually cheery greeting died unspoken. Coffee, hot and strong, appeared as if by magic. He drank the first cup down in one throat-searing gulp. While he worked on the second, he unfolded the morning's papers.

His story had gotten front-page placement, of course. If Osbald had read it, he was spitting nails by now. The piece revealed past business dealings between Osbald and the prosecutor, Hargreave, that should have disqualified Hargreave from involvement in the trial. The dealings were all several years back, but substantial enough to raise doubts about Hargreave's motives in keeping the trial's focus on the events of the night of the killing and not the two men's past dealings. Nobody else had dug up so much as a hint of the relationship.

J.R. grunted and gulped more coffee. It was a first-class piece of investigative reporting that would make folks sit up and take notice, but it brought him no satisfaction. He tossed the *Tribune* aside and picked up the *Times*.

Beautiful Woman Caught Between Two Rivals. Jealousy And Animal Lust Lead To Murder. ''Exclusive to the *Times* by C.A.''

His mouth twisted in distaste. He'd have to make a point of complimenting Caroline on her lurid headlines. He couldn't think of anything that would infuriate her more.

The second story made his stomach churn.

Conspiracy? Questions Raised About Conduct Of Trial.

For that one, Caroline had abandoned any attempt at balanced reporting. Instead, she'd opted for a series of inflammatory questions that, without coming right out and saying it, accused Osbald of cold-blooded murder and Hargreave of conducting the trial so that a verdict of not guilty was virtually guaranteed.

Despite his warnings, she'd the same as waved a red flag in the bull's face and dared him to charge.

* * *

By the time J.R. got to the courthouse, a small crowd had gathered waiting for the doors to open. At the center of the crowd, surrounded by a pack of gossipy fools, Caroline held court. She hadn't seen him.

For a moment he simply stood there watching her and listening to the conversation. He had to give her credit. She was using the opportunity to gather information. Most new reporters would have wallowed in the attention, forgetting that their job was to keep the public informed, not entertained. Then she turned and caught sight of him and he forgot about the crowd and newspaper reporting and his fears for her. All he thought of was how glorious she was, and how glad he was he'd married her, even if she did drive him crazy.

She said something to the people around her, then pushed through the crowd to stand in front of him. As though they were mere acquaintances, she coolly extended her hand.

"Mr. Abbott," she said.

He took her hand in his and wished he could drag her into his arms, instead. "Mrs. Abbott."

"That was a fascinating piece in the *Tribune* this morning."

His grip on her hand tightened. He leaned closer and lowered his voice so only she could hear. "And that was a damned dangerous one in the *Times*."

She laughed. "How nice of you to say so."

"Caroline..." Her hand felt warm and soft in his. Her laughter made his heart catch, and he'd swear he caught a whiff of her perfume.

What would she do if he swept her into his arms and kissed her as he'd kissed her yesterday?

Before he could find out, the courthouse doors were flung open and the crowd surged forward. Caroline slipped out of his reach to shove her way through the pack with an unladylike determination that left him gaping. By the time he got into the courthouse, his seat at the front was taken and the only available seat at the back with a decent view of the proceedings was smack dab beside the opinionated lady from Donnelly's.

"I notice your *wife* managed to get here early enough to get *her* seat," she said, clasping both hands over the enormous handbag on her lap as if she thought he'd steal it.

J.R. propped his right ankle on his knee and perched his hat atop the peak. Short of spitting on the floor, he couldn't get much ruder.

"And a good morning to you, too, ma'am," he said, forcing his sweetest smile. "Lovely day for a trial, isn't it?"

She huffed and muttered something under her breath, then pointedly ignored him.

The morning's proceedings began much as he'd expected them to—dull and clearly designed to get the whole thing over with as soon as possible, and with an acquittal for the defendant.

Bored and angry that he'd come into this story too late to make a difference, J.R. fiddled with the brim of his hat, then shifted his position on the chair. He stared at the ceiling, at the back of the heads in front of him, at the toe of his shoe, then fiddled with his hat again.

This was a damned poor way to end a scandal. After all the buildup in the press, he didn't want to write so drab an ending to it. Unfortunately, things sometimes worked out that way. He didn't have to like it, but he'd been a reporter long enough to know that when it happened the best you could do was write "The End" and go on to something else.

Would Caroline understand that? He craned to one side, as far as he could go without landing in the lap of the man beside him, but couldn't catch so much as a glimpse of his wife. Too many heads and burly shoulders in the way.

How many toes had Caroline stepped on to get to the front? How many of those burly men that now sat between them had she elbowed or prodded or shoved to the side in order to reclaim that coveted front row seat? Three months ago, she wouldn't have dreamed of being so rude. This morning, she hadn't hesitated for a second, and hadn't expected him or anyone else to help her get what she wanted, either.

Ignoring the muttering of the woman beside him, J.R. settled back in his chair. He was going to have to face it. His wife was a reporter. A good one— clever, resourceful, and bright. She liked what she was doing. She *believed* in it. She might love him, but she wasn't going to give up the challenges of this new world she'd grabbed hold of, no matter what he thought or said.

Truth to tell, he wasn't sure he objected. Not like he would have a few weeks ago, anyway. He wanted the best for Caroline. He always had. Only now he was beginning to understand how different what he'd wanted for her was from what she wanted for herself.

"This is outrageous! You can't do this! These entire proceedings are a disgrace! A joke! A blatant travesty of justice!"

J.R. looked up to find an indignant woman standing at the front of the court shaking her fist at the judge.

"You ought to be ashamed of yourself!" Caroline continued fiercely, ignoring the buzz from the public behind her. "Call yourself a judge. Hah! No judge worth his salt would permit this mockery in his courtroom! You should be demanding *all* the truth—every bit of it!—not sending the jury off with nothing but testimony from an accused murderer's friends!"

The buzz turned into a low roar of excited approval. The judge, red-faced with fury, pounded for quiet. Caroline ignored him.

"What about Mr. Osbald's past dealings with Josiah Walker? What about their quarrel over ownership of the Summit mine?" she demanded, shouting now to make herself heard over the tumult. "What about the court case that Walker won at Osbald's expense? What about Osbald's less than sterling reputation here in town? What about *that?*"

"That's telling 'em!" said the stout woman beside him, pounding her fist on her knee with glee.

Someone behind them gave an ear-piercing whistle of approval.

J.R. clapped his hand over his eyes and slumped back in his chair with a groan.

Caroline shouted louder. "How can you pretend to call this a court of law if—"

"Sheriff!" the judge roared. "Throw that woman out!"

J.R. sank deeper into his chair.

Shouts and objections from the crowd drowned out the response, but Caroline's indignant shrieks carried clearly over the commotion.

"Let me go! Unhand me, you beast! Let...me... *go!*"

From between his fingers, he watched as his wife, a sturdy deputy at either elbow, was carried bodily out of the courtroom, kicking and screaming all the way.

The deputies deposited Caroline at the foot of the courthouse steps. Before she could catch her breath, they'd shut the courthouse doors behind them, locking her out on the street. She could hear the uproar even out here.

And so could the dozen or so passersby who had gathered to see what was going on. Ignoring their stares, she tugged her clothes into place, checked to be sure her hat was still securely pinned atop her head, then set off up the street, headed to Mary Walker's house.

The widow listened to her angry recounting of the trial's proceedings, nodding and sniffling into her handkerchief, but in the end, she had nothing to offer. Osbald had murdered her husband and there wasn't a thing she could do about it, Mary assured her from behind her sodden hanky. Justice was something for men to worry about. All she wanted was her husband back.

Since Caroline drew the line at trying to rouse the dead, she eventually quit arguing and took her leave. She wasn't ready to give up, however. Mary Walker deserved justice, for her husband and herself.

But what could she do? The articles she'd written hadn't been enough. J.R.'s stories revealing the details of Walker's and Osbald's past associations hadn't been enough. Osbald had clearly bought Hargreave's complicity and, possibly, the judge's. Mere good intentions couldn't stand against that kind of corruption.

What would J.R. do?

The question made Caroline stop dead in her tracks. J.R. would know what to do. He'd fought against that kind of corruption before and won. He would—

She thought of him, slumped in his seat, his face covered with his hand so he couldn't see her carried out shrieking like a fishwife, and winced.

No, he wouldn't.

No mere apology was going to get her out of this one. J.R. wasn't likely to be understanding about her behavior in the courtroom this morning. Now that her temper had cooled, she wasn't too proud of it, either. She hadn't accomplished anything except make a spectacle of herself.

But if she *could* accomplish something…

Frustrated, oblivious to her surroundings, Caroline scratched at her neck and pondered.

If only she could convince some of the ladies in

town to help. The men seemed to see this trial as just one more in a long run of underhanded games played by men with money and few scruples, but the women like Elizabeth Carter and that strong-minded lady in Donnelly's yesterday were on the side of justice and Mary Walker. Even meek little Georgianne was unhappy with the turn events were taking. If she could just get them and others like them to speak out...

An idea blossomed. It would involve her creating another rumpus, but maybe *this* time a good rumpus would make a difference.

Of course, it was also going to get her even deeper in hot water as far as J.R. was concerned but—

A second idea hit, even better than the first.

Caroline grinned, dazzled by the brilliance of it all, and started walking faster. She knew exactly how to make J.R. forget about another rumpus, but that would have to wait. First, she had to talk to Elizabeth and her friends.

Chapter Seventeen

J.R. had a bad feeling about this.

He watched as yet another lady, bristling with determination, bustled up the walk to Bonnard's Boardinghouse. That made nine. And that was just in the last fifteen minutes. God knew how many more were forted up in there.

The screen door swung open to admit the new arrival. Elizabeth Carter paused a moment in the open doorway to wave mockingly at him, then retreated, latching the door behind her.

J.R. chomped down on his cheroot in disgust.

By the time he'd escaped the courthouse, Caroline had long since disappeared. When he'd showed up here, that Carter woman had refused to admit him, claiming that Caroline was busy and couldn't take time to speak to him. He'd heard the hum of excited female voices coming from the house but hadn't been able to sift Caroline's from among them. And now nine women, each more eager than the last, had joined that busy, secret gathering.

Caroline was up to something. But what?

Frustrated, he ground out the stub of his cheroot, then kicked it into the dirt of the street. Whatever she was planning, he was quite sure he wasn't going to like it. He wasn't going to like it one bit.

He didn't.

The judge had called for court to reconvene at two o'clock, but Caroline had made sure no one would make it on time, not even the judge. She and at least thirty other women were parading up and down in front of the courthouse steps bearing placards that said things like, Justice For A Widow! and Stop Corruption In Our Courts! and What About The Truth? The one that really made him wince was scrawled in bright red paint on the biggest placard of all—When It Comes To Murder, Ask The Ladies!

"Like it?" Elizabeth Carter asked, brandishing the sign as she walked past. "This one was my idea." When he growled, she laughed.

Caroline's "Is Justice For Sale In Cripple Creek?" wasn't much better. Despite her squawk of protest, he dragged her out of the parade and away from prying ears.

"This is *not* a good idea."

"Do you have a better one?"

"Caroline," he said, dragging out each syllable in unmistakable warning.

She arched her eyebrows mockingly. "Mr. Abbott?"

He threw up his hands, torn between the urge to drag her off by her heels, safely out of trouble, or wrap her in his arms, right there in front of God and everyone, and kiss her till she was deaf and blind and mad with desire.

"All right," he snarled. "Fine! Have it your way! But you'd better keep that pistol of yours handy because the way you're going, you're damn sure going to need it."

He figured she'd stomp off in a snit. She didn't. She did something far more unnerving. She laid her hand on his chest, right over his heart, rose up on tiptoe, and kissed him.

"I love you, J. Randolph Abbott the Third," she said, beaming up at him. She dragged her hand off his heart and gave his tie a tweak. "Even if you *do* drive me crazy."

"*Me?* Drive *you* crazy?" he sputtered.

She didn't answer. She'd already marched off to rejoin her parade.

For an instant, he considered going after her, but the thirty-plus steely-eyed, placard-bearing females watching him with avid speculation stopped him like a wall.

J.R. stalked off in the opposite direction, cursing and hoping to hell nobody noticed the damage that one quick kiss had done to his self-control.

At half past four, after the combined efforts of the court clerk, the sheriff, two sheriff's deputies, a heckling crowd, and a coldly disapproving Augustus Snead had failed to budge the demonstrators, the judge sent word the afternoon's session was canceled.

Elizabeth led the ladies in a rousing cheer, but Caroline couldn't quite drum up the enthusiasm to join in. J.R.'s warning still echoed in her head. Worse, the physical effects of that quick, spontaneous kiss hadn't quite worn off, leaving her distracted and prey to confusing thoughts and even more disconcerting desires.

She hadn't meant to kiss him, not in public like that, but being that close to him and wanting him as she did—

"Think you're somethin' special, don't you?"

Caroline knew who was behind the sneering words even before she turned to confront an angry Murray.

"Were you addressing me?"

"What do *you* think?"

She shifted her grip on the handle of her placard in case she had to smack him. For the first time that day she longed for the elegant shoes she'd tossed at J.R. last night and the extra two inches in height they would have provided.

"I think, sir, that you are an ill-mannered boor and a fool to boot."

That made him blink. As the words sank home, his face darkened. She'd seen beets that weren't so red.

"You'll be sorry. You keep this up, I'll show you. I'll get even."

"You can try, I suppose, but if that pathetic little article on the fourth page of this morning's *Times* is any indication, you're going to have to work a lot harder than you have even to come close."

"*I* was the one supposed to report on this trial," he snarled, low so the other women couldn't hear him. "Just me. You horn in on me like this, I'll show you how the game's played. And I guarantee you won't like it if I do."

It wasn't the anger in his voice that stopped her from replying, but the desperation in his eyes. A flash, no more, then the anger hid it. But it had been there, and for the first time she understood just what her impulsive decision to cover this story had done to him.

Judging by the articles he'd had published so far, Murray was neither a good writer nor a good reporter, but it *was* his work, a part of his identity. Without intending it, she had deprived him not only of an income, but the respect that went with it. He would not easily forgive her for it.

She might have said something then, apologized, even, but Elizabeth and a couple of the other women, evidently sensing trouble, were advancing on them.

Murray's upper lip curled back over his teeth in an animal snarl, and then he was gone, scuffling off across the dust-dry street like an angry, impotent bear that couldn't quite find the courage to break the chains that bound him.

Caroline watched him go and wondered how many other men had lost themselves because of the work they'd chosen. She thought of the dandy from Boston and the unwashed hulk from Chicago, neither of whom had hesitated to steal another's work, or thought to apologize for it. She thought of the things she'd done these past few days that she wouldn't have dreamed of even a week ago, things that would shame her father and horrify her mother and that J.R., somehow, had understood, even if he hadn't completely forgiven her for them. All for pennies a word and the arrogance to meddle in something that was none of her business to begin with.

She frowned at the placard she carried, then reluctantly hoisted it over her shoulder. Not even four days since she'd arrived, yet the world was vastly different, somehow. She wasn't the same person who had climbed aboard that train in Denver early Monday morning, and never would be again. And right at the moment, she wasn't at all sure that was such a good thing.

Caroline made her excuses to the ladies, vague ones that brought knowing looks and approving nods. They thought she was off on another interview. She didn't disabuse them of the notion. She had other things to do.

The box of bullets took a sizable chunk out of her dwindling reserves. A jar of her favorite scented bath salts and some new silk hose took even more.

To her relief, Elizabeth and Georgianne were still out when she got back to the boardinghouse, no doubt celebrating the afternoon's triumphs and plotting the next day's assault on Cripple Creek's courthouse in case it should be needed.

Because she didn't want them to catch her here and delay her with more chatter, and because she was afraid she'd lose her courage if she lingered, she hurriedly gathered the things she'd need and stuffed them in her small traveling bag. The gun went in her purse, followed, after a moment's hesitation, by the hotel key she'd never gotten around to returning to J.R.

Just the feel of it was enough to bring back the

memory of that brush of his breath on her ear, there in that doorway, the quick flick of tongue that had almost melted her bones. Muscles low in her belly clenched involuntarily.

This time, she used the side door of the National and the servants' stairs at the back rather than the lift or the grand staircase at the front. The upper hall was quiet, yet her heart was hammering hard enough it seemed as if everyone in the building ought to hear her.

At the door to J.R.'s room, she stopped, her hand half raised, almost dizzy with the thought of what she'd planned. Her nerves, stretched between doubt and anticipation, jangled unpleasantly.

It wouldn't go wrong. It *couldn't*. But then again…

Drawing a deep breath, she raised her hand and knocked.

Damn the woman! Where in hell had she gone?

J.R. stormed through the National's lobby. He collected his key, then took the stairs two at a time, too impatient to wait for the lift.

He should have watched her more closely, been there at the courthouse when the ladies finally disbanded. By the time he'd gotten there, all he'd managed was to corner a couple of stragglers who said she'd gone off on some interview, they supposed. They didn't know where.

He'd spent the last hour combing Cripple Creek for her. She wouldn't have ventured onto Myers Avenue. Not this late when business was beginning to pick up. She hadn't been anywhere near the telegraph office.

He'd asked. The way the clerk's eyes had lighted at the mention of his wife had made him want to slam his fist in the fellow's face. He'd poked into eateries and shops, but hadn't seen so much as the hem of her petticoat, whisking out the door. Elizabeth Carter said she didn't know where Caroline had gone, and this time he believed her.

Where in the hell *was* she?

Not that he really had to worry, he assured himself as he strode down the hallway. Murray wouldn't do anything and Osbald's threats were so much bluster. He might have gotten away with killing Josiah Walker, but too many people would ask uncomfortable questions if he made the mistake of harming Caroline.

Bold words, yet his hand shook, ever so slightly, when he slipped the key into the lock of his hotel door.

J.R.'s teeth clenched. If Osbald so much as touched her, he'd strangle the bastard personally.

The key clicked in the lock. The knob turned easily beneath his hand.

He'd collect his derringer from his bags, then he'd keep on looking until he found her. And when he did, he was, by God, going to lock her in her room and keep her there until Osbald was either convicted or set free.

He was two steps into the room before his brain registered the wreckage left by the miniature tornado that had evidently swept through the place.

First inside the door were two stout walking shoes, laces still tied as if they'd been wrenched off their owner's feet and hurriedly tossed aside. Then came a pair of socks still tangled in the garters that had held them up, a belt, then a lady's jacket crumpled on the floor. A lady's hat that had been aimed at a chair, and missed. A shirtwaist, dangling from one arm of the chair. A skirt, hem black with dust, untidily draped over the end of the bed. A lacy petticoat, hem similarly soiled, that hadn't quite made the bed and had ended up in a heap on the floor, instead.

Slowly, one piece at a time, J.R. followed the trail of discarded garments that led toward the half-open door of the bathroom.

A lacy corset carelessly tossed on the rug made him suck in his breath. The corset was followed by a pair of women's drawers made of the finest lawn, then a frilly camisole.

Slowly, breath catching in his throat, J.R. bent to pick up the camisole.

The delicate garment, crushed from the constriction of the corset, was so sheer he could see the outline of his hand through it. A hint of dampness from her skin still lingered in the fabric. The narrow satin ribbon at the top, wrinkled now from the bow it had once made, slid across the inside of his wrist, making his pulse jump.

Because he could not help himself, he lifted the garment and drank in the scent of her—floral soap and the darker, muskier scent of her favorite perfume. And beneath that, the dangerous scent of a woman.

His head swam. His knees went weak.

His arousal came as fast and hard as any he'd ever known.

His fingers closed in a fist, crushing the camisole. He took a deep breath, fighting for control.

Three more steps brought him to the door of the bathroom. He pushed the door all the way open, then stopped in the open doorway, stunned and fighting for air.

Caroline smiled at him, then lifted the big bath sponge and squeezed water over her arched throat and down her breasts. She could hear the quick intake of his breath even from here. Her smile widened.

"What kept you?" she asked, turning just enough so the tip of one breast showed above the bubbles.

She thought his eyes crossed, ever so slightly, but instead of rushing across the room and diving into the tub with her, J.R. propped one shoulder against the door jamb, crossed his arms over his chest, cocked one foot over the other, and smiled right back.

"I was looking for you."

Her camisole draped over the sleeve of his coat, startlingly white against his dark suit.

"I wanted to wash my hair."

This was, in fact, the second bath she'd taken in the past half hour. The first had been to wash out the dirt and grime. The second was for the sheer pleasure of it.

"You must have been in quite a rush." He held up the camisole so it dangled from the tip of his fingers, satin ribbons trailing.

"I was." That came out low and just a little breathless. The thought of his hands on her body, of his fingers tracing fire across her damp skin, made her head spin.

She shoved the long, wet tendrils of her hair back from her face, achingly aware of the way his gaze traced their slide over her shoulder and down her breast and back. She half closed her eyes, tilted her head back, and slowly squeezed more water down her throat. From beneath her lashes she watched his reaction.

If he didn't breathe soon, he'd pass out right there in the doorway.

She didn't bother to brush away the bubbles that clung to her cheek and jaw.

Her voice dropped lower still. "Care to join me?"

Without a word, he tossed the camisole away. Slowly, his gaze fixed on her like a sharp-tipped, glittering sword, he took off his coat and tossed it aside, then his vest, and his tie, and his belt. Using the door jamb for a prop, he pulled off one shoe and flung it atop the growing heap of discarded clothing, then the other.

Muscles deep within her squeezed tight in anticipation. She tried to catch her breath, but for some reason her lungs didn't seem to want to work.

"Can't you move any faster?" This time the words came out rough and a little edgy.

He laughed and, slowly, one by one, removed his cufflinks and shirt studs and set them down on the edge of the wide, white porcelain sink. The tiny clink as each one hit made her pulse spike in anticipation.

The opening of his shirt widened, exposing first the strong, masculine lines of his throat, then the hard ridge of his collarbone, the broad expanse of smoothly muscled chest, the tight, flat muscles of his belly.

When he unbuttoned the waistband of his trousers, she stopped breathing altogether.

Her gaze slid lower. Her tongue flicked out to lick lips suddenly gone dry. The rest of his trouser buttons ought to be springing open of their own accord, but despite the strain, they remained firmly fastened. He made no move to undo them.

She forced her gaze away, back up to safer ground.

Slowly, deliberately, he rolled up his sleeves. Heart pounding, Caroline watched the progress of that starched linen up each perfect, golden forearm.

And then he stopped, crossed his arms over his chest, and once more propped his shoulder on the door jamb.

"I want to thank you," he said, "for keeping everyone distracted this afternoon. Because of you, I got my story in early, with plenty of time for a long, long lunch."

Caroline bit down hard on her lower lip to keep from screaming. She hadn't had anything to eat since breakfast, but it wasn't that kind of hunger that was tormenting her right now.

"I even had time to work up a few good headlines. What do you think of, Cub Reporter Bears Watching?"

She gave a low growl, deep in her throat.

"No? Well, how about, C.A. Cans Court? I thought that one had an especially nice ring."

"J.R...."

He might have been deaf for all the heed he paid to the warning in her voice. "Or then there's—"

She abandoned the sponge for the more effective means of defense that she'd left on the small table with the towels, right by the tub.

At the sight of it, he shoved upright, but didn't move an inch from the doorway.

"That," he said on a friendly, informational note, "is a gun. What are you doing with a gun?"

"Pointing it at you."

"I can see that. But, why?"

She shifted her grip. With her hands slick with water and foaming floral bath salts, the metal was a great deal slipperier than normal.

"I don't want to talk about newspaper headlines," she said.

The corner of his mouth twitched, ever so slightly. "All right."

"I intend to keep working as a newspaper reporter no matter what you say."

One eyebrow arched delicately. "Then there's not much use in me saying anything, is there?"

"No."

"No. I didn't think so." He propped his hands on his hips. "What else?"

Caroline frowned. He looked dangerously handsome like that, barefoot and half dressed. Despite the gun, his trouser buttons were still suffering from that intriguing strain, which made it a little hard to concentrate.

"You're giving in much too easily," she said.

"I tend to do that when I have a gun pointed at me."

"No, you don't."

He cocked his head and smiled at her. Her mouth went dry. All that seductive advantage she'd been sure was hers had washed away in the flood of heat that had claimed her when he'd undressed.

If only he'd take off the rest of his clothes—

She gritted her teeth and narrowed her eyes. She had to forget about sex for a minute or she'd never win this argument. And she was absolutely, positively determined to win.

She shifted her grip on the gun. "I take care of my own financial affairs," she said. "Neither you nor my father has any say in the matter. My money is mine to do with as I please. I pay my own way, now."

"Great. As soon as we get home, I'll figure up the costs for the house and electricity and phone and the carriage and Mrs. Priddy's wages and food and whatnot. We'll divide it all, straight down the middle."

She flinched. She hadn't thought about that possibility. It would put a real crimp in her clothes budget, but with what she'd be earning from the *Times*…

"All right," she said. "That's fair."

"That's all?"

"No." She shifted so she could prop the hand holding the gun on the side of the tub. It was amazing how heavy the weapon got after you'd held it for a while. "I want you to promise that you'll quit playing nanny. I'm a big girl, now. I can take care of myself."

"Is that so?" Oblivious to the threat of the gun

pointed at his chest, he abandoned the doorway to perch on the edge of the tub. "You sure about that?"

"Yes," she said, a little breathlessly.

This close, she could smell that hint of starch in his shirt, even with the floral bath salts. Starch and shaving soap and J.R. Her very favorite scents.

It was damnably distracting.

"J.R.?"

"You might want to stir a few more bath salts into the water," he said helpfully. "The bubbles are…um… a little thin."

The way he said it, thin bubbles were a good thing.

Caroline glanced down at the water, then abruptly scooted back in the tub, all the way back so her spine was pressed against the curve at the end of the tub. The bubbles were thicker there.

This time she wrapped both hands around the gun. It was that or drop the thing in the bathwater, which Elizabeth wasn't likely to appreciate.

"Darn it, J.R.! Will you pay attention?"

He flashed her a wicked grin. "I *am* paying attention."

Before she realized what he planned, he'd plucked the gun out of her soap-slicked hands and tossed it on his pile of discarded clothes.

"Next time, you might want to cock it. In case you really *do* want to shoot someone."

Irritated, she flicked water at him. "I didn't think you'd notice."

"My dear, you wound me. Not notice a critical little detail like that? Have you no faith in my investigative talents?"

"I don't trust you as far as I can see, Abbott."

Those trouser buttons couldn't stay fastened forever.

He propped one hand on the opposite side of the tub and leaned closer. Dangerously close.

Her heart skipped a beat. She poked a bubble-tipped finger at his chest. "There's still one more thing we have to settle, you know."

He leaned closer still. "I know," he said, and smiled.

How could one little smile play such havoc with her heart and breathing?

She wrenched her gaze off that tempting, sensual mouth. "You have to promise to quit being so darned overprotective. I can take care of myself."

"Really?" His gaze dropped.

She drew her knees up abruptly. "J.R.!"

"Give me a minute, here," he said. "I'm thinking."

With the tip of one finger, he delicately brushed away the froth of bubbles atop one knee, then followed its slow, sliding progress down her thigh.

She gasped and grabbed his wrist.

"Darn you, Abbott," she said, and pulled him over the edge and into the tub with her.

Chapter Eighteen

"More champagne?"

Caroline giggled. "Yes, please."

J.R. took a sip, then bent to kiss her. The wine was sweet and slightly tangy on his lips and tongue. She liked the taste.

She liked the taste of him a whole lot better.

They'd run out of bath salts, towels, and energy an hour ago. Rather than buzz for service and wait for someone to appear to find out what they wanted, J.R., being chivalrous, had pulled on enough clothes so he could pad barefoot down the hall to the phone and order up dinner and champagne for two.

She'd collected her discarded garments, mopped up the water on the bathroom floor, and dumped the soggy towels in the bathtub—which looked quite a bit bigger when there weren't two of them in it—then claimed his dressing gown for her own.

His sodden clothes were still draped over the edge of the tub, slowly dripping dry. His trousers would never be the same.

She'd been right about the trouser buttons, though, even if they had needed a little help from her.

They'd turned the big bed into a picnic spot. There was little left of the picnic now but the bones of an excellent roast chicken and most of the second bottle of champagne. Her energy was coming back and, judging from the glint in J.R.'s eyes, so was his.

She claimed another lingering kiss, then refilled both their glasses. There was still that little matter of his not trying to be her nanny to resolve and then—

The timid knock on the door startled them both.

"Grrrr," said J.R. "Damn waiters."

He gave her a quick peck, then rolled off the bed and, champagne glass in hand, went to open the door.

He'd scarcely turned the knob when Dolly James shoved through the door and straight into his arms. Or, rather, onto his chest. J.R. was too busy trying to keep from slopping his champagne to grab her.

"Oh, Mr. Abbott!" she exclaimed breathlessly, clutching at his shirt. "I don't know what to do and—"

She jumped back as Caroline set her wineglass down and hopped off the bed.

"Oh, my! I didn't know—"

Caroline gave her a tight smile that came with a lot of teeth. "Remember me? I'm *Mrs*. Abbott."

"Yes?" said Dolly doubtfully. "Oh, yes!" She gave a dainty, dismissive shrug. "But I wanted to talk to *Mr*. Abbott."

J.R. blinked. "About what?"

"About Andy. You know. Mr. Osbald?" Her mouth curved downward in an enchantingly feminine frown. Her chin dropped until she was coyly gazing up at him from beneath her lashes. She sidled a couple inches closer. Her hand fluttered to her breast.

Caroline gnashed her teeth and tugged on J.R.'s dressing gown, which tended to gape over her breasts. He'd appreciated the display earlier. Now, he didn't even notice.

"I thought you ought to know," Dolly purred and moved still closer. She didn't so much as glance at Caroline. "He's very angry with Mr. Hargreave 'cause Mr. Hargreave says Andy owes him more money."

"What?" cried J.R. and Caroline in chorus.

J.R. gallantly took Dolly's elbow. "Why don't you sit down here, Miss James, and tell me all about it."

"Us," said Caroline. "Tell *us* all about it."

Dolly gave J.R. a wavery little smile as she did as she was bid. Tears seemed to hover just behind her lids, waiting for the right moment to fall. "Why, thank you, Mr. Abbott. You are *so* kind."

"What about Hargreave?" Caroline demanded burning to hear what Dolly had to say about the prosecutor.

"I came to you, Mr. Abbott, because you're the only one I can trust," Dolly said, suddenly clutching J.R.'s hand and making him spill the champagne.

He set the glass on the floor, safely out of reach, then closed his free hand over hers and gave her a reassuring pat.

"Tell me about Mr. Hargreave," he coaxed.

"Mr. Hargreave is *very* angry. He sent Andy a perfectly *awful* letter demanding more money."

"What?" cried J.R. and Caroline in chorus.

"It's 'cause of all the fuss over Andy shootin' Josiah."

Fuss? Caroline stared. *Fuss?*

"I wouldn't have bothered you," Dolly tearfully assured J.R., "but Andy was so *mean* to me, and when I asked why he was so upset, he *hit* me!"

"Don't you worry," J.R. soothed, giving her hand another pat. "He can't hurt you now."

Dolly gave him a soulful, slightly dewy smile.

Caroline gritted her teeth. "So, what did the letter say?"

Dolly sniffed. Even sniffling, she looked good. "I don't know, but Andy said he'd have to meet the bastard—oh, sorry, Mr. Abbott. I know nice men like you don't use that kind of language."

She batted her damp lashes at J.R. and smiled. Again. J.R. smiled back. Caroline wore off a little more tooth enamel.

"Anyway, Andy said he'd have to meet with Mr. Hargreave and…and settle things."

Caroline elbowed J.R. aside. "Where? When? Tonight? Is it going to be tonight?"

"Well, I—"

"How much money? Is Osbald going to pay it himself?"

"Oh, Mr. Abbott!" Dolly leaned so far forward that her breasts brushed the back of J.R.'s hand. "You don't think he's going to *kill* Mr. Hargreave, do you? He wouldn't do that, would he?"

"No. No, of course he wouldn't kill Hargreave,"

J.R. reassured her. "But why don't you tell me all about it so I can make sure he doesn't?"

Caroline was dancing with impatience by the time Dolly, with many sighs, sniffles, and soulful looks— every one of them for J.R.'s benefit—got the whole tale out.

"Why would they risk being seen together?" she objected. "Just because the meeting's in a...a brothel—"

"But nobody will see them! They don't have to go in the same house, you know."

"They don't? But—"

"Of course not." Dolly frowned at her stupidity. "Andy's got a door that goes from the back of his saloon to the back of The Ranch House."

"The Ranch House?"

"That's Maggie Dolan's place. On Myers Avenue."

"Oh," said Caroline blankly.

"And Maggie's got a door that goes from her cellar to Lola's. And Lola's got a door—"

"I see," said Caroline. "I didn't realize—"

Dolly turned to J.R. "You know about all that, don't you, Mr. Abbott?"

He patted her hand. "Of course."

"You do?" Caroline stared. "How do *you* know about that sort of thing?"

J.R. frowned. "Caroline..."

"You *know* about these sneaky—?"

He smiled at Dolly. Again. "I can't tell you how much I appreciate your telling me—"

"*Us,*" said Caroline firmly.

"*…us* about all this, Miss James," he said, helping the woman to her feet. "You can be sure I'll—"

"We!"

J.R. cast her a withering look over Dolly's shoulder. "That *I* will do everything possible to stop Mr. Osbald."

"You'll make sure everybody knows?" There wasn't a tear in sight now that Dolly was sure she had J.R. wrapped around her finger.

"Everybody. I promise."

"I want the whole damned *world* to know what he's up to." Dolly gave her head an angry toss. "Nobody hits me. *Nobody.*"

How about a good, swift kick, instead? Caroline thought.

Before she gave in to temptation, she wrenched the door open. "It was so kind of you to stop by, Miss James. Good-bye."

Dolly ignored her. She laid her hand on J.R.'s shirt-sleeve and leaned close. "Thank you, Mr. Abbott. You've been so kind."

She was halfway through the door when Caroline said, "One thing, Miss James. Why didn't you come to *me* with this information?

Dolly looked at her blankly. "Why would I do that?"

"*I'm* the one who bought you lunch."

"Well, yes, but he's a *man.*"

J.R. suddenly developed a vicious cough.

"Though I did like the headline. Beautiful Woman Caught Between Two Rivals. That was real nice."

Dolly beamed. "'Specially the beautiful woman part."

She'd turned the corner in the hall and was out of sight by the time Caroline recovered her wits enough to shut the door.

J.R. had already buttoned his shirt and had one foot propped on the edge of the dressing table so he could lace up his shoe. When Caroline snatched up her skirt and petticoats, he set his foot down.

"You're not going, Caroline."

"Hah!" She grabbed her drawers and corset. "You can't stop me."

Since he didn't have his arms filled with bulky feminine clothes, he got to her shoes first.

"Oh, yes, I can," he said, and opened a window and tossed them out.

"Hey!" She started to fling her corset at his head, then realized he might send it sailing after the shoes. "I'll wear your shoes, then."

"I doubt there's enough socks to keep them from falling off your feet." He pulled an unrumpled coat out of the chifforobe and slipped it on.

"I'll go barefoot."

He flashed her a taunting smile. "Be my guest. But watch where you put your feet. In the dark, and with all those horses around..."

Caroline shuddered. "Your bedroom slippers, then."

His smile widened. "Didn't bring any."

His derringer went in his pocket. He didn't bother with a tie.

He was halfway to the door when he abruptly spun

on his heel and headed back to the bathroom. "Almost forgot!" A moment later, he emerged with her gun in one hand and three bullets in the other. "These all your bullets?"

"That's all that's left from what Elizabeth gave me," she grudgingly admitted.

"Good." The bullets went in his pocket. He tossed the gun on the dressing table, then collected the extra room key she'd left there, half buried under her hairpins. "I'll take this, too. Just in case."

He was reaching for the doorknob when she flung her clothes on the floor and threw herself between him and the door. "You can't leave me here! This is *my* story. I'm the one who invited that woman to lunch! I'm—"

"Likely to get hurt, dammit!" He slammed his open hand on the door not two inches from her head, eyes burning with a furious blue fire. "I've given in on the reporting, Caroline, but I'm not giving in on this. I will *not* let you charge into any situation where you might be harmed. Do you hear me?"

He was so close he seemed to suck all the air out of the room.

She tilted her chin defiantly upward. "You don't have any say in the matter. No nanny, remember?"

His other hand slammed onto the door. "Dammit, Caroline! Do you really think I'll stand idly by while you run that beautiful, obstinate head of yours into trouble? God knows why, but I love you. I'll do almost anything to keep you happy, but I'd give my life to keep you safe. Fairness be damned! You're my wife!"

And then he shoved her against the door and kissed her till her head spun on her shoulders and her heart pounded like thunder and her knees turned to jelly beneath her.

She was on the point of dragging him to the floor and making love to him right there in front of the door when he abruptly wrenched away.

"Stay here and be a good girl," he said. He gave her a quick kiss on the cheek, then was out the door before she could catch her breath or get her knees to working properly again. The key was already sliding out of the lock when she gathered her wits enough to scream.

The only answer was the sound of his footsteps fading away down the hall.

Panting with frustration and fury, Caroline glared at the unyielding door and plotted vengeance. Glorious vengeance that would somehow include his being in her power for hours and hours and hours.

But first, she had to bring down Osbald.

She'd brought clean clothes with her, but no extra shoes. When she went digging in the chifforobe for a pair of J.R.'s she could use, she found the high-heeled pair she'd flung at his head. A small lump formed in her throat—instead of leaving them on the street, he'd had them cleaned and polished until they gleamed. Only a man who loved her would have done that. But then she remembered why she'd flung them at his head in the first place, and happily snatched his best pair of dress hose to replace the bulky socks he'd made her buy.

She reloaded her gun with the bullets she'd bought that afternoon, then shoved the gun into her pocket and set her purse aside. At least she hadn't lied when she'd told J.R. the bullets he'd confiscated were the last that Elizabeth had given her.

The locked door was a problem, though. No matter how she jiggled the knob, it wouldn't open. Hairpins, a dinner knife, and J.R.'s favorite tie pin were equally useless. Caroline glared at the keyless lock, then eyed the button for the service bell uncertainly. If she rang for help, it would be a few minutes before anybody responded. Then they'd have to go back for the key, come back up…

She pressed her ear to the door. Nothing but silence.

Wait? Or take more drastic measures? Caroline chewed her lower lip, debating, then dragged the gun out of her pocket and shot the lock off.

She was halfway down the stairs and gaining speed when she heard the first excited, disbelieving shout from behind her.

It took over an hour for J.R. to roust first the sheriff, then the judge and a couple of deputies out of their beds and convince them to accompany him. As he led them toward Osbald's Golden Diamond Saloon and the back door into Maggie Dolan's, he did his best to stifle his doubts about Dolly James's information. Better to worry about Dolly's motives, though, than worry about all the mad stunts Caroline might pull in trying to escape the National.

One thought carried him through—if Dolly James

had lied to him, if she was playing Osbald's game and not her own, then tomorrow morning he would, by God, sic Caroline on the woman.

J.R. gave a small, grim smile and opened the door to the Golden Diamond. Of course, he'd have to face his wife's wrath first. If Caroline got her hands on him first, there was no guarantee he'd still be alive to deal with Dolly afterward.

It was late and time was short, but Elizabeth, fairly bursting with enthusiasm, managed to gather three of her most stalwart supporters.

Caroline eyed the assembled recruits dubiously. There was a plump, pink-cheeked lady named Delilah who wouldn't reach five feet in heels, a mournful scarecrow of a woman in an ill-fitted, rusty-looking black dress that was twenty years out of fashion, and a fiery-eyed widow who walked with a cane and who, so she informed Caroline with relish, was rarin' to show those fool men what's what. And then there was a nervously glum Georgianne, who would have stayed at home if Elizabeth hadn't vehemently insisted she join the expedition. All of them had participated in the march this afternoon and all save Georgianne looked eager and ready for a fight.

Witnesses, Caroline silently assured herself, trying to stifle her growing doubts as she led the eager ladies toward Myers Avenue and Maggie Dolan's Ranch House. She patted the pocket where Elizabeth's gun lay. The hard, cold lump of metal wasn't nearly as reassuring as she'd expected.

This time of night, the only life visible in Cripple

Creek besides themselves was a stray dog and an occasional solitary man. On Bennett Avenue, the saloons were the only places open this late, the light from their windows the only illumination.

J.R. should have gathered help by now. The sheriff, probably. Maybe the judge. *Someone.*

"We'll show those men!" Elizabeth said beside her, brandishing her fist. "Mary Walker is going to have her justice in spite of them!"

The ladies cheered. All Caroline could manage was a wavery smile. This was exactly the sort Adventure with a capital *A* that she'd come West to find, she reminded herself sternly as they turned the corner onto Myers Avenue.

The idea had sounded a whole lot better back in Baltimore.

Caroline's troops took Maggie Dolan's by storm.

"Don't bother about us," Elizabeth said cheerily to the astonished servant who opened the front door. "We won't be long. We're just here to collect a murderous bag of scum."

She sailed through the open doorway before the servant could gather her wits to shut it. The others, eyes popping at the thought of where they were, crowded in right after her but came to a screeching halt five feet inside the door.

"Donald MacIntyre! What are *you* doing in a place like *this?*" The scarecrow in rusty black gaped at a crimson-faced gentleman doing his best to disappear under the sofa cushions. She stiffened in indignation. "Just *wait* till I tell your wife!"

The gentleman gave up trying to hide and fled. Three more would-be customers bolted out the door after him. The fourth, a scrawny old codger in need of a good set of dentures, calmly circled the room in their wake, gathering up the abandoned liquor glasses and dumping their contents into his.

The ladies ignored him. Their eyes were glued to a rather crude painting of a naked woman that took up most of the opposite wall.

"My!" said the scarecrow.

"My, my, my!" said Delilah, elbowing the scarecrow aside so she could get a better view.

"Hah!" said the widow, and thumped her cane on the floor.

"Pay attention, Georgianne!" Elizabeth snapped. "We have more important things to worry about right now."

"Of course," said Georgianne regretfully. "It's just I never—"

"I would hope not!"

"Whoever posed for that must be *very* tall," said Delilah wistfully.

Ignoring the flutters in the pit of her stomach, Caroline started up the stairs. From somewhere on the floor above, she caught the rhythmic squeak of bedsprings.

She was three quarters of the way up with her troops right behind her when a tall woman possessed of a massive bosom and startling red hair suddenly appeared at the top.

"Who are you? What is the meaning of this?" the

woman shrilled. ''You have no right—! Thomas!'' That last came out in an enraged bellow.

Caroline missed a step, but kept on climbing.

''Thomas!''

Heavy footsteps sounded in the lower hallway. An instant later, a man with the lugubrious mien of a weary undertaker lumbered into sight.

Caroline's heart sank. Thomas was the size of a mountain.

''Throw these women out!'' the redhead ordered.

Without changing expression, Thomas started toward the stairs.

''Over my dead body!'' cried the widow, who was bringing up the tail. The instant Thomas set foot on the stairs she stabbed him in the chest with the rubber-tipped end of her cane. ''Stand back! Don't come any closer or I'll have to hurt you!''

Thomas blinked and froze right where he was, staring at her like a bewildered sheep.

''Thomas!''

''Not one step farther!'' cried the widow.

''That's telling him, Emma Lou!'' cheered the scarecrow.

Thomas glanced up at the redhead, clearly perplexed. ''Miz Dolan?''

''Throw 'em out!'' Maggie Dolan roared.

A door in the hall behind her opened. An extraordinarily bald head popped out. Its sweating, round-faced owner glanced their way, whimpered, then vanished. The door slammed shut.

The rhythmic squeak of bedsprings coming from behind another door on the opposite side of the hall stopped abruptly. From another room came the sound of bare feet hitting the floor with a thump.

Caroline set her jaw and took the last steps in a rush.

Startled, Maggie Dolan jumped out of her way, narrowly missing a vase on a carved pedestal near the head of the stairs. Before the madam had a chance to regain her wits, Elizabeth had bulled past her, too, then Georgianne and Delilah, panting slightly from the climb.

Next to the last room on the right, Dolly had said.

They were two doors away when the door they were aiming for opened and Hargreave stepped out.

Caroline stopped so abruptly that Elizabeth almost ran her down.

Hargreave froze, his hand still on the knob of the half-open door. Color drained from his face. "Mrs. Abbott."

"Mr. Hargreave."

"Swine," snarled Elizabeth beside her.

"Oh, my!" said Georgianne, cautiously peeping around Elizabeth.

"Thomas!" Maggie Dolan screeched behind them.

Without taking his eyes off them, Hargreave calmly shut the door.

"You ladies taking up a new career?" the prosecutor asked, deliberately insulting.

"You might say that," said Caroline, deliberately misunderstanding. *Where in the devil was J.R.?* "And how about you? It must be very inconvenient to conduct your business from the upper floor of a whorehouse."

She wasn't sure, but she thought she could hear a window being dragged open in the room Hargreave had just left.

The gun in her pocket suddenly weighed a ton.

Hargreave's eyes narrowed. He glanced at the door as if expecting it would provide an answer, then hastily looked away and forced a sneering smile.

"You'll forgive me if I don't introduce you to the young lady in there," he said. "I'm afraid she's…not quite ready for guests."

Elizabeth snorted and lowered her head, ready to charge.

At that moment, J.R. strode around a corner at the far end of the hall where the servants' stairs must be. The sheriff followed, then the judge. At the sight of the assembled crowd in the hall, the two men stopped short, staring.

With a little sigh of relief, Caroline swallowed the lump of fear that had been threatening to choke her. J.R. didn't even glance her way. His attention was all on the man standing between them.

"Hargreave!" he said pleasantly. "I'm delighted to see we aren't too late. We'd have been here sooner, but it took us longer to convince Osbald's men to let us through that door of his than I'd expected."

Hargreave stiffened. "I don't know what you mean."

"No? Oh, but I'm forgetting! You didn't come in that way, did you? People might have talked if anyone had spotted you with Osbald, given the trial and all."

"Don't be ridiculous! Why would I meet with the man here?"

"Unfortunately for Mr. Osbald," J.R. added in the same friendly, informative tone, "there's a deputy posted under the window of this room, which is a tad inconvenient if he was planning on leaving that way."

Even from five feet away, Caroline could see that Hargreave was beginning to sweat.

"Enough of this!" snapped the judge, shaking himself out of his stupor and stepping forward. "Open that door, Hargreave."

Hargreave backed up against the door. "I—"

"Open the door, Hargreave," said the sheriff, "or I'll do it for you."

The door opened so abruptly that Hargreave almost fell backward into the room. He staggered, fought to keep his balance, and went sprawling on his knees when Osbald stormed out of the room, gun in hand.

"You son of a bitch," Osbald snarled. "I'll kill you for this, I swear it." His gun was pointed straight at the middle of J.R.'s belly.

Caroline's stomach twisted and her knees threatened to give out from under her. J.R. didn't even blink.

"I wouldn't advise it," he said evenly. "This time, the witnesses won't be nearly so easy to buy off."

"Drop the gun, Hargreave," the sheriff ordered.

"Don't be a fool, Osbald," the judge snapped. "Here in Colorado, we hang murderers."

J.R. smiled, but the smile didn't reach his eyes. "That's a fact I suspect Mr. Osbald already knew."

Osbald gave an animal snarl and swung the gun on the judge. "Back off, damn you! *Back off!*"

The three men glanced at each other, then at Caroline and the women behind her. Reluctantly, they backed up. Caroline had the sick feeling that they would have drawn their guns and started shooting if she and the other women hadn't been there. Hargreave moaned and tried to scuttle away. Osbald kicked him so hard he yelped and rolled into a ball, instead.

Osbald laughed, then stepped over him and, gun still trained on J.R. and with his back to the wall so he could keep his eye on all of them, came toward her.

Caroline stepped back, putting herself as far out of his reach as possible. After a moment's hesitation, the other women followed suit. Maggie Dolan, hand fisted on her hips, was still standing at the top of the steps, watching them grimly. At the sight of the gun in Osbald's hand, she cursed, then reluctantly stepped aside, as well.

Neither the widow nor the scarecrow had appeared, which meant either Thomas had gotten up the courage to evict them, or they were still holding him pinned at the bottom of the stairs. And that meant Osbald would run right over the top of them on his way out the door.

Osbald sidled closer. His gaze swung to Caroline, pinning her to the wall. "I'll get even," he snarled. "I just want you to know that. I'll get even."

Beside her, Elizabeth sucked in air. Caroline couldn't breathe at all. She pressed her hand to her stomach, fighting against the sudden nausea and dizziness, and felt the hard bump of the gun in her pocket.

Something in her expression must have caught his attention because Osbald hesitated, then a slow, wolfish grin spread across his face.

"Better yet," he said, very softly, "I'll get even now."

He turned to face J.R. and raised his gun.

Caroline wasn't sure how it happened, but suddenly her gun was in her hands and pointed at Osbald's head.

"Stop!" she shouted, and cocked the gun.

Osbald froze. His heavy head swung back to her.

In the dim light of the hall, his eyes glittered dangerously.

She wrapped both hands tight around the gun, then lowered the barrel until it was aimed straight at his heart. "Put the gun down, Osbald, or I'll shoot."

The words sounded too strained and distant to be hers. From the corner of her eye she saw J.R. shift on his feet. Osbald's gun didn't waver an inch. The pressure in her chest sharpened, squeezing her heart.

"Put the gun down," she said, and shifted her grip on the gun.

That's when he charged. Caroline stumbled backward. His free hand closed around her wrist, forcing it up. She tried to wrench free but he was too quick and far too strong. She tried to let go of the gun, to throw it to Elizabeth. Instead, she shot a hole in the ceiling. In the narrow hallway, the sound was deafening.

Caroline couldn't tell if any of the screams were

hers. She couldn't think. Panic clawed at her throat. The world had narrowed to the gun she still held and Osbald's crushing hold on her wrist, to pain and fear and the smell of liquor on his breath as he slammed her against the wall.

"Bitch! Goddamned bitch!" He gave a vicious twist to her wrist and dragged her hand down even as he shifted his hold on his gun to bring the butt crashing down on her head.

J.R. grabbed Osbald's arm and twisted it back, forcing the man around. Before Osbald could let go of her, J.R.'s fist slammed into his face, snapping his head back. Osbald grunted and staggered back, dragging Caroline with him. She stumbled and fell against him, whimpering in pain and fear. And still, somehow, she kept hold of the gun.

J.R. hit Osbald again, then again.

She tried to get to her feet. Osbald abruptly let go of her wrist and she went sprawling, instead. She dropped the gun. Someone—Osbald, J.R., she couldn't tell which—kicked it and sent it spinning along the polished wood floor, out of her reach.

Above her, the two men struggled to gain control of the gun Osbald still held, raining blows on each other with their free hands, grunting and cursing and scrabbling to keep on their feet. With tears streaming unheeded down her face and her blood roaring in her ears, Caroline wrapped her arms around Osbald's legs and rolled, dragging him down on top of her.

Quick as a cat, J.R. let go of the man's arm and danced out of the way, then pounced again, grabbing for Osbald's gun.

Caroline wasn't quite sure what happened next. She heard grunts, curses, and the horrible dull thud of fists striking flesh. An elbow hit her, then someone kicked her ankle. She got in a good punch to Osbald's kidneys, and a sound kick on what she hoped was his knee, then they rolled away, off her, and she scrambled out of the way.

Still locked in combat, the men tumbled back, J.R. on top. Somehow, J.R. slipped out of Osbald's grip, then reared back to give him a vicious chop to the chin, then another. Osbald's grip slackened enough for J.R. to grab the gun, then roll away and to his feet. He wasn't quite fast enough.

"J.R.!" Caroline screamed. "Watch out!"

The warning was wasted. Osbald was still coming up when there was a dull thud and the vase that had so recently stood on the pedestal at the head of the stairs shattered against the back of his skull. He grunted, and then his eyeballs rolled up in his head and he toppled over like a rotten tree chopped off at the base. The floor shook when he landed.

For a moment there was nothing but stunned silence, then Georgianne gave a little squeak of dismay and dropped the rim of the shattered vase that she was still holding.

"Oh, dear," she said. "I hope I didn't hurt him."

"Thomas!" Maggie Dolan bellowed. "Throw the bastards out, dammit! Every blasted one of them!"

Chapter Nineteen

"So, what do we do next?"

J. Randolph heard the words but he was having a hard time concentrating on the sense of them. In fact, he was having a hard time concentrating on anything other than his wife and the biscuit she was slathering with thick, rich strawberry jam.

"Do?" he said, watching her lick a tiny dab of jam off the tip of one finger. "Hmm."

She brought the biscuit to her lips. Her lips parted, exposing perfect, pearl-white teeth. The teeth opened exposing a delicate pink tongue that flicked out to catch a stray dollop of jam.

Something low in J.R.'s belly grabbed him and squeezed hard and he wondered if he'd tied his tie too tight that morning because he was suddenly having a hard time breathing.

"Should we go home?" his wife asked. "Back to Denver? Or should we stay for Hargreave's trial, too? Elizabeth says they'll probably have it the end of next week. And you know Elizabeth. She's never wrong about that sort of thing."

She took another bite of biscuit and J.R. said "Hmm" again and then her tongue flicked out to catch a dab of jam at the corner of her mouth and he said "Mmm" and felt his body harden and his eyes glaze over.

He ought to be a little less susceptible by now, but after months of separation, two weeks with his wife hadn't even come close to filling his hunger for her. He was pretty sure a lifetime wouldn't suffice, but he was willing to find out.

While they'd waited for the new trial that, in just one day, had handed Osbald a verdict of guilty of murder and conspiracy, they'd done their best to make up for lost time. Not just physically, either. In bed at night, or on long rides into the hills around town, over dinner or, as now, over breakfast in their new suite at the National, they had talked over their differences and what Caroline's new career would mean for her, and for them.

Little though he liked it, she was well on her way to being the *Times'* star reporter. Murray, still spouting empty threats, had been recalled to Denver. The only byline on those front-page articles now was hers.

The brawl in Maggie Dolan's had killed whatever interest she had in guns, but it hadn't dented her determination to keep on writing. He hadn't really expected it would. He was growing accustomed to the idea that she was going to get into trouble now and then whether he liked it or not. Which was only fair, since she'd have to get used to the fact that he was going to do his damnedest to protect her whenever she ran into danger, whether she wanted him to or not.

"J.R.?"

The laughing query dragged his attention back to his wife and the breakfast in front of him. "Yes?"

"You haven't answered my question."

"Ahhh…" He tried to remember what she'd asked him, but she was slathering another biscuit with that damned jam and his body was playing havoc with his brain.

"Denver?" she said, and took a bite of biscuit. "Or here?"

He dragged in air, then threw his napkin down and shoved his chair back.

"Here," he said, and came around the table. "Definitely. Right here, right now."

She laughed, and when he dragged her out of her chair and down to the floor with him, she came willingly. She tasted of strawberries and something sweeter and far more tempting. Beneath the heavy silk of his dressing gown, which she'd commandeered the minute she'd moved in with him, her body was soft and warm and dangerously tempting.

"Did I ever tell you how much I like you in that dressing gown?" His hand slipped through the gaping front of it to claim her breast.

"Yes?" She moaned and arched against him.

He grinned, watching the way her eyes grew hooded and dark. "Yes."

Her tongue flicked out to slide across her lips provocatively. She smiled and dragged him closer.

"If you like this gown," she said in a husky voice

that made his skin prick and the muscles in his belly seize, "you ought to see the one that Lola's dressmaker is sewing for me."

He laughed and tugged the gown away.

"I love you," he said, "And I don't think I can wait."

A heartbeat later, he proved he really meant it. Every single word of it.

Escape to a land long ago and
far away when you read these thrilling
love stories from Harlequin Historicals

On Sale September 2002

A WARRIOR'S LADY
by Margaret Moore
(England, 1200s)
*A forced marriage between a brave knight and
beautiful heiress blossoms into true love!*

A ROGUE'S HEART
by Debra Lee Brown
(Scotland, 1213)
*Will a carefree rogue sweep a headstrong young lady
off her feet with his tempting business offer?*

On Sale October 2002

MY LADY'S HONOR
by Julia Justiss
(Regency England)
*In the game of disguise a resourceful young
woman falls in love with a dashing aristocrat!*

THE BLANCHLAND SECRET
by Nicola Cornick
(England, 1800s)
*Will a lady's companion risk her reputation by
accepting the help of a well-known rake?*

 Harlequin Historicals®
Historical Romantic Adventure!

Princes...Princesses...
London Castles...New York Mansions...
To live the life of a royal!

In 2002, Harlequin Books lets you escape to a
world of royalty with these royally themed titles:

Temptation:
January 2002—*A Prince of a Guy* (#861)
February 2002—*A Noble Pursuit* (#865)

American Romance:
The Carradignes: American Royalty (Editorially linked series)
March 2002—*The Improperly Pregnant Princess* (#913)
April 2002—*The Unlawfully Wedded Princess* (#917)
May 2002—*The Simply Scandalous Princess* (#921)
November 2002—*The Inconveniently Engaged Prince* (#945)

Intrigue:
The Carradignes: A Royal Mystery (Editorially linked series)
June 2002—*The Duke's Covert Mission* (#666)

Chicago Confidential
September 2002—*Prince Under Cover* (#678)

The Crown Affair
October 2002—*Royal Target* (#682)
November 2002—*Royal Ransom* (#686)
December 2002—*Royal Pursuit* (#690)

Harlequin Romance:
June 2002—*His Majesty's Marriage* (#3703)
July 2002—*The Prince's Proposal* (#3709)

Harlequin Presents:
August 2002—*Society Weddings* (#2268)
September 2002—*The Prince's Pleasure* (#2274)

Duets:
September 2002—*Once Upon a Tiara/Henry Ever After* (#83)
October 2002—*Natalia's Story/Andrea's Story* (#85)

Celebrate a year of royalty with
Harlequin Books!

Available at your favorite retail outlet.

Makes any time special ®

Visit us at www.eHarlequin.com

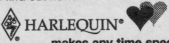

New York Times **Bestselling Author**

Stephanie Laurens

Four in Hand

The Ton's most hardened rogues could not resist the remarkable Twinning sisters. And the Duke of Twyford was no exception! For when it came to his eldest ward, the exquisite Caroline Twinning, London's most notorious rake was falling victim to love!

On sale July 2002

HARLEQUIN®
Makes any time special®

C'mon back home to Crystal Creek with
a BRAND-NEW anthology from

bestselling authors
Vicki Lewis Thompson
Cathy Gillen Thacker
Bethany Campbell

Return to Crystal Creek

**Nothing much
has changed in
Crystal Creek...
till now!**

The mysterious Nick Belyle has shown up in town,
and what he's up to is anyone's guess. But one
thing is certain. Something big is going down in
Crystal Creek, and folks aren't going to rest till
they find out what the future holds.

*Look for this exciting anthology,
on-sale in July 2002.*

HARLEQUIN®
Makes any time special ®

Visit us at www.eHarlequin.com

PHRTCC